A PLACE TO CALL HOME

CHEROKEE ROSE

AL & JOANNA LACY

Multnomah® Publishers *Sisters, Oregon*

CHEROKEE ROSE
© 2006 by ALJO PRODUCTIONS, INC.

published by Multnomah Publishers, Inc.
International Standard Book Number: 1-59052-562-0

Cover design by the DesignWorks Group, Inc.
Cover image by Steve Gardner, www.shootpw.com

Scripture quotations are from:
The Holy Bible, King James Version (KJV)

Printed in the United States of America

Multnomah is a trademark of Multnomah Publishers, Inc.,
and is registered in the U.S. Patent and Trademark Office.
The colophon is a trademark of Multnomah publishers, Inc.

For information:
Multnomah Publishers, Inc., 601 North Larch Street, Sisters, Oregon 97759

Library of Congress Cataloging-in-Publication Data
Lacy, Al.
  Cherokee Rose / Al and JoAnna Lacy.
    p. cm. — (A place to call home ; bk. 1)
  ISBN 1-59052-562-0
  1. Cherokee Indians—Fiction. 2. North Carolina—Fiction. I. Lacy, JoAnna. II. Title.
  PS3562.A256C48 2006
  813'.54—dc22

                    2005033671

06 07 08 09 10 11 12 — 10 9 8 7 6 5 4 3 2 1 0

preface

I n the sixteenth century, the Cherokee Indians occupied mountain areas of North Carolina, Georgia, Alabama, and Tennessee. They had a settled, advanced culture based on agriculture. They were visited by the Hernando de Soto expedition in 1540, and the Spanish explorer later reported that he was impressed by the Cherokee people.

In 1820, the Cherokees adopted a republican form of government, and in 1827 they established themselves as the Cherokee Nation. In 1832, gold was discovered in Cherokee territory, resulting in pressure by whites to obtain Cherokee lands. This, coupled with Andrew Jackson (who was known to be prejudiced against Indians) being president of the United States at the time, spelled doom for the Cherokees as pressure mounted for the removal of all Indians to the West. There were five tribes known as the "Civilized Tribes": the Cherokee, the Chickasaw, the Choctaw, the Creek, and the Seminole. These five tribes were slated to occupy the land known as Indian Territory.

The Cherokee nation's leading chief, John Ross, a mixed-blood Cherokee, struggled hard against Jackson's administration to keep his people from being put off their land. His struggle continued when Martin Van Buren became president in 1837. The opposition was too great, however, and in the winter of 1838–1839, some fifteen thousand North Carolina Cherokees were forced by the U.S. Army to make the one thousand-mile journey known as the "Trail of Tears" to Indian Territory, which is now the state of Oklahoma. Many Cherokees of Georgia, Alabama, and Tennessee as well as the people of the other four Civilized Tribes had already been forced to go to Indian Territory.

Forced to surrender their lands, the people of the Cherokee nation were hoping to find in Indian Territory *a place to call home*.

In 1888, some fifty years after the Cherokee Indians of North Carolina had made their journey to Indian Territory, President Grover Cleveland announced that he and Congress were working on a plan to open up land in Indian Territory for white people. The Indians occupied only a small portion of the Territory, leaving some two million acres where white people could establish their homes. Besides, oil had recently been discovered in north Texas, as well as in many parts of Indian Territory.

With this plan in mind, President Cleveland legally changed the name of Indian Territory to Oklahoma District.

In the national election of November 1888, however, Benjamin Harrison was elected president of the United States and Territories. Immediately after taking office in January 1889, President Harrison took up where President Cleveland had left off on the plan to open up land in Oklahoma District for white people.

In the second week of February, President Harrison announced to newspapers across the country that he and Congress had devised a plan to set boundaries for the habitation of the Indians in what had been their territory for over half a century. The land the Indians would occupy within the boundaries would be called "reservations."

The government would then allow white people to enter Oklahoma District and claim the two million acres known as "unassigned lands." Under the provision of the Homestead Act of 1862, white settlers would be allowed to claim 160 acres of land, and those who lived on and improved their claim for five years would receive title to it.

President Harrison also made it known that he would be sending army troops to Oklahoma District to make sure the Indians moved onto the land assigned to them and settled there.

The president advised the newspapers that very soon he would give them a date when the prospective settlers could come and look at the 160-acre plots, then in a "land rush" a few days later, they could make their claims.

When the "land rush" took place in April 1889, a great number of people from many parts of the country were there to lay claim to choice 160-acre plots. For most of them, their lives had been unsettled and unhappy, and they were hoping to find in Oklahoma District *a place to call home.*

prologue

n the period of history covered by the story of Cherokee Rose, there were two outstanding Cherokee chiefs whose names are still revered today by the Cherokee people: Chief John Ross and Chief Sequoyah. As our readers will see, both men play important parts in this novel, and we pass along here some significant facts about these men.

John Ross was born October 3, 1790, near Lookout Mountain in the Smoky Mountains of North Carolina. He died August 1, 1866, in Washington, D.C.

Born of a Scottish father and a mother who was part Cherokee, the blue-eyed, fair-skinned John Ross (whose Cherokee name was Tsan-Usdi) grew up as an Indian. In the nineteenth century, Ross, courageous and highly intelligent, became the leader of the Cherokee resistance to the white man's planned acquisition of the land they had lived on for centuries. From 1819 to 1826 Ross served as president of the National Council of Cherokees.

When the United States government sought to take the Cherokees' land and move them west, Ross—still a Cherokee chief—put up a spirited defense for his people. His petitions to President Andrew Jackson, under whom he had fought in the Creek War (1813–1814), went unheeded. The U.S. Congress, under Jackson's leadership, established the Indian Removal Act.

In 1838–1839, when Martin Van Buren was president, Ross had no choice but to lead his people, escorted by soldiers of the U.S. army, toward an unknown western prairie called Indian Territory.

In the West, Chief John Ross helped write a constitution (1839) for the United Cherokee Nation in their new homeland. He was chosen chief of the new Cherokee government, an office he held for the remainder of his life. He often traveled by rail to Washington, D.C., as representative of his people, and it was in that city where he died.

Sequoyah was born around 1773 in North Carolina, and died in August 1843 in Oklahoma District. At his birth, he was called Sogwali by his parents. After both parents died while he was yet a youth, Bible-preaching missionaries named him Sequoyah.

Having been a Cherokee chief for some five years, in 1809 Sequoyah began working to develop a system of writing for his people, believing that increased knowledge would help the Cherokee nation maintain their independence from the whites. By

1821, he had developed a system of eighty-six symbols which made up the Cherokee alphabet. The simplicity of his system enabled students to learn it rapidly, and soon Cherokees throughout their nation were teaching it in their schools and publishing books and newspapers in their own language, printing them on their own presses.

Chief Sequoyah had a great interest in the Bible, which was introduced to him in English by the same missionaries who renamed him. By 1823, he had translated the entire Bible into the Cherokee language, and thousands of copies were printed.

In 1825, Sequoyah was presented a silver medal by the General Council of the Cherokee Nation for these accomplishments.

Chief Sequoyah was so admired by the government leaders of the United States that in his memory, the giant redwood trees of California's Pacific Coast and the Sierra Nevada Mountain Range were named after him. Sometime before his death, white men began spelling his name *Sequoia*, thus the giant redwoods are called *Sequoia sempervirens*. California's 386,000-acre Sequoia National Park was also named after him.

The six-month-long journey of the North Carolina Cherokee Indians to what is now the state of Oklahoma has been well named the "Trail of Tears." Of the fifteen thousand Cherokees who began the forced trek, over four thousand died along the way. The suffering of the Cherokees on this journey at the hands of cruel soldiers, along with severe winter weather, hunger, much sickness, and leaving over four thousand graves along the way, leaves a dark blot on the pages of our nation's history.

Let us begin, now, with the heart-stirring story of Cherokee Rose.

one

t was midmorning, October 3, 1790, in the Great Smoky Mountains of North Carolina, and a hint of autumn nipped the air.

In the Cherokee village led by Chief Pathkiller, a seventeen-year-old boy named Sequoyah was slowly riding his black and white stallion along a path that ran past a string of weather-worn cabins. The path was deep in dust, and the cool wind whipped up little puffs.

The rugged mountains on both sides of the village cut into the brilliant blue sky above, which was dotted with many small white clouds.

Sequoyah felt pride well up within him as he looked around the neatly kept village. "I love my home," he said in a half whisper to himself. "I love the wind in my face and these rolling mountains. I hope I will always live right here in the Smokies. I can't even imagine living anywhere else."

Lost in his daydreams, Sequoyah was jarred to awareness when he heard a loud groan. He pulled rein and looked around at the array of cabins. A few yards ahead of him, he caught sight of a young expectant mother named Molly Ross, who was seated on a wooden chair near the front door of her cabin, doubled over in pain.

Sequoyah hurried the horse to the spot, slid off its back, and dashed to Molly, bending low so as to look into her pallid face. "Molly! Is it your time?"

She straightened up, and the long shower of her black hair fell glistening over her shoulders. She ejected a small gasp and tried to speak between the stabbing pains. "Y-yes, Sequoyah…it…it is time."

Another pain struck her. She grimaced and held her breath and waited for it to pass.

Sequoyah found himself holding his own breath as he waited for her to breathe again.

Molly released a tiny moan and said, "The baby is coming quickly. Will you go tell the three midwives, Catana, Binjie, and Eliana, that I need them now?"

A frown lined the young Indian's brow. "Molly, let me help you into the cabin, then I will ride for the midwives."

Molly gave him a tiny smile. "Good idea. I would not want to give birth right here."

She winced with another pain, and when it let up, Sequoyah

took hold of her arm, gently helped her off the chair, and helped her inside the cabin. He eased her down on the edge of the bed and said, "I will hurry, Molly."

Molly doubled over with another pain as she heard Sequoyah's horse gallop away. When the pain eased up, she lay down on the bed; then she closed her eyes and clenched her teeth when another pain lanced her. She wished her husband was there, but Daniel was at his store in Whittier.

Only a few minutes had passed when she heard voices and opened her eyes. Catana, Binjie, and Eliana hurried through the door and went to work to prepare for the baby's delivery.

Outside, Sequoyah stood at the cabin's door, telling people who were passing by what was happening inside.

At one point, Sequoyah saw Chief Pathkiller strolling toward him, escorting his longtime friend Chief Elami from a Cherokee village in the Appalachian Mountains of Tennessee. As the two chiefs drew up, Pathkiller smiled and said, "Sequoyah, you remember Chief Elami."

Sequoyah returned the smile. "Oh, yes, though it has been quite some time since I have seen you, Chief Elami. It is nice to see you again."

Elami nodded as the two of them shook hands Indian style. "It is nice to see you too, my boy."

"Chief Pathkiller, Molly Ross is giving birth to her baby," Sequoyah said. "Her three midwives are with her."

"Oh! It's too bad Daniel is not here with her." Pathkiller turned to Elami. "Molly is a half-breed Cherokee who is married to a Scotsman named Daniel Ross. Daniel owns the general store in the town of Whittier, which is some five miles south of the Smokies."

"I see," Elami said. "The white man is happy living here in your village?"

"Yes, quite happy. When he and Molly married five years ago, Daniel knew she loved her Cherokee people. He offered to make their home in the village, and she gladly accepted the offer."

Elami grinned. "Not many white men would do that."

A crowd had gathered outside the cabin as Sequoyah made everybody aware of what was happening inside. Almost an hour after the midwives had entered the cabin, everyone heard a loud moan from Molly, followed by a slapping sound and the welcome wail of a newborn child.

Seconds later, Eliana came out of the cabin, smiling, and said, "I have good news! Molly's baby is a healthy boy!"

Elation showed on all faces as some of the crowd cheered.

When the cheers faded, Chief Pathkiller asked Eliana, "Does the boy have a name yet?"

Eliana nodded. "The happy mother just told us that she and Daniel had agreed if the baby was a boy, they would name him John. And they also have given him a Cherokee name: Tsan-Usdi, but his parents will call him John."

Eliana stepped up to the seventeen-year-old boy, whose copper-colored face was shining in the sunlight. "Sequoyah, Molly asked that you ride into Whittier and tell her husband that she has given birth to little John Ross."

Sequoyah turned and looked at his chief, questioningly.

"For this occasion, you may ride into Whittier," Pathkiller said. "If anyone stops you before you get to the general store, tell them why you have entered their town and take them directly to

Daniel Ross. He will handle the situation when he hears the good news."

Sequoyah looked back at Eliana and smiled. "Tell Molly that I will go immediately." He dashed to his stallion, swung up on the broad bare back, took the reins in hand, and galloped away.

"Eliana, may I come inside and talk to Molly?" Chief Pathkiller said.

"Just as soon as we have her all cleaned up and the baby in a blanket in her arms, I will return and let you know so you can come in."

Chief Elami turned to Chief Pathkiller. "I must head back to my village."

The chiefs talked for a brief moment while the crowd dispersed, then bid each other farewell. Pathkiller watched Elami as he rode away, and just as he passed from sight, Eliana appeared at the cabin door and said, "You may come in now, Chief."

Chief Pathkiller entered the Ross cabin and followed Eliana as she led him toward the bed where Molly was holding her baby and gazing adoringly at his fair-skinned face and blond hair. She caressed his downy cheek with her fingertips and kissed his smooth brow, then looked up at her chief and smiled.

Catana and Binjie stood on the far side of the bed and looked up as their chief and Eliana drew near.

Chief Pathkiller stepped up to the bed, matched Molly's smile, and said softly, "He is a fine boy, Molly."

"Yes, he is," Molly said, once again caressing the sleeping baby's face. "I hope there will be little brothers and sisters for him, too."

"I understand from Eliana that his Cherokee name is Tsan-Usdi. That is a good name. I also think the name John Ross fits him well."

"Thank you, Chief Pathkiller."

There was a moment of silence as the chief fixed his attention on the baby. Then he said, "Molly, I have a feeling about little John Ross."

Molly's brow furrowed slightly as she looked up at the chief. "What kind of feeling?"

"I believe your son will one day be a leader among the Cherokee people…an honorable and a gallant chief."

A smile spread over Molly's face. "Chief Pathkiller, this is amazing."

"What?"

"The same thoughts you just expressed were going through my mind when you came into the cabin. I know that one day John Ross will make Daniel and me very proud."

The midwives were smiling now, whispering to each other. When Molly and the chief looked at them, they stepped up close to the bed. Catana said, "We want you to know, Molly, that we agree with you and Chief Pathkiller. When little John Ross grows up, he is going to make us all very proud!"

Time passed.

On Sunday, May 10, 1801, Chief Pathkiller granted permission to missionary Edgar Sloan to preach to a crowd of Cherokees who desired to hear what "white man's Bible" had to say. The village shaman did not attend the service, and neither did about half the people of the village.

In the crowd was ten-year-old John Ross, who always dressed in the buckskin clothing of his Cherokee people. He was sitting on the ground close to his parents, who had his seven-year-old brother, Lewis, between them. Sitting beside young John was his friend Sequoyah, the man he admired most after his father.

Sequoyah was now twenty-eight years old, and just the month before, the authorities of the Cherokee nation had made him a Cherokee chief.

Edgar Sloan read many Scriptures to the people from his English Bible, then translated them into Cherokee. In the Cherokee language, he told them of God's Son, the Lord Jesus Christ, coming to earth many years ago to pay the price for the sins of mankind in His death, burial, and resurrection.

The Indian people sat quietly as they listened to this white man. Some just shook their heads in disbelief, thinking of the teachings of their shaman, but others were fully absorbed in the news the missionary shared with them.

Sloan carefully went over the gospel message, explaining that we have all sinned against God and that the penalty for our sin is death. He then told his listeners that repentance is sorrow for sin and a change of mind that results in a change of direction. They must change their mind about their sin and their man-made religion and turn to Jesus to save them.

"I know that to most of you, this is all new. But if you will give the Lord the opportunity to speak to you in your hearts, His Holy Spirit will convince you that it is true. I have already been told by Chief Pathkiller that I can return and speak to you again. I want you to think about what you have heard, and I will be back in two days and help those of you who wish to receive the Lord Jesus Christ into your hearts as your Saviour. Of course, if any of you feel you are ready today, come to me after the service."

Tears of compassion were in Edgar Sloan's eyes as he said, "Let me tell you a story from the Bible and give you one more verse before I finish my message."

The Cherokees listened intently as Sloan told them the story of the woman at the well in Samaria, and how she believed in Jesus and her sins were forgiven. Then she went and told the people in her town about Him.

Sloan ran his gaze over the faces of the people and said, "Many of the Samaritans came to Jesus because of the woman's testimony and believed in Him. The Holy Spirit had convinced them that Jesus was the only one who could save them from dying in their sins and facing the wrath of God. After they became believers, they said to the woman, 'Now we believe, not because of thy saying: for we have heard him ourselves, and know that this is indeed the Christ, the Saviour of the world.'

"You are part of this world. The only one who can save you is Jesus Christ, the Saviour of the world."

Edgar Sloan closed in prayer, asking the Lord to show them their need to know Jesus.

When the service was over, John Ross accompanied Chief Sequoyah, who went to the missionary and said in English, "Sir, I have heard things today from your Bible that I had never heard before. May I tell you something?"

Sloan smiled, glanced at the ten-year-old, fair-skinned boy in Cherokee attire, then looked back at Sequoyah. "Of course."

Sequoyah said that he planned to one day develop a system of writing for the Cherokee people because he believed that increased knowledge would help them maintain their independence from white man's government.

Sloan nodded. "I cannot blame you and your people for wanting to remain independent. It is only natural. I hope you'll be able to accomplish your desire to produce a system of writing for your nation."

Sequoyah looked at the Bible in Sloan's hand and said, "Another thing...when I have developed the writing system, I want to translate the Bible into the Cherokee language so my people can read it for themselves."

"That would be wonderful. Where did you learn to speak English?"

"From another missionary who spent some time here in the Smoky Mountains when I was living in another village. He taught me well."

"I should say he did."

"He taught me much from the Bible, but you still brought out things today that I had never heard before. I will be listening for more when you come back."

Sloan smiled. "Good. And young man, I sincerely hope you'll accomplish your desire to translate the Bible into the Cherokee language."

As Chief Sequoyah and John Ross walked back toward John's parents, John said, "Sequoyah, when I grow up I want to do all I can for the Cherokee people, too."

Sequoyah set kind eyes on him. "John, I have no doubt that you will one day become a chief."

John looked at him incredulously. "But I'm only a quarter Cherokee, and I have white skin, straw-colored hair, and blue eyes. Are you saying that I could still be a Cherokee chief?"

"You are a good boy, John Ross, and you have shown everyone

in our village that you are *all* Indian in your heart. Yes, I know you can become a Cherokee chief, and I am sure you will."

A smile lit up the boy's face. "Well, Sequoyah, nothing could make me prouder than to be a chief in the Cherokee nation."

John's parents heard their son's words to Sequoyah and smiled at each other. Then Molly said, "John, I have never told you what Chief Pathkiller said to me on the day you were born."

"What did he say?"

She then told John the words Chief Pathkiller had spoken at her bedside about his feeling that one day her baby boy would become a leader among the Cherokee people…an honorable and gallant chief.

John's eyes were wide. "Chief Pathkiller really said that, Mother?"

"Yes, he did."

Daniel stepped up and placed a hand on John's shoulder. "Chief Pathkiller said those words to me also, son, when I came home with Sequoyah, who rode to Whittier to tell me you had been born. The *exact* same words."

John's chest swelled up and his eyes sparkled. "I sure hope he's right!"

Daniel patted his oldest son on the back. "I have no doubt that Chief Pathkiller is right. Though you are still very young, there are certain qualities about you that indicate you have what it takes to be a leader."

John ran his gaze between his mother and father. "If…if I become a chief, will I have to go by my Cherokee name?"

Daniel looked to Sequoyah for an answer.

"As a Cherokee chief, I can tell you that if you want to be

known as Chief John Ross, it will be all right," Sequoyah said.

John turned and smiled at his father. "I'm glad, because I want to honor you, Father, by keeping your last name."

Tears misted Molly's eyes, and Daniel gave John a big hug.

two

n that same Sunday, May 10, 1801, in Gatlinburg, Tennessee, near the base of the Appalachian Mountains, Dale Muller and his wife, Betty, along with their little daughter, Rosie, were having Sunday dinner in the home of their close friends, Guy and Clara Evans.

Little blond, blue-eyed Rosie was seated in a highchair next to her mother, who was feeding her while attempting to eat her own meal.

Clara brought up how much she enjoyed the male quartet that sang in the church service that morning, and the others agreed that the quartet was excellent.

"And wasn't that a great sermon the pastor preached this morning?" Dale said.

"He brought out things about Jesus' death on the cross that I had never realized," Guy said.

"Tremendous truths," said Betty, giving little Rosie a drink of water.

There were a few seconds of silence as the adults and little Rosie enjoyed their food, then Dale said, "Guy…Clara…you remember that Betty and I told you we're both from Whittier, North Carolina."

Clara nodded, and Guy said, "We've never been on that side of the mountains, but didn't you say Whittier is about thirty miles from here?"

"That's right. We wanted to tell you that we're going to take little Rosie to Whittier so she can celebrate her first birthday with both sets of grandparents this coming Thursday. We'll go over the day before."

Clara reached over and patted Rosie's chubby cheek. "I'm so glad Rosie will get to be with her grandparents when she turns one year old."

Guy looked at the baby with an admiring gaze. "I just love her pretty hair and those big blue eyes. It just doesn't seem possible this sweet baby could be a year old already."

As the meal progressed, Guy said, "You know, thinking about you traveling over the mountains, I've always been impressed with the Appalachian and Smoky Mountain ranges."

"We've crossed them many times since we moved over here," Dale said, "and I never cease to be amazed at their beauty and at the wildlife in those mountains. All kinds of birds and rabbits and other little furry creatures, plus brown bears and black bears, and

lots of deer. The deer supply the Cherokee Indians in those mountains with plenty of buckskin for their clothing."

Guy chuckled. "And plenty of venison, too!"

"Yes, that also! Actually," Dale added, "there are more deer in
the Appalachians than in the Smokies."

"Oh? I wasn't aware of that."

"That's why many of the Cherokees who live in the Smokies
go deer hunting in the Appalachians."

"Makes sense." Guy paused, then said, "Dale, I've heard that
people crossing over the mountains have sometimes had encoun-
ters with bears. Some travelers have even been attacked by them."

Dale took a sip of hot coffee and set his cup down. "I know it's
happened, but only when the mama bears have felt that their cubs
were in some kind of danger. Such incidents are quite rare, but like
always, when we make this trip over the mountains, I'll be carrying
my rifle in the wagon just in case."

"I'm so glad there's no danger of attack from the Cherokee
Indians who live in those mountains," Betty said. "The Cherokees
are different than the savage Apaches, Cheyennes, Sioux, and those
other tribes out West."

"The Cherokees are peaceable," Dale said, "even though many
years ago our government drove them from the lowlands and
made them live in the Smokies and the Appalachians."

"I marvel at how peaceable they are toward white people,"
Guy said, "especially since they aren't even allowed to come out of
the mountains and enter any of the towns on either side of them."

While Clara, Guy, and Dale discussed the Cherokees, Betty
was busy ladling more creamy mashed potatoes into Rosie's
mouth. Smacking her rose-bud lips, the baby opened her mouth
wide, waiting for more.

Betty crinkled her nose at Rosie and whispered, "You're eating your potatoes faster than I can spoon them in."

The others watched bemused as Betty took a cloth and wiped the baby's potato-smeared face. Rosie giggled and pointed a chubby finger at the mound of potatoes on her mother's plate.

Betty chuckled. "Okay, sweetie, just give Mommy a minute."

Betty popped a spoonful into her own mouth as Rosie watched, then Rosie pointed again at her mother's plate.

"Well, I guess this is one way to stay thin," Betty said. "This little girl wants everything on my plate!"

Clara, Guy, and Dale laughed. Rosie clapped her hands and reached again for her favorite food.

Soon the baby was full and satisfied, and Betty saw a familiar sleepy look come into Rosie's eyes. Betty lifted the baby from the highchair and gathered her close to her heart. "Please excuse me. Rosie is about to take a nap. She's finally got a full tummy, and sleepy time has claimed her."

Clara stood up. "Let's take her to the first bedroom down the hall. The bed in there is large enough that she won't be falling off of it in her sleep."

As Clara led the way from the kitchen, the little girl laid her head on her mother's shoulder, popped her thumb into her mouth, and closed her eyes.

After Rosie, who was already fast asleep, had been placed on the bed, Clara looked down at her and a yearning look crossed her face. When she saw that Betty noticed, she said softly, "One day, the Lord willing, I'll be putting our little one to bed. I sure hope it will be soon."

Betty smiled. "When it's God's time, He'll make it so you can tell Guy he's going to be a father."

Clara took hold of Betty's hand as they headed for the bedroom door, and whispered, "I can hardly wait!"

When the two women returned to the kitchen, the men were already eating the apple pie Clara had left on the cupboard. Guy had placed pieces of pie on small plates at their places.

As the women joined the men for dessert, Clara ran her gaze to Dale and Betty and said, "Speaking of Rosie having her first birthday, you two will be celebrating your first birthday soon…your *spiritual* birthday! How well I remember. It was June 8 last year when you came to church and went forward to receive the Lord Jesus as your Saviour."

"How wonderful our lives have been since we were born again," Dale said, "born into the family of God! We both have the peace of knowing that whenever the time comes for us to leave this life, we'll be in heaven forever with Him."

"I know we have thanked both of you many times for witnessing to us and inviting us to come to church," Betty said, "but we want to thank you again. What a blessing you've been in our lives."

"The pleasure is ours," Guy said.

Soon dinner was over, and after Guy and Dale helped their wives clean up the kitchen, the four of them went to the parlor. The Evanses sat on a small sofa facing the Mullers, who were on a matching sofa.

Dale looked at Guy. "When I mentioned the pastor's sermon a while ago, you said he had pointed out things about Jesus' death on the cross that you had never realized. What jolted me was what it says in that verse in 2 Corinthians chapter five."

Dale picked up a Bible that lay on a small table next to the sofa. He flipped to the chapter he had just mentioned and ran his finger down the page.

"Here. Verse twenty-one, where it tells what the Father had done: 'For he hath made him to be sin for us, who knew no sin; that we might be made the righteousness of God in him.' Just think of that! Jesus had to become *sin* on the cross so we guilty sinners might be made righteous. Oh, I'm so glad when I opened my heart to Him, He made me righteous before His Father. I could never do it myself."

"When Pastor Wilson first read that verse," Betty said, "and I saw that the Father made Jesus become *sin*, it boggled my mind. It helped when he told us we must take this by faith because our finite minds could never grasp it."

"Yes," Guy said. "Somehow, for that powerful moment on the cross, Jesus was *sin*! Since He never sinned, no wonder he cried out in Gethsemane for the cup to be removed."

"Praise His name," Clara said as tears filmed her eyes.

Betty was dabbing at her cheeks with a handkerchief she had pulled from the sleeve of her dress. She sniffed and said, "What a wonderful Saviour! What a wonderful Saviour! Thank You, Lord Jesus. Thank You for Your great love for us."

Even the men were wiping tears. "Let's have a word of prayer together before Betty and I have to head for home," Dale said. "I've got some cows to milk and some other chores to do before we go to the service this evening."

"How about you lead us?" Guy said.

"All right. It will be my pleasure."

Tears were still flowing when Dale closed his prayer of praise and thanksgiving, and all four were wiping their faces.

At that moment, they all heard Rosie making noises. Betty rose to her feet and said, "I'll go get her. Be right back."

When Betty entered the bedroom, Rosie was sitting up, yawning, and rubbing her eyes. Her face beamed as she looked at her mother and raised her arms.

Betty picked her up, snuggled her close, and enjoyed the sweet baby smell. *I love these moments,* she thought, and kissed Rosie's downy blond curls. "Okay, pumpkin, it's time we head for home."

Rosie giggled and clapped her pudgy hands together.

When Betty stepped into the hallway, she saw Dale and the Evanses standing near the front door of the house, watching her and Rosie coming toward them.

Rosie squealed when she saw her father and held out her arms toward him. Dale took her and kissed her cheek. "Well, sweet stuff, it's time to go home."

Guy stepped up, smiling. "How about a kiss from Uncle Guy, Rosie?"

The baby giggled and reached for him. Guy took her in his arms, kissed her cheeks three times, then handed her to Clara, who snuggled her and kissed her and handed her back to Dale.

Guy and Clara followed the Mullers outside to their wagon. Dale used his free hand to help Betty climb onto the wagon seat, then handed Rosie to her. He made his way around the team to the other side of the wagon and climbed up on the driver's seat.

"Thanks for the great meal," he said, smiling at their friends. "We'll see you at church this evening."

Clara waved. "Bye-bye, Rosie!"

The baby giggled and waved.

"We love you both so much," Betty said.

"That goes both ways," Guy said. "See you this evening."

⁓

On Tuesday morning, May 12, in Bryson City, North Carolina, seventeen-year-old Jack Zobel and his closest friend, Wally Hopper, mounted their horses in front of Jack's home. Jack's father, Weldon, was standing on the front porch of the house and called out, "Where you boy's going?"

"Just takin' a little ride, Pa," Jack said.

Weldon frowned. "A ride to *where*?"

"Oh, just into the country a ways. We'll be back in a couple of hours."

Weldon nodded. "Just don't get into any kind of trouble."

Wally grinned. " *Us* get into trouble, Mr. Zobel? How can you even think that?"

Weldon made a mock scowl and laughed. "'Cause I know that boy of mine!"

"Well, I'll make sure he's a good boy and stays out of trouble, sir," Wally said.

The boys rode away, and Weldon Zobel shook his head, grinning.

As the two friends rode eastward out of town, Wally said, "You still want to ride up there into Indian territory, Jack?"

"You bet. I want to see what it looks like where those Cherokees live. I mean, more than just ride up to the base of the mountains and look into the woods like we've done a million times. I want to ride into the mountains and get a good gander at Cherokee land."

"You'd better be glad the Cherokees ain't like those wild redskins out West. We'd lose our scalps if the Cherokees were like that."

Jack grinned at his friend. "I plan to keep my hair."

―ᦆ―

At the same time Wally Hopper and Jack Zobel were riding toward the Smoky Mountains, four teenage boys—Shoro, Yonwi, Coya, and Chula—were leading their bridled horses through the Cherokee village headed by Chief Bando. Each one carried his bow in hand and wore a tubular pack on his back that held several arrows.

The boys mounted up at the edge of the village just as Chief Bando and two other Cherokee men came riding into the village toward them. Bando wore his full chief's headdress, and the other men had their headbands on, each sporting an eagle feather on the back side that pointed straight up. The chief raised a hand for the boys to stop.

"Where are you boys going?" Chief Bando asked.

"We're going rabbit hunting in the forest down that way," Shoro replied, pointing southward. "We always find rabbits there."

The chief nodded with a smile. "I wish I could go with you. I hope you come home with lots of rabbits."

Yonwi waved his bow. "We will bring some to you, Chief."

The chief laughed. "I will accept them only if your parents get a large number first."

"We will do our best," Shoro said.

The chief nodded, and the boys rode around the three men and headed south.

Some two hours later, they came to an area where they had often found rabbits, and they slid off the bare backs of their horses. The forest was heavy with tall red spruce trees. Among the spruce were also silver bell and yellow birch trees. Long chains of mountain peaks stretched to the northeast and the southwest, all clad with heavy timber.

As the boys were tying the reins of their horses to the slender trunks of the silver bell trees, Jack Zobel and Wally Hopper were leading their horses through the forest close by. Suddenly Jack stopped and said in a hushed voice, "Hey, Wally! Look! Indians!"

Wally quickly brought his horse to a halt and looked in the direction Jack was pointing. "Looks like they're goin' huntin'."

"Uh-huh. Let's go over here into the shade so they don't spot us."

Even as Jack spoke, each of the Cherokee boys took an arrow from his pack and strung it in his bow, then headed into the dense forest.

"Hey, I've got an idea," Jack said in a half-whisper. "Let's take one of those Indians' horses into town."

"What for?" Wally said.

"Well, just maybe they'll track us and come lookin' for the horse and get into trouble for enterin' Bryson City. You'd like to see 'em get into trouble, wouldn't you?"

"Yeah, I'd love to see those pesky redskins get into trouble. Let's do it!"

The four Cherokee boys were almost out of sight from their horses when Shoro happened to glance back and caught sight of the two boys untying the reins of Yonwi's bay gelding. Eyes wide, Shoro stopped and said in a low voice, "Yonwi, look! Those white boys are stealing your horse!"

Yonwi looked just as the two boys were leading his bay gelding away. He scowled and let out an angry groan. "Let's stop them! We have weapons!"

They dashed toward the spot where Jack and Wally were mounting their horses. Wally had the reins of Yonwi's horse in his hand when he settled in the saddle. As he looked back at the bay, he saw the four young Indians running through the forest toward them, waving their bows and shouting for them to stop.

"Let's get out of here!" Jack said.

They spurred their horses and galloped toward town with Yonwi's horse trailing behind them.

"You will ride on my horse with me, Yonwi!" Shoro said. "We must catch them!"

The Cherokee boys ran hard to their horses, mounted up, and with Yonwi riding double with Shoro, they galloped after the thieves.

The white boys had a good head start, however, and though the Indians kept them in sight, they were unable to catch up to them. Soon Bryson City came into view, and the galloping Indians watched helplessly as the white boys rode into town a mile ahead of them.

Soon the thieves passed from view, and Shoro signaled for Coya and Chula to stop. Even as he gave the signal, Shoro pulled rein, and all three horses skidded to a halt.

Yonwi gripped Shoro's biceps from behind and said, "We must go and get my horse back!"

"I was about to say the same thing," Shoro said. "I wanted to see if we are in agreement."

Coya shook his head, his eyes bulging with fear. "No! We cannot go into the town!"

"But those thieving white boys should not have stolen Yonwi's horse!" Chula said. "We must go after them and get the horse back."

"No matter what the white men's law says about Indians never entering their towns," Shoro said, "we would not have to go in there if those white boys had not stolen Yonwi's horse."

The fear in Coya's eyes had been replaced by fury. He nodded stiffly. "Let's go get Yonwi's horse back."

The Cherokee boys put the three horses to a gallop and headed for Bryson City.

ack Zobel and Wally Hopper
slowed their horses to a walk
on Main Street, and Wally
said, "We should stop and tie the Indian's
horse to one of the hitch rails. It's best we
don't take the horse to either of our homes.
That would just get us in trouble with our
parents."

Jack nodded. "Yeah, I'm already living on
the edge. You heard what my pa said about
me tending to get in trouble. And since you
told him you'd make sure I was a good boy
and stayed out of trouble…you'd be in real
trouble, too. My pa would tell your pa, and
you'd get a good whippin'."

"Yeah. Don't want that," said Wally as he aimed his horse toward an unoccupied hitch rail in front of the town's hardware store.

Wally drew rein, dismounted, and ran his gaze up and down the boardwalk to see if anyone was watching.

"Be quick about it, Wally," Jack said. "Nobody's lookin' at us at the moment."

Wally tied the barebacked bay gelding to the hitch rail and mounted up.

"Let's ride down by the marshal's office, get off our horses, and see if those Indians show up," Jack said. "If they do, we'll run in and tell Marshal Stuart there are Indians in town."

Wally chuckled as they trotted their horses down the street. "Yeah. And if anybody did notice us leave the Indian's horse at the hitch rail, we just found him wanderin' alone at the north edge of town and brought him in so whoever owns him could find him. We sure didn't know he was some Indian's horse."

At the same time Jack and Wally pulled up to the hitch rail in front of the town marshal's office a half-block from where they had left the bay gelding, Shoro, Coya, and Chula rode their horses slowly into Bryson City with Yonwi riding double on Shoro's horse. They did not see the two horse thieves down the street, but had their eyes on the townspeople along the boardwalks, in buggies and wagons, and on horseback who were looking at them in disgust.

Abruptly, Shoro pointed ahead and said, "Look, Yonwi! There's your horse tied to that hitch rail."

Yonwi looked past Shoro's shoulder and saw his horse at the

hitch rail. "Hurry! I will get on him, and we can ride out of town fast!"

When Jack and Wally dismounted at the hitch rail in front of the town marshal's office, they stayed close to their horses and peeked around them, looking back where they had left the stolen horse.

"Well, lookee there, Jack," Wally said. "See 'em?"

"Yeah, I see 'em. They really are brazen, aren't they? Just ride into a white man's town like there wasn't no law against it. You watch 'em. I'll go tell the marshal before they have a chance to get away."

Marshal Hal Stuart was at his desk, going over some papers, when the door of his office burst open, and Jack Zobel appeared, his eyes wide.

"You look a bit shaken, Jack," he said. "What's going on?"

"Marshal Stuart, there are four Indians in town!"

Stuart leaped to his feet. "Where are they?"

"Down Main Street in front of the hardware store! Wally's out there watchin' 'em to make sure they don't leave before you can arrest 'em!"

The marshal put on his hat and bolted toward the door, whipping his revolver from the holster. Jack was on his heels.

When they stepped off the boardwalk, Wally looked at them and said, "They're still there, but one of 'em's untyin' that bay horse you and I found at the edge of town, Jack."

The marshal had his eyes fixed on the four Cherokee boys. "You two found that bay and tied it there?"

"Yes, sir," Jack said. "We were ridin' out on the north edge of town, and found the bay. We brought him in and tied him there in plain sight so his owner could spot him."

"Okay, you boys go to the army office down the street and tell the soldiers that Indians have dared come into town. I'll have 'em at gunpoint. Hurry!"

In front of the hardware store, Yonwi swung aboard his bay gelding, patted the horse's neck, and said, "I sure am glad to get you back, boy."

Shoro tightened his reins. "Let's go!"

Suddenly a sharp voice cut the air behind them. "You ain't going nowhere! Get off those horses!"

All four looked around to see a short, stocky man with a silver mustache that matched what hair they could see under his hat. A badge on his vest reflected the bright sunlight. He had his revolver cocked and held it steadily on them.

"I said get off those horses! You *do* understand English, don't you?"

Shoro met the marshal's hard gaze. "We do, sir. There were two white boys about our age who stole this bay gelding in a forest at the south edge of our mountains. We saw them do it. The horse belongs to our friend, Yonwi, here. We followed them and found Yonwi's horse tied to this hitch rail."

"You know there's a law against Indians entering white men's towns, don't you?" Marshal Stuart said.

"Yes, sir," Shoro said. "We only wanted to get Yonwi's horse back. We did not mean to cause trouble. We—"

"Shut your mouth, Indian! I want all four of you on the ground right now! Get off those horses!"

As the four boys slid off the horses, they noted that a crowd was gathering nearby, looking on, and some were pointing at eight men in army uniforms coming up the street on foot. Seven of them carried rifles. The eighth was an officer who wore a holstered revolver. Jack Zobel and Wally Hopper were with them.

The Indian boys exchanged glances, and all four faces showed the shadow of fear and uncertainty.

The marshal saw it and said, "Don't move, boys."

As the soldiers and the two teenage boys drew up, the captain ran his gaze over the Indian faces and ordered his men to confiscate the boys' bows and arrows. The boys gave them up silently.

Shoro struggled to keep his temper in check as he looked at the captain. "May I speak?"

"My name is Captain Ronald Barry! Try asking your question again."

Shoro swallowed hard. "May I speak, please, Captain Ronald Barry?"

"All right. Speak."

Keeping his voice soft, Shoro told the captain what happened in the Smoky Mountain forest earlier, explaining how they followed the white boys hoping to get Yonwi's bay gelding back.

When the captain and the town marshal looked at the two white boys, Jack's face flushed and he shouted, "He's lyin', I tell you! We found that horse at the edge of town and figured he belonged to someone in town. So we brought him in and tied him here at this hitch rail so the owners could find him."

"That's right!" Wally said. "These redskins are lyin'! You know how Indians are!"

"Captain Ronald Barry," Yonwi said, "if you will come to our village and ask Chief Bando whether the bay horse is mine or not, he will settle this matter. Would you do this, please?"

The captain looked at Marshal Stuart. "My men and I will

take these Cherokee boys to their village and see what the chief tells us. But even if this *is* his horse, they had no business coming into Bryson City. They must be punished."

The town marshal nodded and gave the Cherokee boys a stern look. "You're right, Captain. They broke the law, and the best thing to do is to have their chief see that they are punished."

Late that afternoon, at the village led by Chief Bando, the chief was talking in front of his cabin with ten men who were planning to go into the Appalachian Mountains to hunt for deer. The band of hunters were led by the chief's younger brother, Aluski, who was telling Bando that he planned to leave with his men at sunrise.

Suddenly, one of the village men came running up, breathing hard. "Chief Bando!" he gasped. "White soldiers have come into the village. They have four of our boys in custody!"

Bando's features tightened. "Four boys of *our* village, Nadani?"

"Yes. Shoro, Yonwi, Coya, and Chula."

"Why are they in custody?"

"I do not know," Nadani said, "but their bows and arrows have been taken from them. I told the soldiers I would come and get you."

Bando sighed. "All right. Let us go to them."

The hunters followed the chief and Nadani as they moved hastily toward the center of the village, where they saw the four boys on their horses and eight mounted United States army soldiers. One of the soldiers had the boys' four bows and arrow packs tied behind his saddle.

A great number of village people—adults and children—were gathering around, looking on.

When Chief Bando drew up, he noted that the soldier on the lead horse had captain's bars on the shoulders of his uniform coat. "Captain," he said, "I am Chief Bando."

The captain dismounted, with a grim countenance. "Chief Bando, I am Captain Ronald Barry. These four boys dared to enter Bryson City. When the town marshal arrested them, they told him a contrived story about two white boys having stolen this bay from a forest at the south edge of the mountains. They said they followed the white boys as they took the stolen bay into Bryson City, where they tied it to a hitch rail."

The chief set his gaze on the four boys. "Is this true?"

"Yes," Yonwi said. "We were deep in the woods, hunting rabbits, and we saw two white boys steal my horse. We followed them to Bryson City, intending to get my horse back, and we found him tied to a hitch rail. The boys had left him there."

"Chief, Yonwi said you would verify that the bay he is sitting on belongs to him," Captain Barry said. "Is this so?"

Chief Bando jutted his jaw. "It most certainly is. And what you called a contrived story is true."

Barry's features flushed.

"The only reason Shoro, Coya, Chula, and I went into Bryson City was to try to get my horse back," Yonwi said.

Only seconds before, the fathers of the four boys arrived on the scene, having been told by people of the village what was happening.

Yonwi's father, Degano, having heard his son's words, stepped up to where Yonwi sat his horse and said, "Son, even though your horse was stolen, the four of you knew you were breaking white man's law to enter the town. You should have come back to the village and reported the theft to me and to Chief Bando. You boys did wrong to enter the town."

The fathers of the other three boys spoke their agreement.

Captain Barry gave Chief Bando a solemn look. "Chief, these boys must be made to understand that under no circumstances are Indians allowed to leave the mountains and enter the white men's cities or towns in North Carolina or Tennessee."

Chief Bando nodded. "I assure you, Captain Barry, that the boys have been taught correctly, and they will be disciplined by their fathers for their disobedience. I would like to add that those white boys should be disciplined, also."

"I am satisfied with what you just told me, Chief Bando," Captain Barry said. "We will return the bows and arrows to these boys, and be on our way."

Chief Bando headed back to his cabin, planning to tell his wife, Nevarra, about the four boys being arrested by the soldiers in Bryson City. She was not there.

With his heart heavy, he left the cabin and walked outside the village to the burial ground, located above the village on a plateau and surrounded by a forest of red spruce trees.

As Bando entered the burial ground, he saw Nevarra kneeling alone beside the grave of their baby daughter, Haylee, who had died from a fever at two years of age less than a month ago. Nevarra's head was bowed low, and both of her hands were caressing the small mound of earth. Her back was toward Bando, and she was unaware of his presence. Bando stopped a few steps away.

Tears slipped from Nevarra's eyes and fell unchecked on the soft earth. Her heart was breaking within her as she remembered her little girl. "Oh, what joy you brought into our home. I miss your happy laughter and your chatter. What will I ever do without you, my sweet Haylee? I tried so hard to keep you alive. I'm so sorry I failed."

Bando slipped up quietly and placed his hands on her shoulders.

Nevarra sniffled, looked up at him, and palmed tears from her cheeks. As she started to rise, Bando took hold of her shoulders, drew her up on her feet, then wrapped his arms around her trembling body, letting her cry as he held her.

Speaking softly, Bando said, "My love, we both know that no one could ever take little Haylee's place. But one day we will have another child who will fill our hearts like Haylee did."

Nevarra nodded, trying to stop crying. When her tears were finally spent, she eased back in Bando's arms and looked up into his eyes, which were also filled with sadness and tears. "Yes, one day we will have another child. But Haylee will always have her special place in our hearts."

Bando sniffed. "Yes. Always."

The two held hands and walked slowly back toward the village. As they made their way along the path, Bando told Nevarra about the four boys who dared to enter Bryson City in an attempt to get a stolen horse back.

Nevarra looked up into Bando's eyes. "I do not like to hear that those boys went into the white man's town, no matter what the reason. White men have no mercy toward Indians who break their rules."

The four Indian boys led their horses as their fathers walked beside them, and the boys tried to persuade their fathers not to punish them.

The fathers reminded the boys that they knew the rules the white men had made about Indians entering their towns.

Degano set his dark eyes on Yonwi. "As I said, you should have come home and told me and Chief Bando that the white boys stole your horse. You should not have gone into Bryson City."

Stethan looked at his son. "Shoro, did you hear what Degano just said to Yonwi?"

"Yes, Father," Shoro said, looking at the ground.

"And what about you, Coya?" Tundo asked. "Did you hear what Degano just said?"

Coya cleared his throat. "Yes, Father."

"And you, Chula?" Keeno said. "Did you hear it?"

"Yes, sir."

Soon the boys and their fathers drew near their cabins in one section of the village.

Shoro looked at Yonwi and said, "I am sorry for what the white boys did to bring this trouble on us. If they had not stolen your horse, none of this would have happened. They are the ones who need to be punished."

Coya and Chula both spoke their agreement, showing their anger toward the white boys.

Stethan looked from boy to boy with solemn eyes. "The white boys did wrong in stealing the horse, yes, but the four of you still knew you should not go into the town. But you did it anyway. You must now be punished for your wrongdoing."

The boys and their fathers split up and headed toward their separate cabins.

When Degano and Yonwi entered their cabin, Yonwi's mother, Aneetla, was sitting at a small table near the front door. She glanced up and saw the look on her son's face. Then she set her eyes on her husband. "Degano, what we were told about Yonwi's horse being stolen and he and his friends going into Bryson City to get his horse back. Is it true?"

"Yes. And as I told Yonwi, he should have come back to the village and told Chief Bando and me about the horse being stolen. He and his friends did wrong to break white man's law. This has only added to the strain the Cherokees and the whites have between us."

Aneetla nodded. "But he *did* get his horse back, did he not?"

"Yes, he did." Degano drew a deep breath. "Now, I must punish Yonwi for entering the white man's town."

Aneetla wanted to plead with her husband not to punish their son, but she reminded herself that mothers in Indian families had no part in disciplining their children when the fathers were involved.

She rose from the chair and moved up close to Yonwi. "My son, I am glad you got your horse back. I am sorry the horse was stolen in the first place."

Yonwi met his mother's gaze. "Me too, Mother."

"Yonwi, you and I will go out behind the cabin now," Degano said.

Yonwi felt himself tighten with the fear of what was coming. "I hate all white men for coming to this country and treating us Indians as they have. I wish all white people would get sick and die!"

Degano looked at his wife, then took Yonwi by the arm and led him toward the back door. He paused long enough to take his leather strap from its hook on the wall, then ushered Yonwi outside, closing the door behind them.

Aneetla hugged herself and turned her back toward the rear of the house. Moments later, she wept as she heard the leather strap strike Yonwi's backside.

four

n Wednesday morning, May 13, Dale Muller was at the corral on his closest neighbor's farm, where Chester Uphoff was repairing a section of the fence one of his horses had damaged the day before.

"I hope little Rosie has a happy first birthday with both sets of her grandparents," Chester said, leaning against a fence post.

"Thanks, Chester, I'm sure she will," Dale said. "And thanks for offering to feed and water our livestock while we're gone."

"My pleasure, Dale. I've lost count of the times you've taken care of our animals when we've had to be gone. You and your family just have yourselves a wonderful time."

"We will," Dale said as he walked away. "See you when we get back."

Chester waved and went back to his task.

Hurrying across the fields, Dale moved onto his own property and headed to the barn. He harnessed up his two horses and hitched the team to the family wagon already loaded for their trip over the mountains to Whittier, North Carolina.

Less than half an hour later, Dale helped Betty onto the wagon seat while holding his little daughter in one arm. When Betty was settled on the seat, Dale placed Rosie into her arms, then went to the front porch and picked up two buckets that were full of water. He carried them to the horses and gave them both a good drink.

It was a glorious spring morning in Tennessee. The fragrant pink and white flowers on the dogwood trees were in full bloom, and a gentle breeze wafted their delightful scent on the air.

Little Rosie loved riding in the wagon, and sat on her mother's lap waiting excitedly for them to start moving.

Dale left the two buckets on the front porch, climbed up beside Betty and Rosie, and put the team in motion.

All three had been up since before daybreak, and Betty was hoping that Rosie would soon fall asleep. She crooned a soft lullaby, holding the baby close to her heart. Very soon, the motion of the wagon and Betty's soft singing worked their magic, and the wee one was fast asleep. Betty shifted Rosie in her arms to find a more comfortable position and settled back to enjoy the scenery.

"I always love this trip," she said in a quiet voice, turning to look at her husband.

Dale glanced at her and smiled. "I do, too."

Dale and Betty soon found themselves lost in their own wool-gathering and reveries as the miles slipped by.

Soon the Mullers were in the Appalachian Mountains, winding their way upward along the well-worn path that white people had traveled for many years through Indian country from one side of the Smoky and Appalachian Mountains to the other.

Both Dale and Betty drank in the clear blue sky; the reflection of the sunshine off rocky shelves; the mountaintops, thick with timber; the hemlock veils in the far ravines; and the fragrance of the red spruce.

Twice, white-tailed rabbits raced each other playfully across their path.

Betty spotted a fox chasing a raccoon, and when the two animals plunged into heavy brush, a wild turkey squawked and burst from the brush, flapping its wings.

It caught Dale's attention, and he said, "Honey, maybe that's why they call those creatures 'wildlife.'"

Betty smiled. "Could be. They fit the description, that's for sure."

As it was nearing noon, Dale said, "There's a creek just over that hill. How about we stop there for lunch? I can let the horses get a good drink while we're there."

When the wagon topped the crest of the hill, Dale and Betty saw the rushing, gurgling creek a few yards off to their right. Gleaming in the sunlight, the creek swung southward between red and yellow borders of Buckeye trees toward a wilderness of lofty mountain peaks.

When they reached the bottom of the hill, Dale guided the wagon to the edge of the creek, positioning the horses so they could drink.

Betty stood up with Rosie in her arms, kissed her cheek, and said, "Sweetie, Mommy's going to put you in your crib while she gets lunch ready."

Directly behind the seat, in the bed of the wagon, was Rosie's crib, which was securely attached to the floor. Betty placed Rosie in the crib and fastened the small strap around her.

Dale started to climb down from the wagon when suddenly his attention was drawn to movement on one of the steep hills they had just passed. He paused when he saw a black bear cub descending a steep, rocky path from the top of the hill.

"Honey, look there," he said without taking his eyes off the cub.

Betty turned and looked where Dale was pointing, when abruptly, another cub about the same size appeared from the brush at the top of the hill and started down the path behind the other one. The second cub stumbled, lost its footing, and plunged down the path. It plowed into the other cub, which frightened it and caused it to tumble head-over-heels. The cubs were entangled and rolling almost as one.

The first cub squealed, and when both bears reached the bottom of the hill, they slammed into a large rock. Both let out a loud wail.

"Poor little things," Betty said to Dale. "Maybe they're hurt."

Both cubs were still wailing as Dale's attention was once again drawn to the top of the hill. "There's nothing we can do for them, honey," he said. "Look!"

The black-furred mothers of the cubs had heard their wails and appeared side-by-side, looking down at their injured babies. Both mothers then put their attention on the humans in the wagon and rose to their hind feet, lifting their four hundred pounds to their full six-foot height, roaring loudly.

Dale took a sharp breath and looked at Betty. "Sit down, honey! Those bears think we had something to do with harming their cubs. We've got to get out of here!"

Just as Dale sat down and took hold of the reins, both mother bears charged down the steep path, their teeth exposed in vicious snarls.

Dale snapped the reins at the horses and got them turned around, but when the team saw the bears, they stiffened, bobbing their heads, and let out shrill whinnies. Dale picked up his rifle and said, "Hang on, honey! I'm going to get us back up on the road and put the horses in a gallop. Rosie's strapped in, isn't she?"

"Yes!" Betty's face was white with shock as she gaped in horror at the bears charging toward them. "Hurry, Dale! Hurry!"

By Wednesday afternoon, Aluski and the other nine hunters had done well in the Appalachian Mountains. They had killed eleven deer with their arrows, and were sure that Chief Bando would be pleased. The dead bucks were draped over the backs of the pack mules the Cherokees used on their hunting expeditions.

The hunters rode down out of the forest to follow the road to the Smoky Mountains and back to their village. They had been on the road only a few minutes when they topped a gentle rise, and Aluski saw an overturned wagon in a shallow ditch alongside the road.

"Look down there," Aluski said, pointing. "Someone may be hurt!"

The hunters put their horses and pack mules to a trot. When they drew closer, they saw the mauled bodies of a man and a woman lying next to the wagon, along with a dead black bear. Lying on the ground near the dead man was a rifle.

The Indians quickly dismounted. One of them pointed to the soft earth at the side of the road and said, "Aluski, two bears must have attacked these people. There are fresh bear tracks leading off toward the creek."

Aluski nodded. "Yes, there was another one, all right. The man was able to shoot this one, but the other bear killed him before he could use his gun on it."

Another hunter said, "The horses must have broken loose from the wagon and galloped away."

"Which caused the wagon to overturn," another said.

The Cherokee hunters were discussing the scene further when one of them lifted a palm toward the others. "What was that sound?"

"What sound?" Aluski said. "I did not hear anything."

"There it is again," said the first man. "It is a baby crying!"

"Yes!" said another, kneeling down beside the overturned vehicle. "There is a baby underneath the wagon!"

Together, the hunters grasped the wagon and tilted it up on its side. In the crib that was fastened to the floor was a blond baby girl. When she saw them, her terrified cries grew louder, her face red with fear and tears.

Aluski loosened the strap that held the baby in her crib and took her in his arms as she continued to wail. He caressed her little face, speaking softly to her.

After a few minutes, the baby's cries tapered off, and only a soft snuffle could be heard. She set her blue eyes on the strange man who held her and smiled at him, patting his dark face with a chubby hand.

"That is a good girl," said Aluski, returning her smile. "Now, what are we going to do with you?" As he spoke, he looked questioningly at the other men.

No one said anything.

Aluski cleared his throat. "Since we are not allowed to enter white men's towns or cities, we cannot take this baby to one and see if anybody knows her. All we can do is take her to our village."

The hunters looked at each other, then Aluski smiled. "I just thought of something. Perhaps my brother and Nevarra might take this baby into their home and raise her as their own."

One of the men nodded. "Chief Bando and Nevarra have grieved very much over their little girl's death. Having this white baby in their home may ease their grief and make them happy again."

"But first, we must bury the bodies of this little girl's parents," Aluski said. "We cannot leave them here for the wild animals to devour."

The Cherokee men traded off holding the little white girl while the others gathered rocks for the burial of her parents. The mangled bodies of Dale and Betty Muller were placed in a low spot in the nearby forest and covered with the rocks.

When the hunters were making ready to pull out, Aluski was holding the baby while he looked through the rubble where the wagon had crashed. He found a quilt and the small basket that held the lunch Betty had packed that morning.

Aluski pulled the quilt free and spread it out on the ground next to the damaged wagon. He placed the little girl in the middle of it, then picked up the lunch basket.

Little Rosie Muller clapped her hands and said, "Da-da…Ma-ma," giving Aluski a toothy grin.

Aluski reached into the basket, broke off a small piece of bread, and offered it to her. She took it and put it in her mouth and started chewing.

Aluski moved back to the wagon and picked up a canteen. He

removed the cap and poured some of the contents on the ground. The water was clear. He returned to the baby and placed the spout to her mouth and tilted it up slightly. Rosie sipped at it greedily, much of the water running down her chin.

Aluski then broke off another piece of bread and placed it in her hand. "Here is some more bread, little one. Eat it up."

The baby gladly accepted the bread. She gave Aluski another of her charming smiles, revealing four tiny teeth.

Aluski patted her blond head. "You will like your new home, little one, I promise. My brother and Nevarra will love you very much."

Soon, leading the burdened pack mules, the Cherokee hunters were riding toward the high peaks of the Appalachian Mountains to cross into North Carolina, descend into the lower elevations of the Great Smoky Mountains, and head for their village.

Riding in the lead, Aluski held the little girl in one arm, cuddling her close. She looked up at him often and chattered with sounds that frequently resembled words. He smiled down at her and said, "I wish I knew your name, little one. But when Bando and Nevarra take you to be their little girl, they will give you a new name. And something else—when you grow older and learn to talk, I want you to call me Uncle Aluski. All right?"

The baby gave him another charming smile and a slight burp.

Aluski chuckled. "Thank you. I will love being your Uncle Aluski."

At the same time Aluski and the other hunters were riding southward in the Appalachian Mountains, Yonwi and his friends Shoro, Coya, and Chula were hunting rabbits in the forest where they had been when Yonwi's horse had been stolen. They had already bagged five rabbits, and were eager for more. Each of them had an arrow strung in his bow, ready for any sign of another rabbit.

Dark clouds were gathering in the sky overhead. There were distant flickers of lightning to the east, and the wind was picking up.

Coya pointed toward the clouds and said, "Maybe we should head back to the village."

Shoro scanned the darkening sky. "It will be some time before the rain comes. We can keep hunting for a while, yet. Then we will take what rabbits we have and head for home."

Yonwi and Chula agreed.

The four boys talked about the punishment they received from their fathers for having gone into Bryson City to retrieve Yonwi's horse. They discovered that the other three had not been whipped as severely as had Yonwi. The welts on his back were still hurting.

The whole incident now fresh in his mind, Yonwi felt rage welling up inside him. "I wish I could have revenge on those two thieving white boys!" he said. "I would like to make them suffer for what they did!"

"Yonwi, you had best forget those white boys," Shoro said. "You are never going to see those two thieves again."

Yonwi thought about it briefly, then sighed. "You are right, Shoro. I will concentrate on hunting rabbits instead."

An hour later, there was lightning and thunder in the black sky overhead as the four boys were coming out of the forest, carrying a dozen dead rabbits. The rain had not yet begun to fall. They were about to mount their horses when they saw movement through the dense trees.

Coya took a sharp breath. "Yonwi, look! Do you see who those two riders are?"

Yonwi focused on the riders through the thick forest, but before he could speak, Shoro said in a half-whisper, "It is the two white thieves who stole your horse!"

Yonwi felt his blood heat up. "Yes, it *is* them! What are they doing on the road that leads up to the Cherokee villages?"

"I do not know, but they don't see us," Chula said.

Yonwi's eyes flashed as he looked at his friends. "I will now have my revenge!"

Shoro shook his head. "No, Yonwi! Leave them alone. It will only lead to more trouble."

Yonwi regarded him with wide eyes. "Shoro, they are on Cherokee property! They must be punished as we were for being on white man's property. I hate white people! Especially those two thieves!" He waved his bow and hissed, "I will take care of them by myself! You boys can wait here."

Lightning flashed above and thunder boomed. The black sky was beginning to sprinkle rain.

Yonwi ran through the dense forest, gripping his bow, which was already strung with an arrow. Yonwi's friends moved slowly toward the road, making sure to stay out of sight within the trees.

On the road, Jack Zobel and Wally Hopper were looking for shelter as the rain began to fall. The wind was growing more intense.

Suddenly two white daggers of lightning cracked overhead. Thunder like a giant bellow of rage shuddered the air. Bending his head against the wind-driven rain, Jack pointed to a heavy stand of trees a few yards from the edge of the road. Wally nodded.

Now the rain was drumming on the hard-packed road and on the foliage of the trees.

Yonwi drew up behind a thick-bodied red spruce. He had to wipe rain from his eyes in order to see clearly.

Just as Jack and Wally turned their horses to head for the stand of trees, a bolt of lightning lanced through Jack and his horse. There was a large puff of smoke, and horse and rider were flung to the ground. More smoke lifted from their bodies, but was soon extinguished by the driving rain.

Wally was terror-stricken by the sight of Jack and his horse lying dead on the ground. He put his horse to a gallop and rode for town in the driving rain.

Yonwi watched him go, then he wheeled about and ran back through the dripping forest to his friends. He was surprised to see them only a few yards from the edge of the road.

"Did you see that?" Yonwi said, gasping for breath.

All three nodded, and Shoro said, "That boy and his horse never knew what hit them."

The four boys hurried to where their horses were tied and their bundles of dead rabbits lay on the ground. They grabbed hold of the bundles and swung up on their horses.

Shoro looked at Yonwi, and said above a clap of thunder, "Are you satisfied that one of the thieves is dead, or are you going to try to find the other one and kill him?"

Yonwi shook his head. "I am not going after the other one. I still hate white people, but my revenge for the horse stealing is satisfied."

Together, the four boys galloped up the road toward their village with thunder and lightning filling the sky and the rain coming down hard.

five

y the time Shoro, Yonwi, Coya, and Chula drew near their village, the rain had stopped and the sky was clearing. Long shafts of golden sunlight shone down from the blue patches in contrast with the dark, drifting clouds.

With the village in sight, Shoro said to the others, "Our parents are going to be happy to see all these rabbits we've brought home."

"Yes," said Chula, "but I do not think we should mention seeing those two white boys who stole Yonwi's horse. I think it is best if we keep it between us about that white boy being killed by lightning."

Yonwi looked at Chula and nodded. "I agree. Let us just keep it between us."

Shoro adjusted his position on his horse's back. "I am glad all of you feel this way. As far as I am concerned, we never saw those white horse thieves today, so of course, we never saw the one who was struck by lightning."

Moments later, the boys rode into the village, and each headed for his own family's cabin.

Chief Bando entered his cabin and closed the door behind him. He heard a sniffling sound and quickly made his way to the bedroom at the rear of the cabin. Nevarra was face down on the bed, a small blanket pressed to her face, and quietly shedding tears. When she heard her husband's footsteps on the earthen floor, she looked up at him and broke into sobs.

Bando sat down on the bed. "I am so sorry our little girl is gone, Nevarra. You know I miss her, too, but I wish there was something I could do to help your heart not to hurt so much."

Nevarra sat up, and Bando folded her into his arms.

Nevarra clung to him and said, "My heart would not hurt at all if I had Haylee back."

He kissed her cheek. "But, my sweet wife, we both know we can never have her back. And as I have said many times since our precious daughter died, one day we will have another child."

Nevarra eased back in his arms and looked into his dark eyes.

"Yes, we will. And that will help ease this pain in my heart."

⤳

Aluski and the other hunters rode into the village with the pack mules carrying the eleven deer. Aluski still held the white girl in one arm.

People began to gather around, looking at the bucks draped over the backs of the mules. They commended the hunters for their success in bagging that many deer and asked them where they had found the little white girl.

Aluski told them how they had found her and about her parents being killed by the two black bears.

"What are you going to do with her?" one older man, who was standing near Aluski's horse, asked him.

"You all know that we cannot take her into any of the white men's towns to see if anyone knows her. Since this is true, she must stay here in the village." Aluski took a deep breath. "I am going to carry this little girl to my brother and his wife and see if they will take her into their home. I believe she would ease their loneliness and grief."

An older woman brushed gray hair back from her face and smiled. "You are right, Aluski. It would help Chief Bando and Nevarra if this little child lived with them."

Others spoke their agreement.

At the edge of the still growing crowd stood Yonwi, Shoro, Coya, and Chula. Shoro leaned close to Yonwi and whispered, "Are you going to be angry if Chief Bando and his wife take the little white girl into their home?"

They all looked at Yonwi as he whispered, "No, I will not be angry. The little white girl is just a baby. She could not help what happened to her parents, nor can she help that she is white."

"I will take the child to my brother's cabin," Aluski said to the other hunters. "I am sure some of the men here will help you skin the deer out and hang the meat up to cure."

Several men volunteered to help the hunters with the task. Aluski thanked them, then rode away slowly toward the chief's cabin, holding the girl in his arm.

He drew up in front of the cabin, slid off the horse's back, and looked into the baby's blue eyes. "I believe you are about to become a white Cherokee."

Rosie smiled at him and made a gurgling sound.

Aluski stepped up on the porch of the cabin and tapped on the door. "Bando? Nevarra? Are you in there?"

Aluski heard mocassined feet shuffling on the earthen floor.

"Yes, Aluski, we are here," Bando said as he opened the door. "Did you kill a lot of d—?" His eyes widened.

Nevarra was at her husband's side. Her own eyes were wide as she set them on the blond baby girl. "Al—Aluski," she stammered, "where…where did you get this child?"

Rosie was studying the new dark-skinned people while keeping one arm around Aluski's neck. Her right thumb was secure in her mouth as she stared at them.

Bando took a step back. "Please…please come in."

"Our hunting party brought home eleven deer," Aluski said as he stepped through the door with the child still clinging to his neck. "They are skinning them out right now."

Bando nodded. "That is good. But…but we are wondering why you have this little white child with you."

Aluski met his brother's gaze, then looked at Nevarra. "I have a story to tell you. May we sit down?"

"Of course," Nevarra said, moving toward three wooden chairs positioned in a semicircle nearby.

When they had sat down, Aluski held Rosie on his lap and told them the story of how he and the other hunters had found her.

The story touched Bando and Nevarra deeply, and it showed on their faces.

Nevarra rose from her chair. "Aluski, may I hold her?"

"Of course," he said, and handed the baby to her.

Nevarra sat down with the girl in her arms and kissed a chubby cheek. "You are very pretty, sweetheart."

Rosie smiled and made a tiny sound with her voice.

A tender look crept into Aluski's eyes as he said, "I thought since your little Haylee is gone, the two of you might want to take this girl into your family and raise her."

Tears misted Nevarra's eyes as she felt a prickling in her heart. Her chest was tight, her throat narrow. She placed her hands under the baby's arms and lifted her up so their faces were only inches apart.

Nevarra looked at her husband with longing in her eyes.

Bando's throat was constricted, but as he caressed the girl's head, he managed to say, "She is beautiful. I would like for us to do as Aluski has said."

Tears spilled down Nevarra's face. She hugged the baby close and said, "Oh, thank you, Bando! Thank you."

Bando caressed the baby's head again and said, "We must both thank Aluski. Thank you, my brother, for bringing her to us."

"How wonderful of you to do this for us," Nevarra said. A beautiful smile that had been absent since the death of little Haylee once again graced her countenance.

"Since we do not know the baby's name, she must be given one," Bando said, touching Nevarra's arm. "Would you like to do that?"

Nevarra nodded, still smiling. "I have already thought of a name." She hugged the girl, kissed a chubby cheek, and looked into her eyes. "I will name you *Naya.*"

"I like that name." Bando leaned close to the baby and kissed the same cheek. "Already I love you, little Naya."

The baby smiled and fondled Bando's nose.

"Nevarra, how old do you think Naya is?" Aluski said.

Still holding the baby so she could look into her face, Nevarra studied her for a moment. "I would say she has to be just about a year old."

"That is what I was thinking," Bando said. "So we will mark this day on white man's calendar as Naya's first birthday—May 13, 1801."

The next morning Chief Bando called a meeting of everyone in the village. When they were gathered in a large half-circle in the center of the village, Nevarra stood beside her husband, holding Naya in her arms.

Chief Bando told them that ever since Haylee had died, he and Nevarra had suffered much grief and loneliness. He then told them the story of the white girl, and he said that he and Nevarra were going to keep her and raise her as their own.

Many of the people had tears on their faces as they waved their arms and called out their agreement with what the chief and his wife were doing.

Chief Bando ran his gaze over the crowd and said, "Thank you. Since we do not know her name, Nevarra has given her a new name. She is now called Naya."

When Chief Bando dismissed the crowd, the Cherokees lined up to get a close look at Naya as they passed by.

Naya watched them with wide, thoughtful eyes. Seeing their smiles and hearing their cheerful voices, she smiled back at them, talking to them in her own gibberish.

The proud new parents beamed at the reception the people gave to their new daughter. Bando and Nevarra were touched by the understanding and the harmony of the village people concerning their adoption of the little white girl.

Naya soon settled into her new home and new way of life. Besides her parents, there was always someone close by willing to play with her and tend to her. She was a happy child, and returned the love that both Bando and Nevarra gave her.

In the days that followed, word spread among the other Cherokee villages in the Smoky Mountains about the violent death of the white couple and the miraculous way their one-year-old daughter was spared. The story was told how Chief Bando and his wife had taken the little white girl into their home to raise her as if she were their own.

Day after day, Cherokees from other villages came to see the fair-haired white girl and to commend Chief Bando and Nevarra for taking the child into their home.

On a warm May afternoon, after a long line of visitors had been there, Chief Bando and Nevarra were sitting in the shade of the tall trees that surrounded their cabin. Bando was holding Naya on his lap, talking to her, when Nevarra said, "Oh, look, Bando. Chief Pathkiller and Miklia are here!"

Bando looked up to see the chief and his wife riding together on Pathkiller's big black stallion. The chief and Miklia greeted people along the path that led to Bando's cabin, then both lifted a hand to wave when they spotted Bando and Nevarra sitting on a crude bench beneath the trees.

Bando and Nevarra rose to their feet and approached them as Pathkiller slid off the horse's back, then helped his wife down.

The new arrivals looked at the baby in Bando's arms and commented on how pretty she was.

Miklia held a cloth bag out to Nevarra. "This is a gift for your new baby. I understand you named her Naya."

Nevarra took the bag. "Thank you for the gift. Yes, her name is Naya."

Bando and Pathkiller shook hands, then Pathkiller pinched Naya's chubby cheek and said, "Hello, Naya. Welcome to Cherokee land."

Naya giggled and touched her cheek where Pathkiller had pinched her.

By this time, Nevarra had the little beaded buckskin dress out of the cloth bag. "Oh, Miklia, this is beautiful."

Miklia smiled. "I think it will fit her all right. I made it yesterday, after Pathkiller and I learned from others who had been here that she was one year old."

"Well, let us go in the cabin and put it on her. It looks like just the right size to me."

While the women and Naya were inside the cabin, Bando filled Pathkiller in on the details of the death of the baby's parents, and how Aluski and the other hunters had found the girl.

Soon the women returned, and Miklia was carrying Naya, who was wearing her new buckskin dress.

Pathkiller smiled admiringly. "It looks nice on her. Now, she looks a little bit like a Cherokee."

After a few minutes, Pathkiller said that he and Miklia needed to be going. Both Miklia and the chief kissed the baby, then Pathkiller helped his wife onto the black stallion's back before he also mounted.

Bando and Nevarra waved as Pathkiller and Miklia rode away, and Nevarra helped Naya wave to them, too.

Chief Pathkiller and his wife were just passing from sight when Bando and Nevarra saw Chief Sequoyah and his friend, ten-year-old John Ross, approaching on their horses from a different direction.

Bando and Nevarra welcomed them warmly, and were pleased when Sequoyah smiled and said, "You two have been blessed. She is such a pretty little girl. I am so glad you have taken this orphan into your family."

Bando's eyes glittered as he said, "Already, we love her so much."

John Ross, whose hair was almost the same color as Naya's, was clad in Indian buckskin as always. He stepped closer to the baby in Nevarra's arms and said, "One day when she grows up and learns what you two good-hearted people did for her, she will be just like me. Even though Naya is not part Cherokee as I am, she will still want to be thought of as *all Indian!*"

The adults laughed, then Chief Bando said, "John Ross, we are proud to consider you *all* Indian!"

The boy blushed and smiled. "Thank you, Chief Bando, for your kind words."

Chief Bando looked at Chief Sequoyah questioningly. "Are you still planning to develop a system of writing for the Cherokee people?"

"I am indeed. But I will not begin until I have prepared myself by studying the English alphabet and language so I can do a proper job with the Cherokee language."

Bando patted his shoulder. "Chief Sequoyah, you just stick to your plan. When you accomplish your goal, it will be a tremendous help to the Cherokee people to maintain their independence from the white people; especially their government."

Sequoyah nodded. "Thank you, Chief Bando. I am not going to let anything or anybody keep me from reaching my goal."

While Sequoyah and John Ross talked with Bando and Nevarra, a long line of other guests was forming.

Soon, Sequoyah and his young friend moved on.

Next in line were teenage boys Chula, Coya, and Shoro with their parents. They also made over the little white girl with smiles and kind words.

Just behind them were Yonwi and his parents. Knowing their son harbored ill feelings toward white people, Degano and Aneetla were pleased to hear Yonwi speak warmly to the white girl and to her new parents.

When they walked away, Degano put a hand on his son's shoulder and said, "Yonwi, I am glad that you seem to genuinely believe that it is good that Chief Bando and his wife have made a home for little Naya."

"I am glad, too, son," Aneetla said.

Yonwi nodded. "Though I still do not like white people, I do like Naya. She is an innocent child. It is not her fault that her relatives hate Indians, as did her ancestors. Now that she belongs to

Chief Bando and his wife, I will think of her as a full-blooded Cherokee."

At the close of the day, when Bando and Nevarra entered their cabin, they talked of how wonderful it was that the Cherokee people were so supportive of their adoption of Naya. They hugged and kissed the baby, who giggled and fully enjoyed their attention.

six

One chilly day in November of 1803, several younger teenage Cherokee boys and girls were gathered at the south edge of the forest just outside the village led by Chief Pathkiller.

The boys had been running races for nearly two hours along the edge of the forest, and the contest was now down to two semi-finalists: fourteen-year-old Landoni and thirteen-year-old John Ross. As the two boys took their places for the final race, the others waited breathlessly, ready to cheer them on.

Landoni and John Ross looked at each other and grinned, then took their stance.

A seventeen-year-old boy named Josho stepped up close to them, holding a fist-sized rock. "Ready?"

Both boys nodded, their eyes fixed on the fallen tree some fifty yards away, which was their turn-around point.

Josho tossed the rock in the air, and when it struck the ground, the two competitors took off, running as hard as they could. The others cheered and shouted as they watched Landoni and John Ross race toward the fallen tree.

John reached the turn-around first, wheeled about, and darted the other way, giving Landoni a big smile as they met and passed. John could hear his competitor behind him as he ran back to the finish line, but he was slowly putting more distance between them.

The shouts from the crowd were loud as John crossed the finish line some twenty feet ahead of Landoni.

Several of the teenagers rushed up to congratulate John, and others met Landoni when he crossed the finish line, congratulating him on taking second place.

Soon the young Cherokees headed for home, and just as they reached the center of the village, they saw a United States army unit riding in from the opposite direction. The soldiers were accompanied by three men in civilian clothing.

Other people in the village were gathering in a group on the path, ahead of the mounted men.

The officer in charge signaled for his men to halt, and the riders drew rein. Then the officer began pointing at different spots around the village as he talked to the three civilian men.

John Ross felt a grinding in his stomach. "I am going to tell Chief Pathkiller those white men are here," he said to the boys closest to him.

John dashed off, and in less than a minute, he stepped up on the porch of the chief's cabin and knocked on the door.

A few seconds later, the door came open, and Miklia smiled at him. "Hello, John Ross."

"Hello, ma'am. Is Chief Pathkiller here?"

"Yes, I am," came a husky reply, followed by the appearance of the chief. "What do you need to see me about?"

"An army unit just rode into the village," John said, pointing back toward the center of the village. "Three other white men are riding with them. The leading officer is telling the three white men something about the village."

A frown lined Chief Pathkiller's brow. He turned to Miklia. "I must go."

When Pathkiller and John Ross drew near the crowd of Cherokees, John saw that the officer in charge was still talking to the three civilians.

By this time, Chief Sequoyah had joined the crowd and moved up quickly to Chief Pathkiller. "I will go with you to talk to them."

Pathkiller nodded. "Come."

John Ross stayed with the two chiefs as they headed toward the mounted men.

When the three Indians drew up to the army unit, Chief Pathkiller set his eyes on the officer in charge and said, "I am Chief Pathkiller. Why are you here, looking at my village?"

The officer looked down at the chief for a brief moment, then dismounted. "Chief Pathkiller, I am Captain Leon Duggan from the army post at Forest City. These three men in civilian clothing are congressmen from Washington, D.C. They have been sent to this part of the country by President Thomas Jefferson to look over the areas the Cherokee Indians occupy in Georgia, Alabama, and

Tennessee, as well as here in the Smoky Mountains of North Carolina."

Making a half turn, Duggan pointed to the closest civilian and said, "Chief, this is Congressman Donald Wagner. The next gentleman is Congressman Charles Stoddart, and the third one is Congressman Reginald Smith."

The three congressmen nodded, each one touching his hat brim in a show of courtesy.

Chief Pathkiller nodded in return, then looked the captain in the eye and asked, "Why have these men from Washington City been sent by President Thomas Jefferson to look over our land?"

"Chief Pathkiller, have you heard of the Louisiana Purchase, which took place several months ago?"

"I have not."

Chief Sequoyah took a step closer to the captain, and John Ross moved up beside him. "Captain Duggan, I am Chief Sequoyah. I have heard of the Louisiana Purchase, but I do not know what it is."

Duggan forced a smile, glanced at the blond boy, then set his gaze on the two chiefs. "Well, let me explain it to both of you. In April of this year, the United States government purchased a vast section of land called Louisiana Territory from a European country called France, which has owned the land for a long time. Have you heard of France?"

"I have," Pathkiller said.

Sequoyah nodded. "So have I."

Duggan went on. "The southern portion of this land acquired in the Louisiana Purchase will soon have a large population of white people. President Jefferson and Congress are considering moving all Indian tribes from here in the southeastern states to a land far away in the western part of the country so there is room for the growing population of white people. If this happens, the government, of course, will see to it that you have a good place to live out west."

Sequoyah frowned at the white man. "Captain Duggan, I have obtained books that have helped me to know what has happened to Indians in the *northeast* states, especially the Delaware Indians."

Duggan's eyebrows arched.

Sequoyah went on. "I can see that the white man's dream of settling the Indian tribes somewhere far from the fertile lands in the East first became known when the white men made a treaty with the Delaware Indians in 1778. In the treaty, the Delawares were to one day head up a state in the far western part of the country composed of all other tribes. They would be rulers of all the other Indian tribes. Are you aware of this, Captain Duggan?"

The captain cleared his throat. "I...know about it, yes."

Sequoyah looked at the three congressmen. "You men know of this promise in the treaty?"

All three nodded.

Sequoyah gave them a thin smile. "Because of this promise, the Delawares fought alongside the Americans in the Revolutionary War against Great Britain. They trusted the Americans." Sequoyah squared his jaw. "When the Revolutionary War was over, the United States government broke their promise to the Delawares. They were told that they would not be rulers over any other Indian tribes. This broke the spirit of the Delawares. The government then decided to allow the Delawares and other tribes of the Northeast to remain in their previously appointed lands. After breaking their treaty, the white man's government at least let the Indians stay on their lands, where they had been since being forced to live there because the white men out-numbered them."

Congressman Smith cut in. "It is true, Chief Sequoyah, that the Indian tribes of the northeast did get to stay on their lands, but President Jefferson and Congress are seriously considering moving the great number of Indian tribes here in the southeast part of the country to someplace in the far west. They want the growing white population here to be able to live in any part of the land, including what the Indians now occupy."

Chief Pathkiller felt rage well up inside him. "It is bad enough," he said, "that many years ago when the white men—who certainly outnumbered the Cherokees—made them leave their homes and farms in the lowlands where their ancestors had been for so long, and live in the mountains. How much worse will it be to force us to make a wearisome journey to the western lands so far away?"

Congressman Smith wiped a hand over his mouth and fixed Pathkiller with piercing eyes. "Don't let your anger get the best of you, Chief. The United States government is strong and powerful. You must not resist anything the government tells you to do. If this plan goes through, the Cherokees and other tribes who are moved out west will have to obey the government, no matter how difficult the journey may be. If the Indians attempt to defy our government, they will be punished severely by the soldiers of the United States Army."

Thirteen-year-old John Ross moved a few inches in front of the two chiefs and said to Smith, "Sir, I realize that I am only a boy, but may I say something?"

Congressman Smith had barely noticed the boy. When he set his eyes on him, he said, "You're white! What are you doing living with the Cherokees?"

"Actually, Mr. Smith, I am a quarter Cherokee. And by my own choice, I will *always* live with the Cherokees. We often have white missionaries come here, and they teach us from white men's Bible. I have memorized some verses from it. One of them is this: 'And as ye would that men should do to you, do ye also to them likewise.' Why do white men like President Thomas Jefferson and the men of Congress and the army soldiers do things to us Indians that they would never want us to do to them? Would you want to be driven from your homes?"

Reginald Smith cleared his throat, glanced around at his fellow congressmen and the soldiers, then looked at Captain Duggan and said, "Captain, we've been here long enough. We really must move on. There is much more Cherokee land to see."

"You're right." Duggan mounted his horse, and without a further word to Chief Pathkiller, Chief Sequoyah, or John Ross, led the others as they rode away.

Sequoyah laid a hand on his young friend's shoulder and smiled. "John Ross, by quoting that Scripture, you stopped the mouths of those white men. One day when you are a Cherokee chief, you will be a great leader of our people."

Chief Pathkiller patted the boy's arm. "Yes, you will, John Ross."

John's face beamed as he ran his gaze between the two chiefs.

Pathkiller then headed toward the crowd of Cherokees who had been looking on out of earshot. Sequoyah and young John followed him. When they drew up to the crowd, Pathkiller told them what the white men had said.

This angered them and put stern looks on their faces, but when the chief told them what John Ross had said, it brought smiles.

One of the Indians, who had come to know Christ as his Saviour a few months previously, said, "Good for you, John Ross. The Word of God will silence them every time with its truth and power."

Other voices, male and female, concurred, and another man said, "You did well, John Ross. I am proud of you."

Sequoyah smiled as he said to the crowd, "It is my belief that someday John Ross will become a Cherokee chief, and that he will be a great leader of our people."

John blushed when the people spoke their wholehearted agreement.

One of the older men, whose name was Bahado, was standing beside his silver-haired wife. He set his weary eyes on Pathkiller. "Chief, do you really think the white men's government will force us to move to the west country?"

Pathkiller took a deep breath and let it out slowly. "Yes, Bahado, I do. Look what they have already done to us since they took over this country. They forced us to move from our homes in the lowland and to live here in the mountains. Now, they want to take *this* land from us. I am sure they will move us out to the west country so they can have this land."

Bahado rubbed his wrinkled chin. "How soon do you think this will happen?"

Pathkiller shook his head. "I have no idea."

"Chief...Bahado...I have long studied white man's ways," Sequoyah said. "This will not be done speedily. Their government leaders are quite slow about things like this. It will be many more years before it happens."

Bahado thought on Sequoyah's words, looked at his wife, then turned back to his chief and said, "Chief Pathkiller, it is my hope that both my wife and I will not be among the living when this horrible thing happens."

Six months passed. In Chief Bando's village on May 13, 1804, the chief and Nevarra were celebrating four-year-old Naya's birthday in front of their cabin. All of the village's men, women, and children were gathered around, smiling. The child was loved by all.

Naya looked at her one-and-a-half-year-old sister, Tarbee, who was in Nevarra's arms, and frowned.

"Sweetheart, why are you frowning?" Nevarra asked.

Naya took hold of her long, blond hair, looked at it, then looked at the fair skin of her hands and arms. "Mother, why is my skin so white and my hair so yellow? My little sister has dark skin and black hair like all these other children, and like you and Father."

Nevarra and Bando exchanged glances, then Bando put his arms around Naya and said, "Sweet Naya, you would not understand if Mother and I tried to answer your question. You are too young. When you are older, we will explain it to you."

"Oh, all right. But make sure you don't forget."

During the next two years, Naya often brought up her white skin and blond hair. Bando and Nevarra told her each time that she was still too young to understand, but they promised that when she was old enough, they would explain it to her.

On Naya's sixth birthday in 1806, when the public celebration was over and the family was inside the cabin, Naya was sitting on Bando's lap while Nevarra was holding Tarbee.

Once again, Naya asked why she was fair skinned and blond, when her little sister, her parents, and all the other Cherokees had dark skin and black hair. She also asked why she had blue eyes, and everyone else had dark-colored eyes.

Bando leaned his head down and kissed Naya's blond hair. "You are still too young to understand, my little one. But just know this—your being different from the rest of us makes you very special."

Naya studied his dark eyes. "Really?"

Bando gave her a big hug. "Yes, really."

A smile replaced Naya's frown, and a twinkle sparkled in her bright blue eyes. "I guess that makes it all right, Father. I can wait till I am old enough. Just don't forget to tell me then, will you?"

Nevarra smiled at her. "We will not forget, sweetheart."

Bando kissed her head again and gave her shoulders a gentle squeeze. "Don't worry. You will know all about it when the time is right."

Bando looked at Nevarra and a wordless message passed between them. *It will not be long now,* they seemed to say to one another.

By 1807 the United States government still had not told the Cherokees that they must move to the West and make their new home.

On Naya's seventh birthday, she was once again on Bando's lap, and little four-and-a-half-year-old Tarbee was on Nevarra's lap.

Bando leaned over and kissed the top of Naya's head. "Well, sweetheart, your mother and I have decided that you are now old enough to be told why you are different from the rest of the Cherokees."

Naya smiled up at him. "I'm so glad to hear that, Father."

Together, Bando and Nevarra told Naya about the overturned wagon in the mountains, how her real parents had been killed by the bears, and how she was found by Aluski and the men hunting deer with him.

Tears misted Naya's eyes. She quickly wiped them away, ran her gaze between her mother and father, and said, "Then...then you are not...my real parents."

Nevarra smiled thinly. "No, dear. But in our hearts, you have been our daughter since you were a year old. We have told you about our little daughter, Haylee, and how our hearts were broken when she died. But now we are able to tell you that you were brought to us by Uncle Aluski, and you filled that empty spot in our hearts."

Bando hugged her close. "Mother and I have loved you as our very own since the day you were brought to us. We are so sorry that your real mother and father were killed in such a tragic way, but we are so happy to have you in our family."

Nevarra rose to her feet, holding Tarbee in one arm. She leaned down and looked into Naya's sky-blue eyes. "Sweet Naya, you have been loved with all of our hearts since the first time we saw you."

Nevarra leaned down, gathered the seven-year-old into her free arm, and kissed her cheek. Bando stood up and took Tarbee into his arms, giving her a kiss on each cheek. Tarbee giggled.

Naya's countenance brightened and she kissed Nevarra's cheek. She looked into her mother's eyes, and then set her gaze on her father. "I love you too, Mother and Father, with all my heart.

Thank you for letting me be your little girl. I won't worry any more, ever, about my white skin, my blond hair, and my blue eyes. I know that I am your daughter for always, and that is all that matters."

Bando kissed Naya's forehead. "Yes, sweet Naya. You are our daughter for always."

seven

n January of 1809, President Thomas Jefferson's secretary of state, James Madison, succeeded him as president of the United States.

On Wednesday morning, February 8, the balding fifty-eight-year-old Madison stood before Congress in the north wing of the United States Capitol Building and spoke to them about important matters they must make decisions on.

When it was almost noon, President Madison ran his gaze over the faces of the congressmen and said, "All right, that takes care of all but one item that needs our attention today. We will break for lunch, then meet back here at one o'clock."

At precisely one that afternoon, the president was on the platform at the lectern, once again facing Congress.

"Gentlemen, I wish to speak to you at this time about a subject you are all acquainted with…especially you men who have been in Congress under President Jefferson, who laid the foundation for it. And that is the plan to remove all the Indian tribes from the states of North Carolina, Georgia, Tennessee, and Alabama to some yet undetermined area in the West."

As Madison went over President Thomas Jefferson's plan, many hands were raised and questions asked. It was almost three-thirty by the time the new president had answered all the questions satisfactorily. Congress then voted by a strong majority to proceed with the plans. Only a few men believed that the Indians should be allowed to stay where they were.

President Madison worked further on the plan, formulating the details of just how the removal of the Indians would be accomplished. In March and early April, he discussed the plan further with Congress, and informed them that he was still working on just where in the West the Indians would be taken. He also told Congress he was going to send four of their members to the areas currently occupied by the Indians. He would choose the four men soon and send them on their way, escorted by an army unit. He wanted the four congressmen to assess the land's potential usefulness in its future occupation by white people, and to advise the Indians that the United States government still planned to one day move them out West.

The next day, President Madison was at his desk in his executive office at the White House when his secretary, Alfred Tinsely, tapped on the door. Recognizing the tap, the president looked up and called out, "Yes, Alfred?"

The door opened, and Tinsely, a small, thin man in his mid-fifties, stuck his head in. "Mr. President, the four congressmen you have summoned to meet with you are here. I realize they are over an hour early, so do you want them to wait until the designated time?"

Madison laid down a paper and shook his head. "There's no need to wait. Bring them in."

Seconds later, the president stood as Congressmen Reginald Smith, Alexander Scott, Harold Finley, and Barton Enfield filed through the door.

"Please sit down, gentlemen," Madison said, gesturing toward a half-dozen straight-backed chairs clustered together across the room.

The president followed them, but none sat down until Madison had first seated himself, facing them.

When all were seated, Madison said, "Mr. Smith, I have chosen you for this assignment because you were one of the three congressmen who visited the Cherokee villages a few years back to announce to them our intentions to move them out West. I need your experience, you understand."

Smith nodded. "Yes, sir."

Madison looked at the others. "I have chosen you gentlemen to accompany Mr. Smith because you have proven yourselves to be quite capable in whatever job President Jefferson assigned you. Mr. Smith, I will let you explain to these men exactly how this tour will function."

"Yes, sir. We'll set up a time to get together, and I'll go over the picture with them so they'll know exactly how we will operate."

"Good." Madison looked at the calendar on his desk. "Let's see…today is April 6. I want you on your way by the first week of

May. I will set it up with the commander of the army post at Forest City, North Carolina, to send a unit of soldiers with you. Let's plan on you taking a train from here to Durham, then you'll take another train from there, which is bound for Asheville and runs through Forest City. The army will provide horses and supplies for you there. I'll advise you shortly of the exact day you'll leave Washington."

Reginald Smith smiled. "That will be fine, Mr. President. I'll have my sessions with my friends, here, so they'll be ready by the first week of May."

In late June, after covering Indian country in Georgia, Alabama, and Tennessee, the four congressmen and their armed escorts moved through the Smoky Mountains of North Carolina. They planned to visit every village and make sure the Cherokee Indians understood that they would be forced to leave their homes and make the journey to a new home far to the west.

Late on Sunday morning, June 25, the four congressmen and their party rode into Chief Pathkiller's village. They noted a crowd of Cherokees gathered in the center of the village, most of them sitting on the ground. A white man stood before them with a Bible in his hand.

"They're having church services," Congressman Enfield said to the others.

Captain Neal Harmon, the officer in charge of the soldiers, drew rein and said, "Let's not interrupt the service."

Each man halted his horse, and one of the soldiers, noting a number of Indians standing outside their cabins, said, "Looks like a lot of the Cherokees don't attend the services."

"Probably the majority don't," Congressman Scott said. "Most Indians look to their shamans for spiritual guidance."

At that time, the preacher brought his sermon to a close, asked the crowd to rise to their feet, and led them in a hymn in the Cherokee language.

While the hymn was being sung, Congressman Smith pointed to an Indian in full headdress who had left the crowd and was walking toward them. "Captain, that's their chief."

"So that's Chief Pathkiller, eh?" Captain Harmon said.

"That's him," said Smith, noting that another Indian was hurrying from the crowd to catch up with Pathkiller. "And that Indian following him is another Cherokee chief. His name is Sequoyah."

"Sequoyah, huh? And where is his village?"

"He doesn't have one. Most of the chiefs aren't in charge of the villages. They just—" Smith noticed a young blond man running to catch up with the two chiefs.

The captain frowned at Smith. "What's the matter?"

"See that young man hurrying toward the two chiefs?"

Harmon's mouth fell open. "Yeah. He's white. I'd say he's probably related to that preacher, but he's wearing Indian buckskins."

"He's only part Cherokee, but he considers himself a full-blooded Indian. When I was here six years ago, he talked about the missionaries who come and preach to them. That fellow with the Bible is no doubt one of them."

The captain nodded and dismounted. "Since you're the leader of the congressional delegation, join me as I talk to Pathkiller."

Reginald Smith swung down from the saddle and stepped up beside Captain Harmon, who was waiting for the chiefs and the blond young man to draw up.

As they did so, Chief Pathkiller set his gaze on the one face he recognized and said, "Your name is Smith, is it not?"

"Yes, Chief Pathkiller. Reginald Smith. And this is Captain Neal Harmon. These other civilians with me are congressmen, as I am."

With Sequoyah on one side of him and John Ross on the other, Pathkiller said, "I know why you have come. Word has already spread from other Cherokee villages here in the mountains that you want to assure us nothing has changed since you were here some years ago. Your government is still planning to force us from our homes and make us take the long journey to the land in the West and live there."

By this time, the missionary and a large crowd of Cherokees had gathered round.

Smith felt John Ross's blue eyes on him. He met his glare, then looked back at Pathkiller. "That is correct. It's going to happen."

"Where in the West will we be going?" Sequoyah said.

"That has not yet been determined."

Eighteen-year-old John Ross's features were stolid. "When is this long journey going to begin, Mr. Smith?"

"That has not been determined, either. We are just here as messengers for President James Madison and the government of the United States to establish in your minds that the day will come when you will be moved out West."

John's jaw jutted. "When you were here before, Mr. Smith, I asked you a question, which you never answered."

Smith's face lost color. "I don't want to hear any of that again."

"What was that, Reggie?" asked Congressman Finley from his saddle.

"I will tell you, sir," John said. "When Mr. Smith and those other congressmen were here six years ago, I quoted a verse from white man's Bible where God's Son, the Lord Jesus Christ, said, 'And as ye would that men should do to you, do ye to them likewise.' I asked Mr. Smith why white men like President Thomas Jefferson and the men of Congress and the army soldiers do things to us that they would not want us to do to them. I ask you, sir, would you want to be driven from your home and forced to make a long, hard journey to some strange land that is nothing like the home you had been forced to leave?"

Finley pulled at an ear and looked at the ground.

John Ross pressed him further. "Why do you congressmen and soldiers go against white man's Bible and do things to us Indians that you would not want done to you?"

Harold Finley looked at John, but did not answer him.

The soldiers and the other congressmen looked at each other in silence.

Reginald Smith set steady eyes on Pathkiller. "Chief, the day is coming when you and all your people are going to be moved to the West. This is President James Madison's message to you. Just remember…the day is coming."

Pathkiller was giving him a stony look when Smith turned and said, "Captain Harmon, our job here is done. It's time to move on."

"But my question has not been answered," John Ross said.

Smith gave him a cold look, then turned and mounted his horse.

Captain Harmon mounted his own horse and said, "Let's go, men."

The missionary and the crowd of Cherokees cheered for John Ross as the soldiers and the congressmen quickly rode away.

—◦—

Word soon spread through the villages in the Smoky Mountains how young John Ross had confronted the congressional delegation in Chief Pathkiller's village. As had happened years before, the congressmen and the soldiers had ridden away without a word, and the Cherokees in Chief Pathkiller's village had loudly cheered John Ross for his courage and for stopping the mouths of the white men.

As the Smoky Mountain Cherokees learned of John Ross's deed, they spoke well of him, with many of the chiefs agreeing that if he were a few years older, they would make him a chief.

One bright, sunny day in mid-July, thirty-six-year-old Chief Sequoyah, who was well-known by all North Carolina Cherokees, rode into Chief Bando's village, accompanied by John Ross. Those Cherokees who were milling about the center of the village saw the two riders and called out words of welcome to them.

Chief Bando, his wife, Nevarra, and their two daughters were talking to a group of men and women when they heard the voices welcoming Sequoyah and John Ross.

Bando glanced that direction, lifted a hand to wave at the two riders, then said to the group, "I need to see why Chief Sequoyah and John Ross are here." He looked at Nevarra and his daughters. "Would you like to go with me? It has been several weeks since we have seen them."

"Yes, Father!" nine-year-old Naya said. "I really like them."

"Me too," said six-year-old Tarbee.

Bando grinned. "All right, then. Let's go."

When Bando and his family drew up, they found the crowd around Sequoyah and John Ross talking to them about John Ross confronting the congressmen and the soldiers in Chief Pathkiller's village.

Chief Bando stepped up to them and shook hands. "John Ross, I want you to know that I agree with what my people are saying about you. I commend you for confronting the congressmen and the soldiers in such a clever manner. The way we heard it, you used Scripture that stopped their mouths…exactly as you did a few years ago."

"That he did," Sequoyah said. "This young man has a brilliant mind and good common sense."

Chief Bando laid a hand on John's shoulder and looked him in the eye. "I will be glad when you are old enough to become a Cherokee chief."

John's brow puckered. "How old do I have to be?"

"You have to be at least twenty-five."

"And even that is rare, John," Sequoyah said. "Very few men have become chiefs in the Cherokee tribe before they were thirty."

"This is true," Bando said, "but I am confident that John will become a chief sooner than that."

Sequoyah nodded. "I have no doubt that you are right. Chief Bando, I have come here to make an important announcement to you and your people. But before I do, I want to hug your daughters."

Bando grinned. "Be my guest."

Naya and Tarbee smiled as Sequoyah wrapped his arms around them at the same time. When Sequoyah released them and stepped back, John Ross moved up, smiling, and said, "Now it is my turn."

Naya and Tarbee responded warmly to John, clinging to him as he hugged them.

Chief Bando then said, "All right, Chief Sequoyah. Your presence here has drawn quite a crowd. Those of us who hear your announcement will tell the others of the village what it is. Please go ahead."

The crowd had formed a semicircle, waiting to hear what Chief Sequoyah had to say.

Facing them, Sequoyah said, "Several years ago I determined that someday I would develop a system of writing for the Cherokee nation. I want you to know that I have now begun to work on that system. You see, when we have an alphabet, books can be written in the Cherokee language. I believe now, more than ever, that increased knowledge will help the Cherokee people to maintain their independence from the whites."

The crowd applauded and cheered. Chief Bando moved up beside Sequoyah and said, "My people and I commend you, Chief Sequoyah."

The wheels turned slowly in the nation's capital concerning the removal of the Indians in North Carolina, Georgia, Tennessee, and Alabama to the West. President James Madison was cautious in the face of extreme opposition from the Indian chiefs. He realized it would take much preparation to have the army equipped and ready to move the Indians westward. He determined to make it happen, but realized he must handle it with great care.

In mid-September 1812, Madison once again sent four congressmen with an army escort to the Indian villages. These congressmen had not made this trip before. The president knew they were good with words, and had sent them to convince the Indians that a move out West would be good for them. They could all start a brand new life out there.

In late October, the congressmen arrived in Chief Pathkiller's village, and he reluctantly granted their request to meet with all of his people. When the crowd had assembled, standing with Chief Pathkiller were Chief Sequoyah and John Ross, who was now twenty-two years of age and married to Quatie, a full-blooded Cherokee woman. She stood close by with some other young married women.

The leading congressman, Raymond Turner, spoke to the people, attempting to convince them that it would be good for them to move out West. It was evident that neither Chief Pathkiller nor his people were convinced.

John Ross stepped forward and said, "Mr. Turner, you can tell by my blond hair and light complexion that I am not a full-blooded Cherokee. I am actually a quarter Cherokee. But, sir, I am *all* Cherokee in my heart. May I speak to you and these other congressmen before the people?"

Turner was hesitant to let the young man speak, but he nodded. "Yes, you may speak."

"Gentlemen, I see no reason why living in the far land of the setting sun would be good for the Indian people," John said. "We are much attached to the land of our forefathers, and even then, have been forced by white man's government to live in restricted areas which the white men chose for us. The grand scheme of moving us west will not make us happy. We are happy where we are. This is our home, and we want to stay here."

There was a rumble of voices, speaking their agreement. Quatie looked at her husband with admiring eyes.

The congressmen exchanged glances, their countenances showing strain.

John Ross continued. "Ever since the white men invaded this country many years ago, we have been made to give up our homes over and over at the command of white men's government."

Raymond Turner cleared his throat and was about to say something when John Ross said, "Gentlemen, let me quote for you what Creek Indian Chief Chitto Harjo wrote many years ago. 'A way back in time—in 1492—a man by the name of Christopher Columbus came from across the great ocean and discovered the country for the white man...but what did he find when he first arrived here? Did he find a white man standing on the continent then? No. I stood here first, and Columbus discovered me.'"

John stepped back, and the people cheered him.

Turner scowled, and he warned them that when the time came that the United States government told them they must move to the West, they had better not resist. If they resisted, they would be sorry. The United States Army would be forced to punish them until they were willing to obey.

There was dead silence among the people as the congressmen and their military escort rode away.

When the white men were out of sight, Chief Pathkiller stood before the crowd and said, "I would like for all of you to wait right here while I talk privately with my friend, Chief Sequoyah."

John Ross made his way to Quatie and stood beside her. She gave him a warm smile.

The crowd watched with curious eyes while their chief huddled together with Sequoyah, speaking in low tones. When the two men had finished their discussion, Chief Pathkiller once again faced his people.

"I have been discussing our young friend, John Ross, with Chief Sequoyah," he said, smiling. "We have talked about his courage and his leadership abilities many times before. After our talk just now, Chief Sequoyah and I agree that even though John Ross is only twenty-two years of age, he should be made a Cherokee chief."

John Ross's eyes widened as the crowd cheered. Quatie squeezed his arm, and he saw that there were tears of joy in her eyes.

Chief Pathkiller set his steady gaze on the young man. "John Ross, is this all right with you?"

A smile spread over John's features. "Chief Pathkiller, I am deeply honored that you, Chief Sequoyah, and these people want me to become a Cherokee chief. It is very much all right with me!"

Ten days later, in Chief Pathkiller's village, Cherokee chiefs from all over the Great Smoky Mountains were there to vote John Ross in as a Cherokee chief. In a solemn ceremony, it was done, and the people warmly welcomed John Ross as one of their leaders.

Standing with Chief John Ross before the crowd, Chief Pathkiller said, "I talked privately with the other chiefs when they first arrived here today, and we have all agreed that John Ross should be given a new Cherokee name, though we expect him to be best known as Chief John Ross. Since he is mostly white man, but in his heart is *all* Cherokee, the new name we have chosen for him is *Cooweescoowee*—Chief White Bird."

The people cheered.

Later that day, when John and Quatie entered their cabin in the village, she looked into his blue eyes, kissed his cheek, and said, "I love you, Chief White Bird."

John folded her into his arms and kissed her soundly. "Since I am White Bird, my private name for you is Little Red Bird."

Quatie giggled. "I love it!"

eight

n early January 1817, at the White House in Washington, D.C., President James Madison was about to turn his two-term presidency over to his close friend, James Monroe, who had won the election the previous November.

Monroe, who had taken the oath of office the day before in front of the Capitol Building, followed Madison into the Oval Office, and they eased into overstuffed chairs, facing each other.

Monroe had pencil and paper in hand. "All right, James," he said, "I'm ready to take notes on those issues you said you would need to fill me in on."

"Well, James, there are three big ones you need to know about," Madison said. "The first is problems I've been facing with the Supreme Court."

Monroe scribbled rapidly as Madison talked about the challenges he had with certain members of the Supreme Court the last two years of his presidency. Madison told Monroe how he had planned to handle them, and answered the new president's questions.

"The second problem you're going to face is one that I've barely had to handle, but it's getting hot. And that's the need to develop a foreign policy toward the European nations that are intervening in the Western Hemisphere."

Monroe nodded. "I've seen that need developing. If you have any suggestions on where I should start, please pass them along."

Madison indeed had suggestions, and talked for an hour as Monroe again took notes.

"Number three is a real tough one. And that is the proposed removal of all Indian tribes from Georgia, Alabama, Tennessee, and North Carolina to some uninhabited area out West. As you know, James, I've been working on this project, which was actually started by my predecessor, all the years I've been president."

Monroe nodded solemnly. "Yes, I know. Fill me in on what has kept this project from moving forward."

Madison explained the difficulties he had faced during his eight years. The first was the army's inability to figure out how to move thousands of Indians the vast distance to the West without great numbers of them, and even many soldiers, dying on the journey. The journey would take so long, there would be no way to avoid winter weather.

The second problem was where to take the Indians so they

could have plenty of space to build their new lives. At this point, none of the government officials in the West wanted the Indians in the areas they governed.

The third problem was the way many of the Indian chiefs were revolting against the move, and the danger of them becoming bold enough to start a war.

Madison took a deep breath and let it out slowly. "James, my friend, you're going to have to find some way to make it work."

"Well, I'm in accord with the project, and I will do my best to get it done as soon as possible. Regarding the threat of war…we need to put fear in the hearts of those Indians about trying to start a war with us. They need to understand that our military power is far greater than anything they can match."

Madison nodded. "You're right. I never thought about using that approach. I guess none of the military leaders did, either."

Monroe eased back in his chair. "I appreciate you filling me in on all of this, James. I know there are many obstacles in each of these items we've discussed, but I assure you, I will work hard to overcome them."

Madison smiled. "I wish you good fortune in your efforts, my friend."

In late May 1817, at Chief Bando's Cherokee village in the Smoky Mountains of North Carolina, his wife, Nevarra, was teaching English to seventeen-year-old Naya and fourteen-year-old Tarbee in a back room of their cabin. After the lesson was over, Tarbee went outside to join in a game with some of her friends.

Having her mother alone for a moment, Naya said, "Mother, can I talk to you?"

Nevarra smiled. "Why, of course, sweet girl. What would you like to talk about?"

Naya bit her lips and put a palm to her mouth. She cleared her throat and said, "Mother, I…I…well, I need to talk to you about me."

Nevarra frowned. "What about you?"

"Well, since I am now seventeen years old and many Cherokee girls marry at this age, I am wondering if you think it is because I am white that none of the Cherokee boys show me any romantic interest. I…I fear that maybe I will never marry and be a wife and mother."

A gentle smiled curved Nevarra's lips. "Naya, I know that your life has been very different from that of other white girls. But you are so special, and here is how I see it. Out there somewhere in Cherokee land, there is a special young man who is looking just for you. He doesn't know it yet, but he will when he meets you."

"Do you really think so, Mother?"

"Yes. Many of the Indian girls your age are already spoken for or are already married. I have no doubt that your time will come, too. Maybe somehow, it will be to a white man."

"But, Mother, I want to marry a Cherokee man. I have lived with Cherokee people since before I can remember. I know the Cherokee traditions and culture. I cannot even imagine marrying a white man and living in the white man's world."

Nevarra took her into her arms. "Sweet Naya, the Cherokee man who chooses you for his wife will have rare and exceptional qualities, I am sure. He will look beyond your outward appearance. He will see the Cherokee heart that beats within your breast. He will know beyond the shadow of a doubt that you are to be his wife, and you will know that he is the love of your life.

Do not fret, little one. It will all come to pass in good time."

Naya eased back in her mother's arms and wiped tears from her cheeks with the palms of her hands. "Do you really think so, Mother, or are you just trying to ease my fears?"

Nevarra hugged her again. "Listen to me. I am sure it will happen. You must simply be patient, sweet Naya."

Naya wiped away more tears, sniffed, and said, "Thank you, Mother. Because you are so sure it is going to happen to me, I will do my best to be patient."

The next day, Nevarra was again giving her daughters an English lesson in the same back room of the cabin. Bando was in the small parlor, whittling sticks into arrows.

There was a knock on the door, and Bando laid down his knife and stick and went to answer it. When he opened it, he was pleased to see a face he had not seen for some ten years.

"Wantana!" he said, eyes wide. "How good to see you! It has been too long, my friend."

Wantana, who wore a full headdress, stepped through the door, and he and Bando shook hands. Bando saw a young man in buckskin move in behind Wantana. He squinted as he looked at the young Cherokee's face.

Wantana let go of Bando's arm and smiled. "Do you recognize him, Bando?"

"He...looks familiar, but—"

"I am Walugo, Chief Bando," the young man said.

"Walugo!"

Wantana chuckled. "My son has grown up in the past ten years, has he not?"

_⌒_

In the back room, Nevarra had left her chair and pressed her ear against the closed door. "There are two men out there talking to your father," she said to her daughters. "I cannot make out what they are saying, but one man is older than the other. The older man's voice is familiar, but I cannot place it."

"You were ten years old when last I saw you, Walugo," Bando said. "You look somewhat like you did then, only more handsome."

Walugo's dark face flushed even darker. "Thank you for your kind words, Chief Bando."

Bando gave him a sly smile. "Tell me, Walugo, is there a young lady in your life?"

"There are many nice girls in my father's village, Chief Bando. But I have not fallen in love with any of them."

"Well, one of these days you will meet that right girl. Perhaps she is in another village, but when the two of you meet, you will fall in love and marry."

Walugo glanced at his father, then looked back at Bando. "I hope you are right, Chief Bando."

"Bando, I have something to tell you," Chief Wantana said. "Do you have time to talk?"

"Of course. Let us sit down in the parlor."

As Wantana and Walugo entered the small parlor, they saw the carving knife, the sticks, the arrowheads, and the feathers Bando was using to make arrows.

Wantana picked up a finished arrow. "These look very good. Maybe I should have you make me some."

"I would be glad to," Bando said, "but I do not know when I could deliver them all the way to your village in Tennessee."

Wantana laughed and laid the arrow down. "I was only jesting, but you just touched on the very thing I wish to talk to you about…my village in Tennessee."

"Oh? What about it?"

"Let us sit down, and I will explain."

When the three men were seated, Wantana said to Bando, "The truth is, my friend, I no longer have a village in Tennessee."

Surprise showed in Bando's features. "What happened?"

"I just moved my entire village of some five hundred people from the Appalachian Mountains of Tennessee to the Smoky Mountains of North Carolina."

Bando's face went slack. "You are joking with me!"

"My father is not joking, Chief Bando," Walugo said. "It is done."

"What caused you to do this, Wantana?"

"The threat we face from white man's government."

"You mean the proposed removal of Indians to the West?"

"Yes. It is going to happen, we just do not know when. President Thomas Jefferson and President James Madison could not get it done, but we have received word that the new United States president, James Monroe, and his Congress are working very hard to make it a reality. Are you aware of this?"

"My people and I are fully aware of it."

"Good. Bando, my friend, I have moved my people here to the Smoky Mountains of North Carolina because I believe the Tennessee Cherokees will be moved out West long before the North Carolina Cherokees are."

"Chief Bando," Walugo said, "my father believes this because the Tennessee Cherokees are closer to the West than you are. Everything we hear about it from white men confirms that they will go ahead of those in the Smokies."

Bando nodded. "I believe you are right. I hope, though, that it is as you just said, Wantana—*long* before we North Carolina Cherokees are forced to leave our homes and make the journey."

"It is this hope that caused me to bring my people here to the Smoky Mountains," Wantana said.

"So where have you located your people?" Bando said.

"On a large piece of land about ten miles northeast of here. It is located next to a large lake shaped like a white man's boot."

Bando nodded. "I know where that is. There is plenty of open space there, and much dense forest close by."

"Yes. We are living in tents right now, but soon we will be cutting timber from that forest and building our cabins."

At that moment, the men looked up to see three women at the parlor door. All three men rose to their feet.

Nevarra dashed to Wantana and said, "Oh, Chief, it is so good to see you! It has been so long!"

"It is wonderful to see you too, Nevarra," Wantana said. "Do you recognize this young man with me?"

Nevarra set her eyes on the handsome young man, then put a hand to her mouth. "Is this Walugo?"

Walugo smiled. "Yes, ma'am."

"The last time I saw you, you were just a boy! Ten years old, I believe."

Walugo nodded. "I am twenty now."

"It is so good to see you," she said, then turned back to Wantana. "Tell me about Careena. How is she?"

While Wantana was telling Nevarra about his wife, Walugo

glanced at Tarbee, then at her sister. Naya met his gaze and smiled. Walugo's heart skipped a beat, and he smiled back.

Bando noticed Walugo and Naya looking at each other. "Chief Wantana…Walugo…I want you to meet our daughters, Naya and Tarbee," he said. "I know you did not see them the last time we were together."

Both men listened intently as Bando told them how he and Nevarra had come to take Naya into their home when she was one year old. When Bando finished the story, Nevarra suggested that they all sit down.

After they were seated, Bando turned to his family and said, "Let me tell you why Chief Wantana and Walugo knocked on our door. They had something very important to tell us."

While Bando recounted for his wife and daughters the purpose of Chief Wantana's visit, Naya found Walugo looking at her every time she glanced toward him. She felt a warmth spread through her heart.

After Bando was finished with his explanation, Wantana looked at Naya and asked, "As a white girl, my dear, how do you feel about living with Cherokees?"

Naya's blue eyes sparkled as she said, "I do not know any other life. As far as I am concerned, Chief Wantana, I am a full-blooded Cherokee. And even though I am sad to know that bears killed my real parents, I am very happy being the daughter of such wonderful people as these. I love them so much…and my little sister, too."

Tarbee smiled at her, then looked at Wantana and said, "Chief, I do not think of my sister as being a white girl. She seems like she is Cherokee to me."

Wantana grinned. "That is good."

"Naya," Walugo said, "your parents will probably be talking to my father for a while yet. Could you and I take a little walk together?"

"If my father gives me permission, I will be happy to take a walk with you, Walugo."

Bando smiled, looking first at Walugo, then at Naya. "You have my permission."

Walugo rose to his feet. "Thank you, Chief Bando. Naya and I will stay close to the village. And we will be back soon."

When the two young people had gone out the door, Bando looked at Nevarra and said, "I think those two have taken a liking to each other."

"Dear husband," Nevarra said, "just yesterday, Naya was asking me why she has not been spoken for yet, since most Cherokee girls her age have been. I told her that her time would come. I can see that she and Walugo do like each other. Wouldn't it be interesting if Naya's time came today?"

Bando smiled and looked at his friend. "Wantana, how do you feel about it? Would you object if your son should choose Naya as his bride? After all, she is white."

Wantana shook his head. "I would not object at all. She is a very nice girl. And she is *your* daughter."

Nevarra set steady eyes on Wantana. "Would the people of your village welcome her? I assure you that her heart and lifestyle are Cherokee, but Bando and I must be certain that she would be well-accepted in your village."

Wantana ran his gaze between Bando and Nevarra. "My son is highly respected by my people, and whoever he chooses for his wife will receive the same respect. Let us just see what happens between them. But I want you to know they would have my blessing, and that of Careena. Even though I have just met your Naya,

I know the two of you well, as do many of the people in my village. She would be most welcome. I give you my word."

Bando smiled at his friend. "Thank you, Wantana. Your word is all we need."

nine

s Walugo and Naya walked away from the cabin, heading for the central part of the village, Naya noted that he was almost a head taller than she was.

Walugo noticed that she was looking up at him with eyes that seemed to measure him. "Is something wrong with my headband?" he said with a smile.

"Oh, no. I was just noticing how tall you are."

"I guess I got my height from my grandfather on my mother's side. By white man's measurements, he was six feet and one inch tall. I am almost as tall as he was."

Soon they were on the main path through the village, and Walugo said, "How about a walk in the forest? We will not go very far. I told your father we would stay close to the village."

"We can do that," Naya said. "I like the forest."

Naya noticed that small groups of young Indian maidens were watching them, whispering to each other and smiling as they pointed to the tall young Cherokee with her. Naya also saw a few maidens looking out the windows of their cabins, openly admiring Walugo.

A feeling of pride filled Naya's heart that Walugo had chosen to spend time with her. She smiled to herself, thinking, *Maybe Mother was right. Maybe my time is about to happen.*

A few more steps and they entered the forest. They were just moving into the shade of the huge trees when a squirrel darted across their path and scampered up a tree. They watched the squirrel until it reached a limb near the top of the tree. Both of them laughed as several birds in the high branches scolded the intruder, then flew away.

They walked a little deeper into the dense forest, and a wild turkey bolted out of some thick brush, flapping its wings and making its high-pitched complaint at being disturbed. Within seconds, it disappeared into another thicket.

Walugo gestured toward a large boulder that stood beside the path just ahead. "Would you like to sit down, Naya?"

"All right."

When they had made themselves comfortable on the boulder, Walugo said, "It is too bad that white man's government wants to force the Indians to live out West."

Naya nodded. "The long journey would be dreadful enough, but then to have to settle in strange new surroundings and get accustomed to them would be very difficult."

"You are right. This move that we just made from the other side of the mountains was bad enough, but to have to travel hundreds of miles through all kinds of weather would be a nightmare. I hope it never happens."

Naya sighed. "I love my home here in the Great Smoky Mountains."

Walugo looked into her eyes for a long moment, then said, "Naya, since you are here, I know I am going to love living in the Smokies, too."

Naya blushed and smiled at him, then looked away.

Walugo waited for her to look back at him, and when she did, he stood up and said, "Well, we had best get back to your father's cabin. I told him we would not be gone long."

As Naya started to rise from the boulder, Walugo extended his hand. "Please allow me to help you."

Her cheeks tinted slightly as she lifted her hand. He took it gently and helped her to her feet.

As they walked along the path, Naya was watching two large birds that were high in a tree, looking down at them. She stumbled on a broken tree limb, and Walugo grabbed her shoulders to keep her from falling.

Naya looked at him and smiled. "How clumsy of me. Thank you."

Walugo smiled back. "That was not being clumsy, Naya. Your attention was simply on those two birds up there."

"Well, if it had not been for you, I would have fallen on the ground."

"I wish I could always be close to you so I could help you whenever you needed me," he said, still holding onto her.

Naya blushed again, this time with a warm commotion stirring inside her.

Walugo cleared his throat and took his hands from her shoulders.

Naya smiled delicately. In a soft tone, she said, "Walugo, it would be very nice to always have you close by."

This time it was Walugo who did not know what to say.

"Father will be wondering where we are," Naya said.

Even as she spoke, she started walking back toward the village, and a happy Walugo moved up beside her.

During the next few months, Walugo came to Chief Bando's village to visit Naya often, with her father's permission. On three occasions, his parents came with him. Nevarra, Naya, and Tarbee were taken with Careena's sweet disposition, and each time they were together, they grew closer in spirit.

One day in late September—also with Chief Bando's permission—Naya rode her horse alongside Walugo and his horse, and visited his parents in their village by the big lake. She quickly sensed the deep respect the people had for their chief, his wife, and his son.

True to Wantana's word, the people in his village were friendly to Naya, though she felt conspicuous with her fair skin and blond hair. Naya had her hair done up in braids, and several little girls came up to her and gently touched the blond braids. Naya smiled and greeted them in the Cherokee language. They were astounded, and giggling, ran to hide behind their mothers' skirts.

After that day, each time Naya visited Wantana's village with Walugo, she felt more at home, and she knew she was being accepted by the people.

One day in early October, Walugo rode up to Chief Bando's cabin, dismounted, and knocked on the door.

Tarbee opened the door, smiled warmly, and said, "Hello, Walugo. How nice of you to come and see me!" Then she broke into a giggle.

"Well, it is very nice to see you, Tarbee, but I am actually here to see your beautiful sister."

"Oh, you mean that blond you are going to marry?"

"That is the one."

"My father told me he had given you permission to marry Naya, but he did not say when the wedding is going to take place."

"Well, he probably did not tell you when because he assumed you knew the Cherokee tradition that one year must pass before the wedding takes place."

"Oh, yes, now I remember." She broke into another giggle just as Naya moved up behind her, smiled at Walugo, and said, "Hello, Walugo."

Walugo's eyes lit up. "Hello, Naya. I have some good news to share with you."

"I will leave you two alone," Tarbee said.

When Tarbee had gone to the rear of the cabin, Naya invited Walugo to sit down in the parlor.

When they had kissed each other and taken seats facing each other, Naya said, "What is the good news?"

"You are aware that with my father's blessing, I have been encouraging the people of our village to make an open stand against the plan of white man's government to one day force them to move to the West."

"Yes, and I am so proud of you."

"Thank you. The good news is that I have been invited to a meeting at Chief Pathkiller's village to help educate young men like me about the controversy. And let me tell you who is going to teach us."

"Who?"

"Chief John Ross. I have heard so much about him, and I am eager to meet him. Have you ever met him?"

Naya smiled. "Walugo, I have known him since I was a little girl. Chief Pathkiller and my father are close friends, and Chief John Ross has lived in Chief Pathkiller's village for many years. He has often been in our village, though it has been a while now since I have seen him. I highly respect Chief John Ross. I am glad you are going to get to meet him. Please greet him for me."

"I will do that."

One day in the spring of 1818, Naya, Walugo, and his parents were sitting on benches in front of the parents' cabin, talking about the wedding, which would take place the following September.

The sound of trotting hooves met their ears, then slowed, and a male voice called out, "Hello!"

"Chief John Ross!" Naya said as she jumped off the bench.

John slid from the saddle and Chief Wantana, Careena, and Walugo rose to their feet. John smiled and spoke to them, then his smile broadened as he moved toward Naya. "Naya, it is so good to see you!" John glanced at Walugo. "Would you put an arrow in my back if I were to embrace your future bride?"

Walugo laughed. "No, my friend. Naya has spoken often in

the past few months of how much she admires you. There will be no arrow."

John embraced Naya discreetly, then held her at arm's length. "You have become even more beautiful than you were the last time I saw you. Are your parents doing well?"

"Oh, yes."

"And Tarbee? Is she spoken for yet?"

"Not yet, but she is still a bit too young for that."

"It will be a fortunate young man who marries her, even as Walugo is so fortunate to have the privilege of marrying you."

"You have that right," Walugo said.

Naya gave her future husband a sweet smile, then said to the blond Cherokee chief, "I have never had the chance to tell you how very much I like the name the Cherokee chiefs gave you—Cooweescoowee. White Bird."

John smiled. "You could be called White Bird yourself."

She giggled. "I cannot argue with that."

John turned to Wantana and Walugo. "I came here because I need to spend a little time with both of you."

Both men nodded, and Naya and Careena went inside the cabin while the three men sat on the benches.

"I thought you would want to know what is happening in Washington City," John Ross said, "about President Monroe's plan to move the Indians to the West."

"We certainly do want to know," Wantana said.

John Ross drew a deep breath, then let it out slowly. "Just two weeks ago, President Monroe presented his plan to Congress. He referred to the Cherokee, the Chickasaw, the Choctaw, the Creek, and the Seminole as the 'Five Civilized Tribes.' He believes that, unlike other tribes, we will not declare war on the United States

Army when they come to take us to the West."

Wantana nodded. "He is probably right. We Cherokees will not risk getting our women and children killed by attacking the soldiers if they come to force us westward."

"Congress believes that, too," John said. "The majority voted for President Monroe to proceed with his plan, and at present, the president is working hard to get the plan going. However, as word of this has spread among the five tribes, the tribal leaders, myself included, are giving him much opposition. And those Congressmen who voted against it are also openly opposing him. They do not want to see the Indians forced from their homes."

"Good for them," Walugo said. "And good for you, John Ross."

Wantana wiped a hand over his mouth. "I fear, though, John Ross, that even with all this opposition, one day we will be forced to leave our homes and make the journey to the West."

John sighed. "I have to agree, Wantana. One day it will happen. But at least because of this opposition, it will take more time to put the plan in action."

Wantana pulled his lips into a thin line. "Of course, I hope that no matter how it looks right now, something will happen that will stop the plan, and we can remain right here."

When September came, Walugo and Naya were making final preparations for their wedding, which would take place in Chief Bando's village on Sunday, September 20. At the request of Chief Bando, Nevarra, and Naya, Chief Wantana would conduct the ceremony.

Walugo had built a new cabin for his bride in Chief Bando's

village, with the help of some of the men in both villages. Walugo had asked Naya not to enter that part of the village until the cabin was done. He wanted to present it to her privately a few days before the wedding.

That day finally came and everything was ready for Naya to see. As they turned a corner onto the path where the cabin was built, Naya's eyes widened and she exclaimed, "Oh, Walugo, it is beautiful!"

When they got closer, she noted the cherry roses that he had planted on both sides of the cabin. She rushed ahead of him and pressed one of the roses to her nose. He drew up beside her, and she told him how sweet it smelled, then wrapped her arms around him and kissed him soundly.

Walugo gave her the tour of the cabin, and when she had seen it all, she told him what a beautiful job he had done. Walugo said he could not have done it were it not for the men who had helped him. She kissed him again, and told him she would personally thank every man who had helped.

On the day of the wedding, everyone in the village gathered at the village center. Chief John Ross and his wife, Quatie, were also there. The groom and his father appeared from behind a cabin and stood before the large crowd in the sunlight.

Behind another cabin, Nevarra and Careena were with Naya, whose face was shining as she stood before them in her wedding dress, which Nevarra had designed and made. It was velvety soft white buckskin with white fringe along the hem and the sleeve edges, and with intricate turquoise beading on the bodice. She wore a woven white headband, which was also adorned with white feathers and turquoise beading. Her father had made her white knee-high moccasins with fringe along the back of them. Naya's blond hair hung down her back, past her waist, and was pulled up on the sides of her head and held there with small combs.

Nevarra and Careena stepped around the corner of the cabin into the crowd's view with the bride following, and as Naya moved toward the groom and his father, she stood out like a beacon amid the sea of dark-skinned, black-haired people.

Walugo had trouble breathing as he looked at the loveliness of his bride. *She is really mine*, he thought as she drew up and smiled at him.

Chief Wantana united them as husband and wife in a simple ceremony as the two of them looked lovingly at one another.

ten

n the morning of Wednesday, February 10, 1819, Chief John Ross attended a meeting of the National Council of Cherokees, of which he had been a member since shortly after he became a Cherokee chief.

The meeting was held in an open area within a forest near the western base of the Appalachian Mountains of Tennessee, providing the Cherokee chiefs of Alabama, Georgia, and North Carolina a central place to meet. The Tennessee chiefs had only a short distance to travel.

Chief Abandi of the Georgia Cherokees, who was president of the National Council of Cherokees, stood before the assemblage of chiefs with a slight breeze ruffling his silver hair. His back was bent, and he was obviously quite weak.

"My friends," Abandi said with a quavering voice, "most of you have known that sometime soon I would have to step aside and let another chief take my place as president of this National Council. I must tell you, that day has come. For health reasons, as well as my eighty-one years, I have chosen to resign as your president.

"I want to tell you the man I believe should follow me in this office." Abandi squinted his eyes and pointed into the crowd. "That man, right there. Chief White Bird, otherwise known as Chief John Ross."

John Ross, who was sitting on the ground between Chief Pathkiller and Chief Bando, blinked and swallowed hard.

Abandi smiled at him and said, "This young man, as you all know, is one-quarter Cherokee, which qualifies him for the position. Other things also qualify him. I recommend him because of his outstanding leadership and his fearless stand in opposition of the white man's government since he became a chief a few years ago."

Chief Pathkiller raised his hand and said, "Chief Abandi, may I speak?"

Abandi nodded. "You may."

Pathkiller rose to his feet, the eyes of the chiefs fixed on him. "As chief of the village where Chief John Ross and his wife reside," Pathkiller said, lifting his voice so all could clearly hear him, "I wholeheartedly agree with Chief Abandi. I have known him for many years. We would be wise if we elected Chief John Ross—Chief White Bird—as president of the National Council of Cherokees."

Chief Bando jumped up and said, "I agree. I know Chief John Ross well, and he is the best qualified man for the position."

There were cheers and voices calling out their words of agreement.

Chief Abandi waited until all had grown quiet, then said, "All in favor of electing Chief John Ross as president of the National Council of Cherokees, stand to your feet."

Within a few seconds, every man in the crowd was on his feet.

Abandi nodded. "It is unanimous." He set his weary eyes on the blond man with the blue eyes and said, "Chief John Ross, you are now president of the National Council of Cherokees. Please come and make your acceptance speech. Afterward, you can lead the Council in other matters that need to be taken care of. I will be at your side to assist you."

Chief John Ross stepped up to Chief Abandi, who shook his hand, then gestured for him to face the crowd.

Chief John Ross expressed his love and devotion to the Cherokee Nation. He assured the gathered chiefs that he would do his best to lead the Nation and to represent the Cherokee people before white man's government.

Late that afternoon, when Chief John Ross and Chief Pathkiller arrived home, Pathkiller sent messengers throughout the village to call all the people together for a special meeting. The crowd swiftly grew as the people came from every direction. John Ross saw Quatie coming toward him and smiled at her.

When Quatie drew up, she took hold of her husband's hand and said, "What is this meeting about?"

"You will find out in a moment," John said.

Quatie nodded and moved into the crowd to stand beside Chief Pathkiller's wife, Miklia.

A few minutes later, the messengers stepped up to Pathkiller and told him that everyone was present. The chief then ran his gaze over the faces of the people and said, "I have a very important announcement to make to you." He glanced to where Quatie stood beside his wife. "Quatie Ross, will you please come and stand with your husband?"

Quatie showed surprise, but she moved out of the crowd quickly and came and stood by her husband's side.

"All of you know that Chief John Ross and I attended the meeting of the National Council of Cherokees today in Tennessee," Chief Pathkiller said. "The Council president, Chief Abandi, resigned his position because of health problems and his age. He strongly suggested that the Council elect Chief John Ross as its president. And we did. It was a unanimous vote. I wish to introduce to you the new president of the National Council of Cherokees, Chief John Ross!"

The crowd cheered, with many waving their arms in jubilation.

Quatie looked up at her husband with tear-misted eyes. "Oh, John, I am so proud of you!" Then she wrapped her arms around her husband's neck and kissed him soundly on the lips.

No one in the crowd took offense. They only cheered louder.

White missionaries Layne and Sylvia Ward, who knew the Cherokee language well, had taken the gospel to twenty-three of the forty-three Cherokee villages in the Great Smoky Mountains of North Carolina. Other missionaries had also worked in these villages, but most of them had moved on to other tribes in the southeastern states.

The Wards had established churches in eleven of those villages, and these churches were pastored by eleven Cherokee men God had called to preach under Layne's ministry. Each of these pastors read and spoke English well, and using the English Bibles Layne provided them, they translated their messages into the Cherokee language.

Shamans in some of these villages opposed the pastors, but they continued to proclaim the gospel and to preach the Word of God to build their church members up in the faith.

Layne Ward was training other young Cherokee men who had felt God's call to preach so they would be ready when additional chiefs allowed churches to be founded in their villages.

One day in March 1819, Layne and Sylvia were talking with Chief Calhondo just after Layne had held a Bible study in Chief Calhondo's village with a number of men, women, and teenage boys and girls who had become Christians two weeks previously. The three of them were sitting on benches in front of the chief's cabin as Layne tried to convince Chief Calhondo to allow him to bring in a young Cherokee preacher to found a church.

Chief Calhondo told the Wards that if he allowed a church in his village, the village shaman, Ridino, would be angry.

Layne looked him in the eye and said, "But God would be pleased if you allowed it, Chief Calhondo."

The chief shook his head. "I cannot allow it. Because of Ridino's mystical powers, I fear making him angry."

Sylvia was sitting beside her husband, praying in her heart. At that moment, she looked up to see Ridino step out of his cabin and head toward them. She tugged at her husband's sleeve and pointed toward Ridino with her chin.

Layne glanced that direction.

"He must have been watching us talking to Chief Calhondo," Sylvia said. "He's probably coming to make trouble."

Calhondo eyed the approaching shaman and nodded. "Ridino does not want someone in the village who contradicts what he teaches the people."

A harried look was etched on Ridino's face as he drew up. "Mr. Ward, I...I need to have a private talk with you. Will you come with me to my cabin?"

Layne stood up. "I will be glad to talk with you." His Bible was still in his hand as he looked down at Sylvia and said, "Wait here for me."

Sylvia nodded, and in her heart, she asked God to protect her husband.

As shaman and missionary entered the cabin, Ridino asked Layne to sit down with him at his eating table so they could face each other.

Ridino fidgeted a bit, cleared his throat, and said, "When you were here two weeks ago and preached to the crowd, I hid close by and listened to the sermon. It...has been bothering me ever since. The story you told about Jesus Christ dying on that cruel cross, and the Scriptures you read have been heavy on my mind. I heard that story from another missionary a few years ago in another village. He read some of the same verses from his Bible that you did."

Layne nodded. "I am glad you have heard it before, Ridino. And I have to say that I'm glad the story bothered you when I told it two weeks ago."

Ridino adjusted his position on the wooden chair and looked squarely at Layne. "The Scriptures you used to show that those who do not receive Jesus Christ as their Saviour will burn forever in a place called hell, but those who do will spend forever in a place called heaven with God and His Son, have come back to me over and over again. They have even kept me awake at night. I cannot get them out of my mind."

Silently, Layne praised the Lord that the Holy Spirit had been at work in Ridino's heart.

Ridino drew a shaky breath. "Mr. Ward, though the Scriptures you read go against everything I have believed, somehow I know they are true. I have been wrong. I—" He choked up, and it took him a moment before he could speak again. "Mr. Ward, I am quitting right now as a shaman. I want to become a Christian."

"That's wonderful, Ridino," Layne said. "You're making a decision you will never regret. May I show you some other Scriptures to help solidify your understanding of the gospel?"

Ridino wiped a tear from an eye and nodded.

Layne flipped pages and stopped at the book of Romans. "Ridino, you speak English well. Can you also read it?"

"Yes."

"Good." Layne handed him the open Bible. "Read me verses twenty-three and twenty-four in chapter three, here."

Ridino took the Bible with a shaky hand and looked down at the page. "'For all have sinned, and come short of the glory of God; being justified freely by his grace through the redemption that is in Christ Jesus.'"

"What is sin, Ridino?" asked Layne.

Ridino frowned. "That other missionary said that sin is the transgression of God's law…His Word that I hold here in my hand."

"That's right. It says all have sinned. Are you included in that 'all'?"

"Yes."

"Do you know what *justification* is?"

"It is having your wrong-doings pardoned so you stand before God as if you had never sinned. You explained that when you preached here two weeks ago."

"Oh. I did, didn't I? Look at that verse, Ridino. Notice it says that we are justified freely by redemption. Tell me *where* redemption—or salvation—is found."

"In Christ Jesus."

"Is it found anywhere else?"

"No. Only in Christ Jesus."

"Not in some religion?"

"No. Only in Christ Jesus."

"Then that is where you need to be, Ridino. *In* Christ Jesus."

Ridino frowned. "How do I get there?"

"By receiving Him into your heart. When you take Jesus into your heart as your personal Saviour, He takes you into Him." Layne extended his hand. "Let me have the Bible." Layne turned to 2 Corinthians 5, then handed the Bible back to Ridino. "Read me verse seventeen here in chapter five."

"'Therefore if any man be in Christ, he is a new creature: old things are passed away; behold, all things are become new.'"

"In order to be a new creature and have all things new in your life, Ridino, where do you have to be?"

"In Christ."

"And how do you get in Christ?"

"By receiving Him into my heart."

Layne looked into Ridino's eyes. "To receive Jesus into your heart by faith, you must believe His gospel, which according to

Scripture is the fact that Jesus died on the cross, was buried, and rose again. Do you believe that?"

"I do." Tears filled Ridino's eyes. "I want to receive Jesus into my heart. How do I do that?"

"All right. We'll bow our heads, and you ask the Lord Jesus to come into your heart and forgive you of all your sins, and to save you."

When Ridino had done so, Layne laid a hand on his shoulder and prayed for him, that the Lord would give him peace and use him for His glory.

Relief showed in Ridino's beaming face as he looked at Layne and said, "Thank you for showing me the way."

"It was my pleasure, Ridino."

The new convert wiped more tears. "Mr. Ward, how did I somehow know that the Bible is true?"

"God's Holy Spirit drove it into your heart. He convinced you that it's true."

"Even though I was a shaman?"

"Even though you were a shaman. You know now, don't you, that shamans are under the power of Satan, and do his bidding?"

"Yes, I do. I know that for a fact."

"And you know that you will no longer have a position of great power and prestige in your tribe?"

"I know that, yes, but I do not care. I have peace, now, about my soul, and I am happy in Christ."

"Let's go tell Chief Calhondo and my wife what you've just done."

Moments later, Layne and Ridino approached Sylvia and Chief Calhondo where they sat on the bench. They both looked up.

"Chief Calhondo," Layne said, "if you will grant me permission to bring a young Cherokee preacher to start a church in your village, you will not need to fear making Ridino angry. He has just become a Christian."

Sylvia's eyes glistened with tears as she whispered a word of thanks to her heavenly Father.

Shock showed in Calhondo's dark features. He stood up and squinted at Ridino. "Is this true?"

Ridino told him his testimony of having received the Lord Jesus Christ into his heart. He also made it clear that he was no longer a shaman.

Calhondo looked at Layne and said, "I want to hear more about Jesus Christ, and I want my wife, Deeda, to hear it, too."

An hour later, the chief and his wife also called on Jesus for salvation. Calhondo wasted no time telling Layne he had permission to bring in one of his young Cherokee preachers to start a church in the village.

Layne smiled. "Chief, the Christians in your village will be happy to hear this."

Ridino touched Layne's arm. "Will you go with me to Chief Bando's village?" he asked with a serious look on his face. "The shaman in that village, whose name is Hoyo, is a close friend of mine. I want to tell Hoyo what has happened to me, and try to convince him to become a Christian also. I will need your help."

"Sylvia and I have not yet been in Chief Bando's village, Ridino," Layne said, "but I have been planning to go to Chief Bando and ask for permission to tell him and his people about Jesus. Sylvia and I will go there with you right now."

Layne then turned to Chief Calhondo and his wife. "I will be back tomorrow with a young preacher, whose name is Cassdi. The new church will start next Sunday."

Calhondo and Deeda joined hands, smiled at the missionary, and the chief said, "May the God of heaven bless you."

When Layne, Sylvia, and Ridino entered Chief Bando's village, some of the people recognized Ridino and spoke kindly to him. He returned their greeting, then led the missionaries to the path to Chief Bando's cabin.

A moment later, Chief Bando heard the knock on his door and opened it. "Hello, Ridino," he said. "And who are these people with you?"

"They are missionaries, Chief," Ridino said.

"I am Layne Ward, and this is my wife, Sylvia," Layne said.

"Oh, yes. I have heard of you." A frown furrowed his brow, and he said to Ridino, "Why would you be in the company of Christian missionaries?"

Ridino let a smile curve his lips. "Chief Bando, I am no longer a shaman."

"What? Why is this?"

Ridino still had his smile. "Mr. Layne Ward came to Chief Calhondo's village with Mrs. Ward, and he preached about Jesus Christ to the people who would listen to him. Many of them have become Christians, including Chief Calhondo, his wife…and me."

Chief Bando shook his head. "Ridino, this amazes me. I have never known of a shaman becoming a Christian." He then turned to the white couple. "Why have you come here?"

"Chief, I have come to ask permission to hold a service and preach to the people of your village about Jesus Christ. Since you have heard of my wife and me, you must know what we do in the villages."

Bando nodded. "Yes, I know. Mr. Ward, I have met many Cherokees who have become Christians. I must say that I see something pleasantly different about them." He paused, looked at Sylvia, then back at Layne. "All right. You have my permission to preach about Jesus Christ to my village. My wife, Nevarra, and our daughter, Tarbee, and I will attend. I am sure that my daughter, Naya, and her husband, Walugo, will attend also."

"Thank you, Chief Bando," Layne said, smiling broadly. "I deeply appreciate the opportunity to preach here in your village."

"Chief Bando, while I am here, I would like to see my friend, Hoyo," Ridino said.

The chief's features stiffened. "Hoyo is going to be angry when he learns that you have become a Christian, Ridino."

Ridino nodded. "I know it will upset him, but I am still his friend, and I care about him. I want to see him become a Christian, too."

eleven

he shaman, Hoyo, stood at the front door of his cabin as Ridino told him he had decided to become a follower of Jesus. Layne Ward was at Ridino's side, but Sylvia stood behind them some distance, unnoticed by the shaman.

Hearing the name of Jesus Christ and the news that Ridino had become a Christian made Hoyo's face burn. His lips quivered as he set his eyes on Ridino and said, "The spirits will punish you for this! They will kill you and send your ghost to drift away forever in the wind!"

"No, they will not," Ridino said, remaining calm. "My Jesus Christ is more powerful than Satan's evil spirits. The Bible tells how Jesus repeatedly overpowered the spirits, rendering them helpless. My Jesus Christ will protect me."

Hoyo's body quivered with rage. "Get away from me! I want nothing to do with you, Ridino! You are a traitor!" With that, Hoyo backed into the cabin and slammed the door.

As Layne and Ridino walked away and drew up to Sylvia, she said, "Ridino, you tried. All you can do now is pray for him."

Solemn-faced, Ridino nodded. "I will do that."

The next day, Wednesday, March 17, Layne Ward stood before the small group of Cherokees who had gathered to hear him preach and read from his Bible about the virgin birth of God's one and only Son. He showed how the religious leaders in Israel despised Jesus and finally were able to get the Roman soldiers to nail Him to the cross. He read of the glorious resurrection, and warned them of an eternity in hell if they did not come to Jesus for salvation.

In the group were Chief Bando, Nevarra, Tarbee, Walugo, and Naya.

While Layne was preaching, a curious Hoyo looked on from behind the corner of a cabin. He was stirred with anger at what he heard.

When Layne finished his sermon and invited those present to receive Jesus as their Saviour, no one came. But Layne was not discouraged, for he knew he was sowing the seed of the Word. After the service was over, he went up to Chief Bando and asked if he could continue to hold services there that week. The chief granted his request, telling him he was interested in the story of Jesus Christ and was sure the others were also.

As the days passed and Layne continued to preach, the crowds grew. Hoyo looked on, but kept himself hidden. Through Saturday, no one had yet come forward at the invitation.

However, when Layne finished his Sunday sermon and invited the people to receive the Lord Jesus as their Saviour, several did...including Chief Bando, Nevarra, Tarbee, Walugo, and Naya.

In his hiding place, Hoyo watched as the new converts rejoiced with Layne and his wife. There was a strange stirring in Hoyo's heart and mind, and there was sweat on his brow. He could almost feel the flames of hell licking at his body. He took a deep breath, left his hiding place, and hurried to the spot where Layne was instructing the new converts from Scripture about what God expected of them.

As Layne was reading a passage, he caught movement out of the corner of his eye, and looked up at Hoyo, who was approaching him.

"What can I do for you?" Layne said when Hoyo drew up.

Tears filmed Hoyo's eyes as he said, "Mr. Ward, I have been hiding out there behind one of the cabins, listening to your sermons since Wednesday. I realize how wrong I have been to be a shaman. I want to be saved."

There was much rejoicing when Layne took Hoyo aside to lead him to Christ, and after they returned, Hoyo announced that he was now a Christian and no longer a shaman.

Late that night, when all the village was asleep, Walugo was awakened by the sound of sniffling. He turned over, raised up on his elbows, and looked at his wife. Naya opened her tear-filled eyes and tried to stifle her weeping, but the sniffling continued.

Walugo caressed her head and said, "What is wrong, dear one?" He then gathered her into his arms. "Naya, why are you awake and crying?"

"Oh, I am sorry. I didn't mean to awaken you, darling. It has just been such an exciting day, and I am rejoicing that I am now a child of God. These tears are happy ones, not sad ones."

Walugo squeezed her tightly. "I am thrilled over my salvation, too. I am so glad Mr. Layne Ward and his wife came here, and that your father allowed him to preach to us."

There was a brief moment of silence, then Naya said, "I was also thinking of something else while I was lying here."

"What was that?"

"It…it just came to my mind as I was thinking about how wonderful it is that you, my parents, my little sister, and I are now Christians and will be together forever in heaven." She swallowed hard.

"And what was it that came to your mind?" Walugo asked.

"Well…I was wondering if my real parents might have been Christians."

Walugo ran his fingers over her face and wiped away her tears. "I suppose that is possible."

"I was barely one year old when my real parents were killed by those bears. I know nothing of where my home was, and nothing about any relatives I might have had. Do you realize if my real parents were Christians, and others in my family were Christians, I will one day see them again in heaven?"

"I certainly hope they are up there waiting for you."

Naya blinked against fresh tears. "Many times I have tried to picture my parents in my mind's eye, but I have no recollection of them at all. I love my precious Indian parents with all my heart, and I am so thankful they took me into their family and raised me. I love Tarbcc so much, too. She is such a sweet little sister."

"You do have a wonderful family, Naya."

"Yes. But there is still a part of me down deep inside that yearns to know my real parents."

"That is understandable."

Naya choked up, and there was a note of desperation in her voice as she said, "Oh, I hope they were saved, Walugo."

"I do, too. But there is no way you can know until you get to heaven. But just the possibility that you will find them there is a wonderful thing to hold close to your heart."

"Yes, it is," Naya said softly. "I guess we better lie down and get some sleep."

Walugo nodded. "Morning comes early," he said around a yawn.

Naya lay close to her husband's side, and soon Walugo was fast asleep. It took Naya a little longer, as she lay there pondering all the possibilities heaven might hold for her.

The next day, with Chief Bando's permission, Layne Ward assigned a young Cherokee preacher named Okluskie to pastor a church in the village.

On the same day, at Chief Calhondo's village, Ridino was on the small front porch of his cabin, washing windows, when he heard a familiar voice behind him call his name. He turned about to see a smiling Hoyo coming toward him.

"Hello, Hoyo. What are you so happy about?" Ridino said.

Hoyo then told his friend what had happened to him at the

preaching service in Chief Bando's village the day before.

Ridino rejoiced at the news of Hoyo's salvation and that his career as a shaman had come to an end.

In November of 1819, Naya learned from one of the midwives in the village that she would be giving birth to a baby sometime the following spring, probably in May.

When Naya told Walugo the news, he was ecstatic. On the spot, he asked that they kneel together so he could pray for Naya and the baby. In his prayer, Walugo asked the Lord to keep his wife and baby safe and well through the coming months.

When they told the rest of the family, there was much rejoicing.

As time moved on, Naya spent many hours sewing tiny little clothes. As each article of clothing was finished, she folded it and added it to the growing stack of baby things, which were stored in a trunk lined with soft cotton.

In the middle of a warm night late in May, 1820, Naya awakened Walugo with a muted moan, speaking his name.

His mind was clear instantly. "What is it, love? Is it time for the baby?"

Naya gritted her teeth and nodded, and another low moan escaped her mouth.

Walugo left the bed, and as he was putting on his buckskins, he said, "I will go awaken Analaya and bring her quickly. Will you be all right?"

Naya smiled weakly up at her husband. "I will be all right. You just hurry and get that midwife here. Once Analaya is here, will you go and tell my family that the baby is coming? I want my mother in here with me."

"I will do that. Are you sure you will be all right while I am going after Analaya?"

"I will be fine. Hurry."

Walugo nodded. "I will run like the wind. You just stay right here."

As Walugo dashed out the door, Naya smiled and said to herself, "I wonder where he thinks I might go."

At that instant, she was struck with another pain.

When the midwife had cleaned up the baby, wrapped her in a small blanket, and placed her in her mother's arms, Walugo bent down, kissed the baby's cheek, and told her he loved her. He then kissed Naya's forehead and said, "I will go tell the chief and Tarbee that we have a precious little girl."

Analaya and Nevarra watched Walugo dash out the bedroom door, and moments later, Bando and Tarbee stood to their feet as Walugo entered the parlor of the cabin.

"We heard the baby crying," Bando said. "What is it?"

Walugo's chest swelled up as he said, "It is a girl! Come and see her!"

Seconds later, the grandfather and the aunt joined the grandmother and the midwife at the bedside, while Walugo stood over his wife and little daughter.

Nevarra frowned slightly. "Have you given her a name yet?"

"We chose a boy's name and a girl's name just a few days ago," Naya said.

"Well, since we have a girl," Bando said, "what name did you give her?"

Walugo looked down at Naya. "You tell them, sweetheart."

Naya held the baby close to her heart and said, "On both sides of this cabin, Walugo planted cherry roses. In honor of those beautiful flowers that God made, we are giving our baby girl the name Cherry Rose."

"Oh, that is beautiful!" Nevarra exclaimed.

Tarbee bent down close, looked at the baby, and said, "I am your Aunt Tarbee, Cherry Rose. I love you, and I love your name!"

"Such a beautiful name—Cherry Rose," Analaya said.

Tarbee moved back from the bed a step, and Chief Bando bent down and smiled at the baby. "Hello, little Cherry Rose. I am your grandfather, and I love you."

Tears filled Nevarra's eyes. She moved up beside her husband and leaned close to little Cherry Rose. "And I am your grandmother, sweet little gift from God. I love you, too."

In March of 1821, President James Monroe was still working on his plan to have all the Indians in North Carolina, Tennessee, Georgia, and Alabama forcefully moved to the West so white people could have their land. Military leaders and many members of Congress warned him to go slow. Monroe was told that if the project was not managed carefully, the situation could get out of hand.

In April of 1821, the National Council of Cherokees met as usual at the western base of the Appalachian Mountains of Tennessee.

Council president, Chief John Ross, led the discussion of various matters that were before the Council. Just before closing the meeting, Ross told the Council that he had brought his old friend Chief Sequoyah with him, and he wanted them to hear what Sequoyah had to tell them.

There was applause as Chief Sequoyah stepped up beside the council president. He smiled at the crowd and said, "My friends, all of you know that I have been working for some time to develop an alphabet for our Cherokee language. I am happy to be able to tell you that the job is done. I have now developed a system of eighty-six symbols that make up the Cherokee alphabet."

John Ross said to the crowd, "Now that this is done, very soon Cherokees throughout our nation will be teaching the alphabet in our schools and publishing books and newspapers in our own language. And we will be printing them on our own presses, I might add."

In late 1821, Chief Sequoyah left his cabin in Chief Pathkiller's village, walked a short distance to Chief John Ross's cabin, and knocked on the door. When the door opened, Sequoyah smiled at Quatie and said, "Hello, Mrs. Ross. Does your husband happen to be here?"

Quatie nodded with a smile. "He is in his office at the back of the cabin. He is reading some papers concerning the National Council of Cherokees. Please come in."

Sequoyah followed Quatie to the back room. She stepped in ahead of him and said, "Dear husband, Chief Sequoyah is here to see you."

John stood up and welcomed his friend, and as Quatie walked

away, John gestured for Sequoyah to sit on a wooden chair, then sat down facing him. "What can I do for you?"

"You are aware of the spread of Christianity here in the villages of the Smoky Mountains because of the preaching and leadership of missionary Layne Ward."

"I am. I think it is wonderful."

"Layne Ward came to me yesterday," Sequoyah said. "He has known for some time that the second ambition I had after developing the Cherokee alphabet was to translate the English Bible into the Cherokee language. He urged me to do so as soon as possible since so many Cherokees have become Christians and need the Bible in their own language. As you know, I have been studying English carefully for quite some time in preparation to do the translating. I feel I am ready, but I need your advice. Do you think it is time for me to do the translating? Is the Cherokee nation ready for this?"

Ross nodded. "Chief, having the Bible in our own language is vastly important. The shamans will be unhappy, but that is too bad. Yes, our nation is ready. I urge you to begin your translation work as soon as possible."

Sequoyah's face showed that he was pleased. "I will begin the work immediately."

"Good! And God bless you in it."

Two years passed, and by mid-1823, Chief Sequoyah's work was finished. He had carefully translated the entire Bible into the Cherokee language. By May of 1824, with the help of Layne Ward and Chief John Ross, thousands of copies had been printed and distributed among the Cherokee people.

In January of 1825, John Quincy Adams became president of the United States. He shocked Congress by telling them he was against the idea of forcing the Indians in the southeastern states to move out West. Congress was split on the issue, but a comfortable majority agreed with the new president, and the plan to move the Indians was dropped. When word reached the tribes, there was much rejoicing.

In June of 1825, the National Council of Cherokees met on Indian land in Georgia. There, Chief John Ross had Chief Sequoyah come before the councilmen, and he presented him with a silver medal for his accomplishments with the Cherokee alphabet and for his translation of the Bible into the Cherokee language.

Sequoyah humbly accepted the medal, saying that only with the help of the God of the Bible could he have accomplished these tasks.

The councilmen smiled and nodded, looking at the chief with admiring eyes.

twelve

ne hot day in July of 1827,
Layne Ward was riding his horse
in the Great Smoky Mountains
along a dusty road, having just visited a
Cherokee family who had come to the Lord
under his preaching a few days earlier.

He looked up to see two riders coming
toward him along the road, and he recognized them as two of the men who belonged
to the church in Chief Bando's village. They
appeared to be on their way back to their village.

When they drew up to each other, they pulled rein, and Layne said, "Ubdi! Guwisdo! Nice to see you! I understand from Pastor Okluskie that the church is doing well."

"It is," Guwisdo said. "We are seeing souls come to Jesus almost every week."

"It is such a blessing to be part of it," Ubdi said. "Thank you for coming here and preaching the gospel to our people."

Layne grinned. "I am so glad for the work the Lord is doing here in the Smokies."

"Mr. Ward, have you heard about Chief Pathkiller?" Guwisdo said.

"No. Is something wrong?"

"Chief Sequoyah was at our village yesterday and told Chief Bando that he is very ill."

"Do you know what it is?"

"Well, Chief Sequoyah said it is his heart. Of course, Chief Pathkiller is getting up in years. His shaman is giving him medicine for it, but Chief Sequoyah fears he will not live much longer."

"I'm sorry to hear this," Layne said.

Ubdi sighed and said, "It is hard to see a man who is not a Christian approach the door of death."

"I have talked to Chief Pathkiller many times in the eight years I've been here in the Smokies," Layne said. "He would not turn from his religion and put his faith in Christ. He would never allow me to talk to his wife, Miklia, either."

"So sad," said Guwisdo.

Layne pulled his pocket watch from his vest pocket and looked at it, then slipped it back in place. "I am going to go to Chief Pathkiller's village right now and talk to him again."

"We will be praying, Mr. Ward," Guwisdo said.

"I appreciate that," Layne said as he put his horse to a trot.

When Layne guided his horse into the village, he was disturbed to see a small group of people standing in the village center. Some of the women were weeping.

The village shaman, Lukosko, saw Layne coming and pointed him out to the others. There was a frown on Lukosko's brow as Layne drew up and swung from the saddle.

Layne ran his gaze to the other men and said, "I have come to see Chief Pathkiller."

The shaman's jaw jutted as he fixed the missionary with cold, black eyes and said, "Chief Pathkiller just died."

"I am so sorry," Layne said. "I will go to the cabin and visit his wife."

"No!" Lukosko said. "Some of the women are with her. You cannot visit her."

"We will not allow you to visit Miklia," one of the men said. "It is best if you leave now."

The other men nodded, their faces like stone.

Layne noticed Chief Sequoyah threading his way through the small crowd. The shaman scowled at Sequoyah, who ignored him and said, "Mr. Layne Ward, I am sorry that you have been treated so coldly by Lukosko and his followers."

"Is Chief John Ross at home, Chief Sequoyah?" Layne asked.

Sequoyah shook his head. "He is at a meeting of Cherokee leaders in Tennessee, and his wife is with him."

Layne laid a hand on Sequoyah's shoulder. "Thank you for

your kindness." Then he turned to his horse and swung into the saddle. He looked down at the group and said, "I am very sorry that Chief Pathkiller has died."

With that, he rode away at a trot, his heart heavier than it had been when he rode into the village.

In 1829, Senator Andrew Jackson, who had been born on the western frontier of the Carolinas, became president of the United States. It was evident during his campaign for the presidency that, if elected, he would work to force the Indians out of the southeastern states and have them relocated in the western part of the country.

The very day Jackson took office in early January, he went to work to promote the idea within the government to remove all the Indians from the deep South to the West. Because of his love for North Carolina and his dislike for the Indians, he especially wanted the Cherokees out of that state. He knew, however, that he would have to convince the majority of the men in Congress to back him.

Jackson worked on his scheme as much as possible during the next year, and in the first week of January 1830, he presented his plan to Congress. He was pleased to find that his year of handing out literature and making brief speeches to Congress had paid off. By a show of hands during this session of Congress, he found that the large majority shared his view and were willing to hear more from him on it.

The next time he addressed the legislators, Jackson urged them to pass the Indian Removal Act, which would allow the government to move all tribes wherever they decided. This legislation would declare that if the Indians rebelled when they were told where and when to move, they would face severe reprisals from the well-armed United States Army.

On May 28, 1830, the United States Congress followed President Andrew Jackson's lead and voted by a strong majority to make the Indian Removal Act a federal law. They stipulated clearly in the Act that the Indians must be warned of the severe consequences if they rebelled.

When the official word of the enactment of the Indian Removal Act reached the Cherokees in the Great Smoky Mountains of North Carolina, and of the warning of the severe consequences they would suffer if they rebelled at being moved to the West, there was much anger in every village.

Many of the village chiefs were at the point of rebellion already.

When word of this pending rebellion came to the ears of Chief John Ross, he sent a message to all the chiefs in North Carolina and to the Cherokee leaders of the National Council of Cherokees in Tennessee, Alabama, and Georgia that he was going to Washington, D.C., and demand to see President Andrew Jackson. He was going to do his best to make the president see the injustice of what he and Congress had done.

In the third week of June, John Ross boarded a train in Asheville, North Carolina, and headed for Washington. He stayed in a hotel that night, and the next morning, hired a buggy to take him to the White House.

—❦—

President Andrew Jackson was at his desk in the Oval Office when his secretary, William Bergen, entered and said, "Mr. President, there is a man out there in my office who insists that you allow him to come in and talk to you."

Jackson looked up from the papers he was reading. "Who is he?"

"His name is John Ross. He's from a Cherokee village in North Carolina."

Jackson's jaw clenched hard. "How did he get in here?"

"The guard who brought him in told me that Chief John Ross, as he called him, has identification papers to prove that he's president of the National Council of Cherokees. But…but he's a white man."

"Go get his papers and bring them to me."

"Yes, sir. I'll be right back."

Less than a minute had passed when the secretary was back with the papers. He laid them on the desk in front of the president and said, "Ross says he is a quarter Cherokee. I guess he has to be at least *part* Cherokee to be a chief…and as these papers show, especially to be the president of the National Council of Cherokees."

Jackson read over the papers carefully. When he had finished, he sighed and said, "Go tell him that Vice-President Calhoun will see him tomorrow. I haven't got time for him."

William Bergen wheeled and left the room with Ross's papers in hand.

President Jackson went back to reading the documents before him, but his secretary soon returned and said with a tight voice,

"Sir, Chief John Ross doesn't want to talk to Vice-President Calhoun. He insists on talking to *you*. In his position, he might be able to cause you trouble you certainly don't need. Maybe it would be best if you granted him a few moments."

Jackson chewed on his lower lip, then said, "All right. It's eleven-thirty. Tell him I will see him sometime this afternoon. I'll make him wait a while."

At four-thirty that afternoon, John Ross was still sitting in the waiting room where William Bergen had taken him earlier, when he looked up to see Bergen come in.

"All right, Mr. Ross," Bergen said, "President Jackson will see you now."

"Thank you," said Ross, rising from the chair with his official papers in hand.

He followed Bergen into the Oval Office, where the president was standing at one of the windows, looking outside. As Bergen was leaving the room, the president moved up behind his desk and pointed to a pair of wooden chairs that sat in front of it.

"Have a seat, Mr. Ross."

When both men were seated, Jackson looked at Ross across his desk and said, "You sure don't look like an Indian."

Ross ran his fingers through his blond hair. "I know, but I am a quarter Cherokee."

"So your papers said. I only have twenty minutes to talk to you. What is it you want?"

John locked eyes with him. "Mr. President, this Indian Removal Act that you and Congress put into law is a grave injustice to all of the Indians you plan to move out West. We are not animals to be forced from one pasture to another. We are human beings. It was bad enough when the white men came here and made our Cherokee people leave the lowlands of North Carolina and have to live on the steep slopes of the Smoky Mountains and do our farming on such difficult land. But at least it is now our home. Please consider the heartbreak it will be for our people to have to give up their homes and go to a strange land. I am asking you to revoke this horrendous law."

John saw the president's face flush. "The Act stands, Mr. Indian Chief John Ross. And I warn you…there will be devastating consequences if you and your people rebel at being made to move to the West. Do you understand what I'm saying?"

John's first impulse was to punch the man in the nose, but he wiped the back of his hand across his mouth and said, "Just where in the West are you planning to send us?"

"The congressmen and I have been working on this, and the place we have selected is a large, uninhabited section of land between Kansas and Texas that covers seventy thousand square miles. I have already dubbed it *Indian Territory.*"

"So, it seems your plan is well set."

"Absolutely."

"When will the removal of the Indians to Indian Territory begin?"

"I'm not sure, yet. It's going to take some time…maybe four or five years. The plan is to take the Choctaw, Creek, Chickasaw, and Seminole tribes there first. Your Cherokee tribe will be the last to go. But it will take some time to get it all arranged with the United States Army since it will involve thousands of soldiers."

John Ross rose to his feet. "Looks like my twenty minutes have expired, Mr. President. I will be going now."

Jackson stood up. "No hard feelings?"

"I would be lying if I said there were no hard feelings." Chief John Ross turned and left the Oval Office as President Andrew Jackson watched him go.

Deeply disappointed, Chief John Ross returned to the Smoky Mountains of North Carolina and spread the word to all the village chiefs, so they could inform their people what President Andrew Jackson had told him. He then sent riders to call for a meeting of the National Council of Cherokees on Tuesday, June 29, at their usual spot on the west edge of the Appalachian Mountains in Tennessee.

When the meeting took place, the Cherokee leaders were very upset, but unanimously agreed with their president that they dare not bring the United States Army down on them by rebelling against the Indian Removal Act.

Ross ran his gaze over their faces and said, "My friends, for the sake of all Cherokees, you have made the right decision. When we are told that we must begin our journey to Indian Territory, we must obey and give up our homeland without resistance. My hope is that we will find a place to call home in Indian Territory."

When the Cherokee leaders returned to their villages, they met with their people and told them what was happening. They explained carefully why the Cherokees must not rebel against the white man's government when they were told to make their move to Indian Territory.

In Chief Bando's village, groups of villagers were standing

around, talking about what Chief Bando had told them. In one group of men, an angry Yonwi, who was now forty-four years of age, said, "I cannot just stand by and let the white man's government make my family and me leave our home." His eyes flashed with wrath. "What I would like to do is go to Washington City and kill President Andrew Jackson!"

Chief Bando happened to be walking by with his family. He stepped up to Yonwi and said, "You must not talk nor think like that. Murder is a sin against God. I agree that the president and the Congress are wrong in what they are planning, but we are greatly outnumbered by the whites. Such an act would not only be a sin against God, but would bring the wrath of the white man's government and their huge army against us. For our own safety, all Cherokees must remain peaceable." Chief Bando looked at Yonwi sternly. "Do you understand what I am saying?"

"I understand," Yonwi said quietly.

Chief Bando managed a smile. "Good."

As Yonwi walked toward his cabin with his close friends, Shoro, Coya, and Chula did their best to calm him down and to make him see that his anger would only bring him trouble.

Walugo, Naya, and Cherry Rose stepped into their cabin, and the ten-year-old looked up at her parents and said, "I do not understand why the white people are so mean. Mother, you are a white person and you are not mean. Mr. and Mrs. Layne Ward are white people, and they are not mean. But why are most of the white people so mean to the Indians? Why do they hate us?"

Naya sighed and looked to her husband for help.

Walugo laid a hand on his daughter's shoulder. "It really is not the majority of the white people who hate Indians, sweet Cherry

Rose. It is the majority of the men who run the government, and the soldiers in the white man's army."

Cherry Rose, who had opened her heart to Jesus when she was eight, said, "Jesus loves all the Indians, doesn't He?"

"He sure does, sweetie," Naya said.

The child ran her gaze between her parents. "Since you told me on my last birthday how Mother was found under the wagon and was brought to live with Grandfather and Grandmother in this village, it has helped me to understand why my skin is not as dark as most Cherokees, and my hair isn't black, but light brown."

"That is right," Walugo said. "You are half Indian and half white."

Cherry Rose looked at her mother and smiled. "I am proud to be half white, Mother, because you are white. But I do love being Cherokee."

Time moved on, and one day in the fall of 1833, when Cherry Rose was thirteen years of age, Walugo and Naya had three Christian girls who were close friends of their daughter in their home for an evening meal. During the meal, the girls began to tease Cherry Rose because she was half white.

"You can tease me all you want to," Cherry Rose said with a grin, "but look at my mother. Though the colors of her skin, hair, and eyes are different than Cherokees, her heart is *all* Cherokee. Cherokees saved her life when she was just a baby, and she loves them." She looked at Naya. "Isn't that right, Mother?"

"You are right, sweet daughter."

Cherry Rose looked at the three girls and said, "As far as I am concerned, I am *all* Cherokee!"

Naya rose from her chair and put an arm around her daughter. "Do you really mean what you just said…that as far as you are concerned, you are *all* Cherokee?"

"Yes, I do!"

"Well, if your father is in agreement, why don't we just change your name from Cherry Rose to *Cherokee Rose*?"

Walugo smiled. "*Cherokee Rose*! I like that!"

The thirteen-year-old girl looked at her father, then at her mother, who were both smiling at her. "Are you sure, Mother? I would not hurt you for anything, but I know you feel as I do. The Cherokees will always be our people."

Naya nodded. "Yes, they will always be our people, and I would be proud to see your name changed to Cherokee Rose."

Tears filmed the girl's eyes. She looked at her father. "Are you sure it is all right with you?"

Walugo's smile spread widely as he left his chair and moved up beside Naya. "It is *more* than all right." He leaned down close and kissed his daughter's cheek. "From now on, you are our little Cherokee Rose."

The three teenage girls smiled and clapped their hands.

Cherokee Rose put her arms around the necks of her parents and said, "Thank you, Father! Thank you, Mother! This makes my heart very, very happy!"

thirteen

n the last day of June, 1835, Chief Sequoyah was talking to a man named Deendo, who lived in the same village. They were standing at the south edge of the village in the bright sunlight when Deendo looked past Sequoyah and said, "Oh, no. Here comes trouble."

Sequoyah turned around and saw riders coming toward them. An even dozen soldiers were escorting two white men in business suits. "It always means trouble when white soldiers ride into our village," Sequoyah said. "And it is usually worse when civilians are with them."

Sequoyah and Deendo waited for the riders to draw up, then the officer in the lead said, "Do either of you understand English?"

"We both do," Sequoyah said. "What do you want?"

"These two men with us are Congressmen Albert Foster and Chester Waltham. They want to speak to your chief. I believe his name is Tisimndo. Correct?"

Sequoyah nodded.

"Isn't this the village that Chief Pathkiller used to head up?" Congressman Waltham asked.

"Yes. Chief Tisimndo became our chief when Chief Pathkiller died eight years ago."

"Is Chief Tisimndo here?" Congressman Foster asked.

"He is. Let us go into the village."

"Chief Sequoyah," Deendo said, "I will hurry ahead and tell Chief Tisimndo these men are here." And he ran toward the center of the village.

As the riders urged their horses forward at a walk, and Sequoyah moved alongside them, Chester Waltham said, "So you are Chief Sequoyah, the one who produced the Cherokee alphabet and translated the Bible into the Cherokee language."

Sequoyah looked up at him and nodded. "Yes."

"Quite some task, I would say."

"It kept me busy for a while."

No more was said as they moved closer to the center of the village. When they reached it, several adults and children were gathered there in a group, looking the soldiers and the congressmen over.

Sequoyah saw Chief Tisimndo in his full headdress coming toward them, with Deendo beside him. As they drew near, Deendo pointed out the officer in charge. Chief Tisimndo stepped up to the mounted officer and said, "I am Chief Tisimndo. You want to talk to me?"

The officer gestured toward the two men in civilian clothing.

"This is Congressman Albert Foster, and this is Congressman Chester Waltham. They have been sent here by President Andrew Jackson to talk to Chief John Ross, president of the National Council of Cherokees. Since you are the village chief, we wanted to talk to you first so you would know why we are here."

Tisimndo nodded. "What do these men want to talk to Chief John Ross about?"

"He can tell you after we have talked to him, Chief," Albert Foster said. "We are short on time. Is he home?"

"Yes, he is home. I will lead you to his cabin."

The congressmen dismounted and followed the chief deeper into the village.

Some thirty minutes had passed when everybody saw Chief John Ross and Quatie coming toward them, accompanied by the two congressmen. The congressmen moved up to the soldiers, and Chester Waltham said to the officer in charge, "We're ready to go."

The crowd watched the men ride away, and when they had passed from view, Chief John Ross said to Chief Tisimndo, "I need to have everyone in the village here so I can tell them what the congressmen told me."

Tisimndo nodded. "I will send some men to announce that we are having a meeting."

Within twenty minutes, every person under Chief Tisimndo's leadership was in the crowd at the center of the village. The chief and John Ross stood together, facing them. Tisimndo told them that two congressmen of the United States government had just been there and talked to Chief John Ross, and now Chief John Ross would tell them what the congressmen had said.

Tisimndo remained at Ross's side.

Ross looked from person to person in the crowd as he said, "Congressmen Albert Foster and Chester Waltham were sent here by President Andrew Jackson to bring a message to me as president of the National Council of Cherokees. They told me that within one week, the United States army will begin to move the Choctaw, the Creek, the Chickasaw, and the Seminole tribes on the long journey to Indian Territory in the West."

A disturbed look came over the faces of all the adults and young people in the crowd. The children were paying little attention.

"Now, as to the Cherokees," Chief John Ross said. "The congressmen told me that it will probably be two to three years before we will be moved to the West. They explained that it is going to take some time to move the other four tribes to Indian Territory and get them settled in their new home. They made it clear, though, that our day will come.

"That is all I can tell you at this point, but I wanted all of you to know what President Jackson is planning for us. I am so sorry that I was unable to convince him to cancel his plans."

Silently the members of the village walked away, each lost in his or her thoughts. Some of the children asked questions of their parents, but were told it would be explained to them later.

The next day, with Chief Tisimndo's help, John Ross gathered men of the village to carry the news to the Cherokee people in

Tennessee, Georgia, and Alabama. John Ross told them that he would ride to every village in the Smoky Mountains of North Carolina and break the news to them.

Chief Tisimndo and Chief Sequoyah stood with John Ross as the messengers rode away. Ross's heart was heavy as he watched the riders until they vanished from view. With a deep sigh, he turned to Tisimndo and Sequoyah. "White man's government has been talking about moving us to the West for so many years, it became like a soft wind. We knew it was there, but paid little attention to it."

Sequoyah nodded. "You have described it well, John."

Ross took a deep breath. "I hoped the removal to the West would never happen. The president and those men in Washington City have no idea what chaos they are creating in our lives. We are a peaceful nation, other than a few renegades here and there. Our nation has never caused any problems nor posed any threat to the white men."

"This is so unfair, but what can we do?" Sequoyah said. "We have no choice but to obey them."

"You are right, Sequoyah," Tisimndo said. "With the power of their army, we dare not resist them. We will have to move to the West when they tell us it is time."

John Ross bowed his head for a moment, then raised it and looked around at the mountains that were his home. "Well, my friends, we Cherokees will not despair. We are a strong people, and we must never let white man's government break our spirit. We will do as they say, and we must help our people to see that our hearts and minds must unite as one. When the soldiers come to move us westward, we will be ready. And may the great God of heaven help us!"

Two days later, after already visiting more than half of the Smoky Mountain villages, John Ross rode into Chief Bando's village. When he explained his reason for being there, Chief Bando assembled all of his people together, and Ross told them what the white man's government intended to do. Chief Bando then told his people not to let their tempers get the best of them. They had known the time was coming, and they must make the best of it.

That evening when Chief Bando entered his cabin, he found Walugo, Naya, and fifteen-year-old Cherokee Rose there. Cherokee Rose was weeping, and Nevarra was trying to console her.

Bando moved to his granddaughter and in a soft voice said, "What is wrong?"

"Oh, Grandfather, I don't want to leave my home here in the Smoky Mountains," Cherokee Rose said with tears running down her cheeks. "It is mean and wicked of the white man's president to do this to us. Our people have lived here for many, many years, and worked hard on this land. How can one selfish white man decide the fate of so many people? It is just not fair!"

Bando took hold of her hand, holding it tenderly. "We have all felt the same way you do, sweet girl. We had hoped that it would never really happen, but now it looks like it is going to take place."

"What will happen to us?" Cherokee Rose sobbed out. "Can we all go to the West together, or will the soldiers break up our families?"

Bando drew her close in his arms. "Hush now, little one. Our God is in control of our lives, as always. He knows how we feel and understands why we are so terribly upset. He is not going to allow the white men to break up our family. Nothing can come into the life of a child of God that does not first get past the great Shepherd who is leading us through this life. The Lord must have a good reason for allowing us to be moved westward to Indian Territory."

Sniffling, Cherokee Rose looked at him through her tears, her lips quivering.

Bando gave her a smile. "Try to look at it as a new adventure, sweet granddaughter. You will be seeing new places and meeting new people. Yes, it will be hard for us, but the Cherokees are a resilient people, and with us in this family also being God's children, He will be right there to help us. He promised in His Word that He would never leave us nor forsake us, and He will keep that promise."

Bando went to a nearby table and picked up his Bible. He handed it to Cherokee Rose and said, "First, I want you to read to all of us what it says in Psalm 18:30."

She took the Bible and opened it to the page where the verse was found. Taking a shaky breath, she read aloud: "'As for God, his way is perfect: the word of the LORD is tried: he is a buckler to all those that trust in him.'" She nodded, and a thin smile graced her lips. "Yes, Grandfather, God's way *is* perfect. And if I have it right, a buckler is a shield."

"That is correct. God is a shield to all those that trust in Him. Now read us Romans 8:28."

Cherokee Rose turned to the New Testament and soon had the right page. "'And we know that all things work together for good to them that love God, to them who are the called according to his purpose.'" She wiped tears from her cheeks. "I have read this before, but together with Psalm 18:30, it means more than ever. I must learn to trust my Lord from now on."

Cherokee Rose's parents and her grandmother formed a tight circle with her and her grandfather, embracing each other with optimism showing on their faces.

Time moved on. In the November 1836 election, Martin Van Buren, who had been Andrew Jackson's vice-president since 1833, was elected president of the United States. When Jackson relinquished his office to Van Buren in January 1837, he voiced his regret that the Cherokee Indians still had not been moved to Indian Territory. Van Buren reminded Jackson that he was in full agreement with his plan to do so, and it would be a priority with him to get it done.

During the first week of July 1837, Chief John Ross rode into all forty-three villages of the Smoky Mountain Cherokees, announcing that their Cherokee brethren in Tennessee, Georgia, and Alabama were being moved to Indian Territory. The Alabama Cherokees were first to begin the journey on June 26. Three days later, the Georgia Cherokees started their journey, and on July 1 the Tennessee Cherokees left their homes and headed west. Each group had a large military escort.

When the people in the villages asked John Ross how long it would be till they were forced to make the move, he told them he figured it would be a year or more. He explained that the white man's government would want to see that all the other Cherokees were well settled in their new home before they brought the North Carolina Cherokees in.

—❧—

In the late summer of 1838, President Martin Van Buren and Congress issued the order under the Indian Removal Act of 1830 for the fifteen thousand Cherokees of North Carolina's Smoky Mountains to be evicted from their homes and forced to travel to Indian Territory, which was over a thousand miles to the west. The journey must begin no later than mid-October.

On Tuesday, August 28, 1838, a platoon of fifteen United States army cavalrymen rode into Chief Tisimndo's village, with the Indians looking on in trepidation. Chief John Ross had told them a few days earlier of President Van Buren's deadline to begin the journey to Indian Territory.

Chief Tisimndo was on the main path that led into the village, in conversation with Chief John Ross, and both men stiffened when they saw the grim-faced soldiers riding toward them.

On the lead horse was a broad and powerful man with stars on his hat and uniform that told them he was a general. There was a malevolent look in his eyes. He had a wide mustache that drooped at the corners of his downturned mouth. He set his gaze on the man wearing the full headdress and said, "I assume you are Chief Tisimndo."

The chief nodded. "Yes."

"I am General Winfield Scott. I am here as a spokesman for President Martin Van Buren, and I need to speak to Chief John Ross."

Ross took a step closer. "I am Chief John Ross."

Scott looked him straight in the eye and said, "I was told you are part Cherokee. You look all white to me."

"I am a quarter Cherokee. What did you wish to speak to me about?"

"I want you to bring together all the men who belong to the General Council."

"This will take some time, General. I will send riders all over these mountains to fetch them."

Scott scowled. "How much time will that take?"

"About two hours. There are forty-two other villages."

"All right. Get them moving."

Just over two hours had passed when all the chiefs of the Council were gathered for the meeting with General Winfield Scott, which was held just outside Chief Tisimndo's village.

"I am here to inform you," General Scott began, "that President Martin Van Buren and the Congress of the United States have issued the order for all the Cherokees in these Smoky Mountains to make preparations for your journey to Indian Territory. The plan is for you to begin the journey on Monday, October 17."

Scott could not miss the angry looks and the fire in the eyes of most of the chiefs. He turned to John Ross and said, "You had better have a talk with these men, Ross. All of the North Carolina Cherokees must obey President Van Buren's orders without the slightest resistance, or they will suffer the consequences. And believe me, they will be severe."

John nodded, and said in a low voice, "I will make sure they understand this. I will talk to them after you are gone."

"See that you do."

The general went on to say that he and seven thousand soldiers would escort the fifteen thousand North Carolina Cherokees on the journey to Indian Territory.

John Ross was stunned to learn that Scott would head up the military unit that would force them to make the journey West. He had heard how vicious General Winfield Scott could be.

Scott went on. "I want you all to know that the tribes that have already been moved to Indian Territory are glad to be there."

Anger and distrust still showed in the eyes of the chiefs.

Noting it, Scott said, "Listen to me! All of you had better accept the Indian Removal Act graciously. Make sure you get it across to your people that any resistance, whether before we leave or while we're on the journey, will bring serious discipline by the soldiers. It is best for you Cherokees if all of you make up your minds to submit to the soldiers. Do you understand?"

There was dead silence.

"I asked if you understand!"

"I will see to it that they understand, General," Chief John Ross said.

Scott burned him with hot eyes. "You'd better!"

When the army platoon had mounted up and were riding away, Chief John Ross stood before the Council and said, "None of us want this awful thing to happen to us and our people. But as you can see, we have no choice. Please put your anger aside. It will only bring suffering at the hands of the soldiers, and very possibly bloodshed. Go back and tell your people exactly what General Scott told you. I know much about his military career, and he is like a wild beast when he is disobeyed. Please warn your people of this."

—⌒—

Soon the men of the Council were on their horses, heading back to their villages. Chief Tisimndo and Chief John Ross walked together to where a crowd had gathered within the village. Every inhabitant of the village was there, and Layne Ward and his wife were also there, having ridden in a short time before the soldiers arrived.

John Ross told the people what they had learned from General Winfield Scott, then turned it over to Chief Tisimndo, who warned everyone not to resist when the soldiers came on Monday, October 17.

When the crowd had dispersed, Layne Ward approached Chief John Ross with Sylvia at his side, and said, "We have something to ask you my friend."

"And what is that?"

Layne took hold of Sylvia's hand. "Sylvia and I would like to go to Indian Territory with you. Would that be all right?"

John Ross gripped Layne's free hand, smiled, and said, "We would all be happy to have you!"

fourteen

awn broke on the cold, rainy morning of October 17, 1838, beneath a heavy sky. The clouds were agitated by high winds. They piled, rolled, and mushroomed while obscuring the peaks of the Great Smoky Mountains of North Carolina.

At the southern edge of the central part of the mountains, General Winfield Scott and his seven thousand mounted soldiers ate breakfast in their tents out of the rain. A few ate inside the wagons that carried their food and supplies.

Rain was still falling when the general mounted his horse and led his men deeper into the mountains, spreading them out toward all forty-three villages to get the Indians ready for their journey.

The North Carolina Cherokees had been preparing for this occasion for many weeks. Every man, woman, and child, although deeply distressed, was ready for the long, grueling journey. Many tears were shed as they made last-minute preparations to follow a pending command that was totally senseless to them.

At Chief Tisimndo's village, Chief John Ross and Quatie were just finishing their breakfast when there was a loud knock on the door, and General Winfield Scott's booming voice announced his presence.

When John opened the door, he noted that the rain was not falling as heavily as it had been. The general looked past John and said, "This is your wife, I presume."

"Yes," said John, looking back at her. "Her name is Quatie."

"Full-blooded Cherokee?"

"Yes."

Scott nodded. "I hope you were able to get it across to all the Cherokees in these mountains that they are to obey every command that I or any of my soldiers give them."

"I have done my best to get this across, General, but I cannot guarantee that everyone will abide by it."

Scott's eyes flashed fire. "They had better abide by it, or they're gonna be sorry!"

In the villages, most of the families were eating breakfast together, dreading the moment the orders would come to climb into their wagons or get on their horses. Some had no horses or wagons of their own, and would have to try to find wagons to ride in. Most, however, would have to walk.

Light rain continued to fall under a heavily clouded sky, and in many cabins, the Cherokees lit lanterns to dispel the gloom in their rooms and the gloom in their hearts.

Some of the families were startled when the doors burst open and they saw the sudden gleam of bayonets as the soldiers commanded them to get ready to move out. Children screamed and tried to hide behind their parents while sobbing loudly, tears running unchecked down their cheeks. The soldiers snapped at the parents and told them to shut their children up.

In one cabin, a soldier shouted above the cries of the children, "Shut up, you bunch of heathens! Just do as you're told, and no one will hurt you!" The father and mother tried desperately to quiet their little ones while the soldier glared at them.

As the hours passed, Cherokee men were seized in their fields while taking one last look at their cattle or while they were moving along the roads. Women were taken from their spinning wheels, and children from their play.

Some of the Indian men resisted, and they were jabbed with bayonets or horsewhipped.

At Chief Bando's village, Yonwi carried boxes and sacks of various items from the cabin to the wagon that stood just outside the front door. His wife, Towanna, sat on a wooden chair near the door and watched her husband come and go. Her face was pale and her eyes were dull. As she watched Yonwi place an armload in the wagon, she told herself it was a good thing they did not have many more belongings, or some would have to be left behind.

When Yonwi entered the cabin for another armload, he

wiped rain water from his eyes and glanced at his wife. Her face was even more pale, and her frail body shook as she rubbed her upper arms.

He stepped to her, knelt down, and took hold of her hands. They were hot to the touch, even though she was shivering. Dread filled his very being as he asked, "Are you feeling worse, Towanna?"

She drew in a shaky breath and said, "I will be all right. Do not worry about me."

Yonwi looked into her dull eyes. "You are not convincing me."

"My husband, we have no choice in this matter. If you would refuse to go on the journey because I am ill, those hateful soldiers would probably kill you. We must be ready to move out when they say it is time. I wish you would let me help you load the wagon. Two of us could do it faster."

"No! The long journey will be hard enough on you. I want you to rest as much as you can. I am almost finished. Only three or four more trips, and we will be ready to go."

A heavy shiver ran through Towanna again. Yonwi grabbed a blanket that lay on a table close by and placed it around her shoulders, tucking it close to her trembling body.

Yonwi moved further back in the cabin to pick up another load of goods, and at the same time, Towanna saw two soldiers moving toward the open front door. A gasp escaped her lips, and she smothered it quickly with her hand.

Yonwi heard the gasp, and when he turned to look at his wife, he saw the two soldiers step inside the cabin. One was a husky corporal, and the other a slender private. Each carried a rifle.

Towanna's eyes were wide with fright as the corporal looked at Yonwi and the pile of goods next to him. He shifted his gaze to Towanna and said, "Get off that chair, woman, and help your husband load the wagon! We must move out very soon! A little rain won't hurt you!"

Yonwi moved toward the soldiers, his dark eyes fixed on the corporal. "My wife is not well," he said. "It was *I* who sat her down and told her to rest."

The corporal shook his head. "She has to help you. We need all the wagons loaded and every Indian ready to go when General Scott says it's time to pull out."

"I will have the wagon loaded in plenty of time. Now go away!"

The corporal pointed a stiff finger at Yonwi. "You're in trouble, redskin!" He turned to the private and said, "Go get two more men, and bring a whip back with you."

The private darted out the door, and Yonwi started toward the corporal, who quickly raised his rifle and cocked it. "Come on, Indian! If you'd rather have a bullet than get horsewhipped, the choice is yours!"

Yonwi froze, and Towanna sat wringing her hands.

A few moments later, the private stepped in, gripping a whip in his hand, and told the corporal he had two men outside.

Yonwi was forced out into the rain at gunpoint. His deerskin jacket and his shirt were removed, and he was flung to the ground. Towanna rose from the chair and moved outside, keeping the blanket around her shoulders.

While the three other soldiers held Yonwi facedown on the muddy ground, the corporal cracked the whip across Yonwi's back repeatedly. Yonwi winced with each hissing blow, gritting his teeth in agony.

Tears mixed with rain on Towanna's face. She threw the blanket aside and ran haltingly to where the soldiers held her husband, screaming for the corporal to stop. He paid her no attention. The whipping went on.

Towanna stepped up to the corporal and hit him on the jaw with her fist. He knocked her to the ground with one swoop of his arm. She tried to rise to her feet, but her body betrayed her, and she fell into the mud.

The corporal began whipping Yonwi again.

Suddenly, Chief Bando was on the scene. He rushed up to the corporal and said, "What is going on here?"

The corporal paused with the whip in his hand. "I told this Indian to make his wife help him load his wagon, and he said she was sick. He refused to do as I commanded him, and he was about to attack me. For that, he gets the whip! His wife tried to interfere, and for that, she got knocked down."

Chief Bando helped Towanna to her feet and steadied her. He looked at the corporal and said, "It is true that Towanna is not feeling well. You had no right to treat her as you did. Any husband would have reacted the way Yonwi did."

The corporal looked at Towanna, then said to the other soldiers, "I've whipped her husband enough."

As the soldiers picked up their rifles, the corporal helped Yonwi to his feet and said, "You'd better not give us any more trouble on the journey, or you will be sorry." With that, the corporal and the other soldiers walked away.

Bando looked at Yonwi's back and said, "We will need to put some root salve on those stripes. I am sorry for what happened to you and Towanna, but you must be careful not to anger the soldiers anymore."

Soon the rain stopped, and each household in the Smoky Mountains was busy with last minute loading of wagons and packing up what those who would be walking could carry. A deep sadness pervaded each village.

By late morning, General Winfield Scott had all fifteen thousand Cherokees gathered in one large field, surrounded by his seven thousand well-armed soldiers. Scott spoke to the crowd in a loud voice and explained the rules to be obeyed on the journey. He used the Cherokee men who had already been horsewhipped or cut with bayonets as examples of the consequences if the rules were not obeyed.

"Are there any questions?" General Scott said.

A tall, broad-shouldered white man and a shorter, thinner Cherokee man stepped out of the crowd and moved up to him.

"General Scott, I am Layne Ward, a missionary to the Cherokees. This man with me is Pastor Jesse Bushyhead. We would like your permission to pray with our people before the journey begins."

General Scott pulled at his droopy mustache. After a moment of silence, he nodded. "All right. Go ahead and have your prayer."

"Thank you," Layne said.

A few soldiers removed their hats and bowed their heads, and a small number of the Cherokees joined them as first Layne Ward and then Jesse Bushyhead led them in prayer. After the last "amen," General Scott announced that the people should go ahead and eat their midday meal. In exactly one hour, they would be on their way.

After lunch, the soldiers hurriedly lined up the Cherokee wagons in a long line, four-abreast. Most of the Indian families had wagons, which were pulled by oxen or horses. Those who did not, and had not found room aboard another wagon, were prepared to walk, carrying their belongings on their backs. Many of the Indian men were on horseback and would ride beside the wagons their families occupied.

The soldiers rode their horses in long lines beside the wagons, and were also grouped at the rear of the long train to keep their eyes on everyone.

Soon, General Winfield Scott and a dozen of his officers were at the head of the line, ready to start the journey. As General Scott put his horse in motion, signaling for the wagons to move out, thousands of heads turned to look back at the mountainous region they had called home for generations. Many memories flooded their minds, and the tears flowed.

On the driver's seat of Walugo's wagon, eighteen-year-old Cherokee Rose sat next to her mother, who was positioned between her and her father. She looked back at their village and wept. "If I live to be a hundred years old," she said, "I will never forget this home of my birth. My heart will always be here."

Cherokee Rose continued to lean from the seat and look back, memorizing every hill and valley, the lay of the land, and her village. Soon a curve in the road blocked her view, and her beloved land disappeared in the distance.

Cherokee Rose turned and faced forward, looking past the long rows of wagons ahead at the inscrutable trail to the unknown. Lost in her thoughts and memories, she continued to weep, and silently prayed for her Cherokee people.

Naya put an arm around her, squeezed tight, and said, "Precious daughter, I know this is very difficult for you, but you must not let it crush you. The Lord could have stopped the white man's government from doing this, but He did not."

"Remember the Bible verses your grandfather showed you," Walugo said. "Psalm 18:30 and Romans 8:28. God's way is perfect, and He has a purpose for everything that He allows to come into your life, or that He *puts* in your life."

Cherokee Rose wiped away her tears and leaned forward so she could look at both her mother and her father. "It is hard, but I know both of you are right. Pray for me, that I will have the faith to trust God for my future."

As the days passed on the long trek, the Cherokee men and women were often whipped or nicked with bayonets when they did not obey the soldiers precisely. Chief John Ross went to General Winfield Scott about it, but Scott told him that the Cherokee people had been warned of the consequences if they broke the rules.

Seeing that he could not convince the general to make his men ease up on the Cherokees, John Ross rode his horse among the long lines of wagons, warning the people not to break the general's rules.

fifteen

n the following Saturday evening, General Winfield Scott chose a large section of open land beside a creek and led the wagons into a circle to camp for the night. Both Indians and soldiers lit fires so they could cook supper, and the smell of smoke soon filled the air.

Layne Ward entered the area where the military men were gathered and approached General Scott. "May I talk to you for a moment, sir?"

"All right. What is it?"

"Well, sir, tomorrow is Sunday, and I would like to have a preaching service in the morning for all who wish to attend. We could hold the service right after breakfast, then move on right afterward."

The general shook his head. "We can't spare the time, Ward. It's a long way to Indian Territory, and we must make use of every hour of daylight. If you're gonna have preaching services, it'll have to be at night. And they'll have to be short so those of us who don't attend can still get our sleep. So make 'em short—fifteen or twenty minutes at the most."

Layne nodded. "As you say, General. We'll have our Sunday service tomorrow evening after supper, then."

"And remember…no more than twenty minutes."

"I'll remember, sir."

On the following Monday afternoon, many of the travelers saw four soldiers angrily drag two older men from the long line of those on foot and beat them with whips.

Walugo and his family were close enough in the line of wagons to see the whole thing. Just as they drew near the spot where the soldiers were forcing the battered old men to their feet, a young lieutenant drew up on his horse, dismounted, and began to rail at the soldiers for what they had just done. The soldiers argued with the lieutenant, saying the old men had dared talk back to them when they were told to walk faster.

Seated as usual beside her mother, Cherokee Rose fixed her gaze on the lieutenant as he snapped at the two corporals and two privates, "I'd better not see you mistreat any of the Indians again, do you hear me?"

Neither Cherokee Rose nor her parents could hear what the four soldiers said in reply, but the girl kept watching the scene until the line of wagons made a slight turn, and they passed from view.

"I like that lieutenant," Cherokee Rose said to her parents. "He has some compassion. Seems I've noticed him before since we started on this journey."

"I have, too," Naya said. "He is a fine young man."

Cherokee Rose giggled. "And handsome, too."

Walugo chuckled. "Oh, so you noticed his good looks, did you?"

She leaned forward and fixed her father with steady eyes. "How could I help but notice, Father? Why, he is almost as handsome as you are!"

As Naya was laughing at her daughter's words, Chief John Ross drew up beside the wagon on his horse. "Hello," he said with a smile. "*Who* is almost as handsome as your father, Cherokee Rose?"

She pointed back along the trail. "That young lieutenant back there who was yelling at those four soldiers for mistreating two older Cherokee men."

"Guess I didn't notice them."

"I wish I knew that lieutenant's name," Cherokee Rose said. "I would compliment him for rebuking those solders."

"You're sure he was a lieutenant?" John Ross said.

"Yes. The insignias on his uniform were easy to recognize."

"Can you describe him?"

The girl smiled. "He is in his early twenties. I would say he stands an inch or two over six feet tall. He is broad-shouldered and appears to be quite muscular. He is also very handsome. Like I said, *almost* as handsome as Father."

"What color is his hair?" John Ross asked.

"It is almost the same color as my hair…light brown. And his eyes are blue."

John Ross nodded. "Your description fits only one lieutenant among these troops that I know. His name is Britt Claiborne."

"Lieutenant Britt Claiborne," Cherokee Rose said. "I like that name."

Walugo and Naya exchanged glances and smiled at each other.

A few days later, when the travelers stopped beside another small stream to camp for the night, Cherokee Rose saw a soldier with sergeant's stripes scolding a young Cherokee woman. When she told him she had not done what he was accusing her of, the soldier slapped her, knocking her down.

Several soldiers were standing nearby, rifles in hand, and the other Indians who were there knew better than to interfere.

Suddenly, Lieutenant Britt Claiborne appeared and said to the sergeant, "I saw what you did!"

The sergeant looked at him with fiery eyes. "She had it comin', Lieutenant!"

Claiborne leaned down and helped the young woman, who was rubbing a large red spot on her cheek, to her feet.

Cherokee Rose rushed up and took hold of the woman's hand, steadying her. "Simanda, are you all right?"

When Simanda nodded, Britt Claiborne turned to the sergeant and said, "It takes a real man to slap a woman, doesn't it, Ed?"

Ed Harrison's face was beet-red. "Shut your mouth, Britt! I'll slap anybody who has it comin'! And she had it comin'!"

"I don't care what she did, you had no right to slap her!"

Sergeant Harrison's mouth went tight and anger flared in his eyes. "Now *you* have it comin'!" he said, and swung a fist at the lieutenant.

Claiborne dodged the blow, and his left fist struck the sergeant's jaw with a solid crack. Harrison staggered backward, and Claiborne followed and landed a roundhouse right. Harrison hit the ground on his back, out cold.

Cherokee Rose, still steadying Simanda, said, "Thank you, Lieutenant, for coming to my friend's rescue. I will take her to her wagon now."

Britt Claiborne looked into Cherokee Rose's dark-brown eyes and smiled. "You're welcome."

The next day, Wednesday, October 31, the travelers were moving westward once again. Walugo and Naya listened as their daughter told the story of seeing Lieutenant Britt Claiborne come to Simanda's rescue.

Walugo looked past Naya at his daughter on the wagon seat, and said, "The more I hear about this young lieutenant, the more I like him."

Just then all three of them were surprised to see Lieutenant Claiborne ride up from behind them and draw close to the right side of the wagon. He smiled down at Cherokee Rose and said, "Hello. Is your friend all right?"

"She is fine. Her cheek is bruised a little, but she is all right."

"I am glad to hear it. I…ah…I didn't get a chance to ask your name, young lady."

She blushed. "My name is Cherokee Rose."

"That's a pretty name. And are these your parents?"

"Yes. My father is Walugo, and my mother is Naya."

"Glad to meet you, folks. You certainly have a lovely daughter."

"We think so, Lieutenant Claiborne," Walugo said.

The lieutenant's eyebrows arched. "Oh. So you know my name."

"Chief John Ross told us your name a few days ago, after we saw you rebuking those four soldiers for mistreating the elderly Cherokee men."

Cherokee Rose looked up at the mounted man and smiled. "Lieutenant Claiborne, I want to tell you how much I appreciate how you protect us from being brutalized by the soldiers."

Britt adjusted his officer's hat and said, "Many of our men go far beyond reason in picking on your people just because they are Indians. It makes me mad, and when I see it happen, I have to step in."

"You are quite young to be a lieutenant," Cherokee Rose said. "The army must like you."

He chuckled. "Well, I'll tell you my age if you will let me guess yours."

"All right."

"I'm twenty-one."

"That is very close to what I would have guessed," she said.

Britt glanced at Walugo and Naya, then looked at the young Indian maiden. "May I venture a guess at your age?"

"Of course."

"Eighteen?"

Walugo chuckled. "You are pretty smart, Lieutenant."

Cherokee Rose giggled. "I turned eighteen on May twenty-fifth."

Britt smiled at Walugo. "Maybe just fortunate, sir. Anyway, you and your wife certainly have a lovely daughter."

As the lieutenant rode away, Naya squeezed her daughter's hand. "I think he likes you."

Cherokee Rose blushed. "Do you really think so, Mother?"

"Something would be wrong with him if did not like our girl, Mother," Walugo said.

One day, after the travelers had eaten their midday meal and everyone was cleaning up in preparation to pull out again, Lieutenant Britt Claiborne led his horse through a thick stand of trees to a nearby brook. He noticed three teenage Cherokee boys a few yards farther down the bank, dipping water from the brook with buckets. They looked at him and smiled, and Britt heard one of the boys say to the others, "That is the nice soldier who likes us Indians."

"What are you boys going to do with that water you're dipping from the stream?" Britt asked, holding the reins while his horse drank from the brook.

One of them replied, "We are getting this water for our mothers so they can use some of it to wash the dishes and the rest of it for cooking later."

"Well, I'm proud of you for being so helpful."

The horse had its fill of water, so Britt began leading him toward the trees. The Cherokee boys waved to him, then started up the bank, each carrying two full buckets.

Britt had just entered the shade of the trees when he heard harsh male voices coming from where he had last seen the boys. He dropped the reins and headed back toward the brook. When he reached the edge of the trees, he saw three soldiers with whips in their hands approaching the boys. He recognized Corporal Bob Isler, Private Glenn Norell, and Private Wayne Curry.

"You boys are not supposed to leave the wagons!" Corporal Isler yelled. "Why are you here?"

One of the boys started to explain, but Isler told him to shut up, saying they had disobeyed the rules and were going to get a whipping.

As the soldiers began striking the boys with their whips, Britt ran toward them, shouting, "Hey! Stop!"

The soldiers glanced his way, but kept on striking the boys, who were trying to shield themselves with their arms.

When Britt drew up, demanding that they stop, the two privates obeyed, but Corporal Isler kept whipping the boy he had down on his knees.

Britt grabbed Isler's wrist, twisted his arm, and jerked the whip out of his hand. "Why are you beating these boys?"

Corporal Isler grimaced as he held his arm. "These boys broke the rules! They're not supposed to leave the wagons at any time!"

"What are you talking about? No such rule exists! These boys were here getting water for their mothers. Now get on back to the wagons while I help them refill their buckets."

Later, as the Cherokees and the soldiers were once again on the move, General Winfield Scott, his eyes blazing, rode up alongside Lieutenant Britt Claiborne. "I want to talk to you!"

Britt's brow furrowed. "Yes, sir?"

"Corporal Isler, Private Norell, and Private Curry just told me you got rough with them because they were disciplining three

Indian boys. You even hurt Corporal Isler's arm. I want to know why you did this!"

Britt calmly explained what had happened. "I had to get rough with Bob Isler, General," Britt concluded, "because he kept whipping the boy even though I told him to stop. Isler accused the boys of breaking some rule by leaving the wagons, and I quickly told him there was no such rule. The boys had done nothing wrong, and they had no right to whip them."

"Well, Lieutenant Claiborne," Scott said, "all three of those soldiers told me that when they approached the Indian boys, they talked back angrily to them; and this was why they whipped them."

Britt looked the general in the eye. "That is a lie! I was still close to the boys when those soldiers accosted them. They did *not* talk back to them in any way. When Isler asked them why they were there, one of the boys started to explain, but Isler told him to shut up, and then the whips started to hiss."

General Scott was silent for a moment, then said, "Lieutenant Claiborne, I know you well enough to know that you would not lie to me about this."

"Thank you, sir."

"I will have a serious talk with those men. You're right—there is no rule that says those boys couldn't leave the wagons to fetch water for their mothers."

That evening, when the travelers were stopped for the night, Cherokee Rose approached Britt and told him she had heard about the whipping incident and that she deeply appreciated how he defended the boys.

Britt thanked her for her kind words and said he was glad he had been there to stop the whippings before they got any worse.

—◌◦

The wearisome journey continued.

One windy day, when the travelers were camped beside Lake Chickamauga in Tennessee, Sergeant Rolf Nichols was walking past Cherokee Rose and another Indian maiden as they were talking to each other. A gust of wind blew his hat off, and it landed in a nearby thornbush. He set his eyes on Cherokee Rose and said, "Your name is Cherokee Rose, isn't it?"

She nodded, brushing a tuft of hair from her eyes. "Yes. And this is my friend, Lolanda."

Nichols nodded toward Lolanda, then said to Cherokee Rose, "I've heard that you're a Christian."

A wide smile spread over her lips. "I am. Are you a Christian, Sergeant?"

A smirk formed on his face and he laughed. "Hah! Absolutely not! Only fools become Christians."

Cherokee Rose felt her throat tighten. "Sergeant Nichols, without the Lord Jesus Christ as your Saviour, you will go to hell when you die."

He laughed again, throwing his head back in a mocking manner. "I don't believe in hell, but isn't it true that you Christians are supposed to love everybody and be kind to them, and to do things to help them?"

"Sergeant, what are you leading up to?"

"Since you're a Christian, I need you to do something for me. Look over there in that thornbush. The wind blew my hat in there, and I want you to go get it for me."

"Sergeant, if I were to get your hat for you," Cherokee Rose said, "I would get all scratched up by the thorns."

"So? You're a Christian. You're supposed to do what I tell you."

She shook her head. "You are misunderstanding this, Sergeant. Just because I am a Christian does not make me your slave. Go after the hat yourself."

Lieutenant Britt Claiborne happened to be walking that direction but had not yet noticed Cherokee Rose and Lolanda in conversation with Sergeant Nichols. Suddenly, Britt's head came up when he heard Sergeant Nichols shout, "Don't talk to me that way, Indian! If you don't do what I told you to do, I'll give you a whippin' you'll never forget!"

Even as he spoke, Nichols was taking off the whip he wore on his belt.

Britt dashed up, jumped between Cherokee Rose and the angry sergeant, and said, "Put your whip away, Rolf!"

"Get out of here and mind your own business!" Nichols said.

"Real tough man, aren't you, getting ready to whip a defenseless young lady?"

Indians and soldiers were drawing up to the scene.

"Yeah, and I still am! But since you're in my way, Claiborne, I'll have to whip you first! Your rank doesn't scare me!"

As he spoke, the sergeant raised his whip to use it on the lieutenant. Britt's fist connected with such force that it sounded like a flat board striking a wooden wall. Nichols staggered back, shaking his head, and threw the whip to the ground. With exceptional speed for his size, he lunged toward Britt, both fists swinging. Britt countered by driving a powerful right fist to his midsection, and the paunchy Nichols doubled over. Two more blows to the head, and the sergeant's knees gave way, and he fell heavily, sprawling full length on the ground.

Two soldiers rushed up and knelt beside the unconscious sergeant.

Britt turned to Cherokee Rose and took hold of her hand. "Are you all right?"

"Yes, thanks to you."

"Why was he going to beat you?" Britt asked, still holding her hand.

"He apparently hates Christians," Cherokee Rose said. "He came up to me and said he had heard that I was a Christian. When I told him it was true, he commanded me to go fetch his hat, which the wind had blown into those thornbushes. When I refused, he became very angry and took the whip from his belt to beat me."

"I'm glad to hear that you're a Christian," Britt said, smiling. "I've noticed that you and your family attend the preaching services, but that doesn't always mean people are Christians simply because they attend. I want you to know that I'm also a born-again child of God."

Cherokee Rose smiled. "I am so glad to hear that! I recall, now, that I have seen you at some of the preaching services, too."

"You have seen me at *some* of the preaching services because sometimes I'm on duty and can't make it to the services. I would be there every time if I could. I especially like Layne Ward's preaching. He's excellent."

"Yes, he is."

"He reminds me so much of the evangelist who was preaching in our church in Atlanta when I was twelve years old. He preached a powerful sermon about the cross, and at the invitation, I walked the aisle and received the Lord Jesus into my heart as my Saviour. How old were you when you opened your heart to Jesus?"

"I was eight. It was after one of the Cherokee preachers had preached a sermon on hell, and when my parents and I went back to our cabin, I was crying. My mother asked me what was wrong, and I told her I did not want to go to hell…that I wanted to ask Jesus to come into my heart and save me. My father went over some verses about salvation in the Bible, and he led me to the Lord."

"Wonderful!" Britt said. "Ah…Cherokee Rose…your mother is so fair-skinned and has blue eyes. She isn't even part Cherokee, is she?"

"No. My grandparents, Chief Bando and Nevarra, adopted her right after her parents were killed when she was about a year old. Sometime I will tell you the whole story."

"I'd love to hear it. So you're half Cherokee?"

"Yes."

"Well, you might be surprised to learn that I'm a quarter Cherokee."

"Really?"

"My father's mother was a full-blooded Cherokee."

"That makes you an even better man, Lieutenant!" said Lolanda, who was still standing nearby, listening in on the conversation.

Cherokee Rose's eyes were filmed with tears. "I am so glad to know you are part Cherokee, Britt. I feel closer to you already."

"I'm glad you feel that way," he said.

Later, when Cherokee Rose told her parents and her grandparents that Britt was a quarter Cherokee, they liked him even better than they had before.

sixteen

he next morning, when everyone in the camp was rising from their crude beds in the wagons and from their bedrolls on the ground, Chief Calhondo sat up on the edge of the bed in his wagon, yawned, and looked down at his wife, Deeda. He saw that she was awake, and her teeth were chattering.

Calhondo leaned close to her. "We should have put another blanket over us. You are cold."

Deeda's voice trembled as she said, "I am not cold from the night air. I...I am very sick. I have a fever, and I am dizzy."

Calhondo laid a hand on her brow. "You have a very high fever, my dear. Let me give you some water to drink. Maybe that will help."

After giving Deeda a full cup of water to drink, Calhondo placed a wet cloth on her forehead.

The chief offered to prepare her some food for breakfast, but she told him she could not eat. She told him he should go ahead and eat breakfast on his own.

By the time the soldiers were moving among the Indians' wagons and telling them it was almost time to pull out, Deeda lay on the bed, mumbling incoherently. Calhondo felt her brow, and it was hotter yet.

He looked through the opening of the canvas top and saw two soldiers talking to Indians in a nearby wagon, telling them to hurry up and get ready. They would be pulling out in just a few minutes.

Calhondo hopped down from the rear of the wagon and called out, "Sergeant Taylor!"

The sergeant turned around and headed toward him. "Yes?"

"My wife is very sick, Sergeant. She cannot travel."

Taylor gave him a petulant look and said, "Sick or not, she must travel. Get your wagon ready to pull out. We'll be leaving in about fifteen minutes."

Calhondo hurried to Chief John Ross's wagon, where John and Quatie were getting ready for the day's travel. They saw Calhondo coming toward them and the look of anguish on his face.

"Chief, what is wrong?" John asked.

"It is Deeda. She is very sick. She has a high fever and is dizzy, and she cannot talk right. She is just mumbling. I told Sergeant Taylor that she is sick and cannot travel, but he showed no concern. He said she must travel, sick or not."

"Quatie, I will go take a look at Deeda," John said. "You finish up here, all right?"

Quatie nodded. "Of course. If there is anything I can do to help her, I will do it."

Calhondo thanked Quatie and hurried away toward his wagon beside John.

When the two men climbed into the wagon, Deeda's brow was shiny with perspiration, and she was rolling her head back and forth, still mumbling.

John felt her brow and shook his head. "Calhondo, I am not a physician, but I have seen many sick people in my time. I cannot be sure, but I think Deeda may have typhoid fever."

Calhondo's hand went to his mouth.

"All we can do is try to keep her fever down. I will have Quatie ride in the wagon and bathe her brow and wrists in cool water, and do her best to get the fever down."

Calhondo nodded. "I appreciate this very much."

John hopped out of the wagon. "I will tell Quatie what I think it is, and she will be here quickly."

John Ross left Calhondo's wagon with a heavy heart. If Deeda did have typhoid fever, she might die. And many others would likely come down with the fever, too, since Indians and soldiers alike had all drunk from the same rivers and streams.

"I hope I am wrong," he told himself.

John told Quatie what he thought Deeda might have and that Calhondo needed her to be at Deeda's side to bathe her brow and wrists with cool water. When Quatie heard this, she hurried away.

Quatie drew up to Chief Calhondo's wagon and was about to climb into it when Layne Ward and his wife, Sylvia, came walking up.

"We just heard about Deeda from one of the soldiers," Layne said.

"I came to offer to ride in the wagon with Deeda," Sylvia said, "but I have a feeling that is why Quatie is here."

Calhondo nodded. "You are right. But thank you for your willingness to help. I very much appreciate it."

Layne and Sylvia hurried back to their wagon, and soon the columns of wagons, riders, and those on foot moved out. The familiar sounds of squeaking wheels, the muffled beat of horses' hooves on the soft earth of the trail, and the creak of saddle leather filled the air.

When they had been traveling for nearly two hours, a young Cherokee woman named Laneena, who lay on a bed in the rear of a wagon, called out to her husband, "Dorudo! My pains are very close together! The baby is coming!"

Dorudo called back to Laneena that he would help her, then got the attention of a corporal riding his horse a few yards ahead of the wagon.

The corporal pulled rein, let the wagon catch up to him, and said to Dorudo, "What is it?"

"I have to stop the wagon. My wife is about to give birth to our baby, and I have to help her with the delivery."

"We stop only when General Scott says we stop, Indian," the corporal said. "Your wife will just have to deliver her baby by herself. She's a squaw. She can handle it. Keep that wagon movin'!"

Just behind Dorudo's wagon was the Layne Ward wagon. Sylvia was on the driver's seat next to her husband. They both heard the exchange between Dorudo and the soldier, and Sylvia called out, "Corporal! Corporal!"

The soldier looked over his shoulder. "Yes, ma'am?"

"If you will give us permission to stop this wagon and that one for only a moment, I will ride in that wagon and deliver the baby."

"All right, lady," the corporal said. "I'll signal the wagons behind you to stop. But make it fast."

Layne stopped his wagon, hopped down, and helped Sylvia to the ground. Dorudo was on the ground, waiting for her. She hurried to him, and as he helped her onto the tailgate, she said, "I didn't think the baby was due yet."

"It was supposed to be born in a little over two months," Dorudo said. "I fear all of the strain of this unwanted journey has been too much for both Laneena and the baby."

Sylvia crawled inside the wagon, and Dorudo closed the tailgate, hurried to the front of the wagon, and climbed up onto the driver's seat.

The corporal waved at the drivers again and shouted, "Move out!" When the wagons were once again in motion, he put his horse to a trot and rode on ahead.

Layne kept his wagon very close to the rear of Dorudo's wagon as Sylvia put her attention on the young Indian woman, who was moaning in agony.

"Laneena, can you hear me?" Sylvia said, on her knees beside the small bed.

Laneena did not respond. There was only more moaning.

Sylvia took hold of her hand and spoke louder. "Laneena, it's me, Sylvia Ward. I'm here to help you deliver the baby. Come on, now. We can do this together!"

Sylvia waited for Laneena to squeeze her hand as the next contraction came, but Laneena's hand lay limp in her own as the contraction took place.

Laneena let out a low moan, and suddenly a stream of blood

and water gushed out of her. Changing her position, Sylvia was surprised to see a tiny baby in the midst of all the blood and water. She quickly picked up the mewling little one and saw that he was not fully formed. She wrapped the baby boy in a towel, but he gave a little sigh and went limp in her hands.

Laneena's breathing was shallow, and there was a pale tinge around her mouth. She barely opened her dull eyes, saw the baby wrapped in the towel, and looked up at Sylvia, who felt her heart skip a beat as she said, "You have a little boy." Sylvia laid the dead baby beside his mother. "He is right here, Laneena."

Laneena lifted a shaky hand. Sylvia took it and guided it to the baby's face. Laneena gently stroked her son's cheek, a weak, wistful smile caressing her lips. Then her head slumped to one side, and her hand on the baby's cheek went limp.

Sylvia took hold of the hand and felt for a pulse. There was none.

Tears began streaming down Sylvia's cheeks. "O Lord," she said in a low voice, "in all of the chaos and heartache of this forced move of these people, I am having a hard time understanding why You are letting it happen."

Suddenly, a passage of Scripture from the fifty-fifth chapter of the book of Isaiah came to her mind. *For my thoughts are not your thoughts, neither are your ways my ways, saith the LORD. For as the heavens are higher than the earth, so are my ways higher than your ways, and my thoughts than your thoughts.*

Sylvia wiped tears from her cheeks. "O dear Lord, please forgive me for my doubts and confusion. Help my unbelief. Please renew within me a right spirit, and give me Your grace and Your strength. Help Layne and me to be faithful witnesses to Dorudo. And help us to be a blessing to all the other precious and bewildered Indians who have been forced to leave their homeland and to head into the vast unknown."

Less than an hour had passed since Sylvia had entered Dorudo's wagon when Layne saw her appear at the rear of the wagon, her face pale. He was about to ask her about the baby when she waved a hand, signaling him not to speak.

Sylvia carefully mouthed that Laneena and her baby had both died, and that Dorudo did not yet know it. Layne nodded that he understood, and mouthed back that he would get the attention of one of the soldiers so they could stop.

When a soldier came riding by less than a minute later, Layne told him what had happened, and that Dorudo did not yet know his wife and newborn baby had died. He asked if they could stop so he could tell Dorudo of his loss.

The soldier scowled. "We cannot stop now, Mr. Ward. You can tell Dorudo when we stop for the noon meal."

Layne had to bite his tongue, for he knew better than to argue. He got Sylvia's attention and mouthed to her what the soldier had said.

Hours later, when they all stopped for lunch, Layne left his wagon and hurried to the front of Dorudo's wagon. Dorudo was just tying the reins to a small post beside the driver's seat when he saw Layne approach. "What is wrong, Mr. Ward?" he asked.

Layne cleared his throat. "Dorudo, I'm sorry to have to tell you that your wife and baby both died a little while ago. Sylvia is still back there with them. She can tell you exactly what happened."

Dorudo climbed into the rear of the wagon from the driver's

seat, and Layne hurried around to the tailgate. Sylvia told Dorudo what happened, and he wept and wailed over the lifeless bodies of his wife and newborn son.

At the same time, Quatie Ross, with her husband by her side, told Chief Calhondo that Deeda had just died.

There was much mourning among the Cherokees as two graves were dug at the side of the trail. The newborn baby boy was buried with his mother. A cold, wind-driven rain began to fall as Cassdi, one of the young preachers trained by Layne Ward, conducted the graveside service. As the rain slanted down on the crowd gathered around the graves, it seemed to some as though the heavens themselves were mourning the loss of the two women and the baby boy.

When the service was over, Yonwi and his friends Shoro, Coya, and Chula spoke their condolences to Dorudo. Then with anger showing in his eyes and his voice, Yonwi said, "Dorudo, the loss of Laneena and your baby boy is the fault of the white men! If I had the means to do it, I would kill every one of those soldiers!"

"So would I, Yonwi!" Dorudo said through gritted teeth.

Many tears were flowing as the columns pulled out. The rain had stopped.

Cassdi rode in Dorudo's wagon with him, trying to comfort him, but Dorudo was seething.

"Yonwi is right, Cassdi," Dorudo said. "If the white man's government had not forced us to leave our home, Laneena would not have given premature birth to the baby. She and my little son would still be alive."

The burning anger in Dorudo only grew worse as the day progressed. When the travelers stopped for the night, and Cassdi had joined his own family, Dorudo reached into a wooden box under the wagon seat and took out a long-bladed hunting knife. He slipped the knife under his belt, covering the handle with his buckskin jacket, and headed in the direction where General Scott would be waiting while the army cooks prepared supper. As he entered the area, cook fires were burning, and he saw General Scott standing by one of the fires alone, looking down into the flames. Scott's back was toward Dorudo.

When Dorudo was within a few feet of the general, he slipped the knife out and raised it above his head to plunge into the general's back.

Just then, a captain happened to look in that direction. He swiftly drew his revolver from its holster on his belt and fired. As soldiers turned that direction, and General Winfield Scott pivoted at the sound of the shot, Dorudo fell down dead with a bullet in his head.

The next morning, when Dorudo was buried, all the Cherokees gathered around the grave, and many tears were shed. The well-armed soldiers watched them carefully. General Scott addressed the Indians, warning them that any Cherokee who would try to kill him or any of his men would end up just as Dorudo did.

As the hard journey progressed, more Cherokees died. More babies were born dead. Others were born alive, but soon died from typhoid and smallpox, which broke out among the Cherokees. Other Indians who resisted the brutality of the soldiers were killed.

Almost every day, when they moved away from where they had camped for the night, they left graves behind.

The Cherokee pastors, Layne and Sylvia Ward, and even Lieutenant Britt Claiborne and Cherokee Rose did all they could to comfort those whose loved ones had died, and had the joy of leading many to Jesus.

Amid the sorrows of the journey, Britt and Cherokee Rose found that they were growing more and more fond of each other.

The weather was getting progressively colder, and both soldiers and Indians knew it would not be long before bone-chilling snow would cover the ground, making the journey even more difficult.

One cold, windy day, as the columns moved steadily westward, Walugo, Naya, and Cherokee Rose were on the driver's seat of their wagon, clad in heavy winter coats.

"It would have been much wiser if the president and Congress had waited until spring to make us begin this horrible ordeal," Walugo said. "This freezing cold and the snow that is coming will only cause more of our people to die."

There was sadness in Naya's voice as she said, "You are right, my husband, but the white man's government, including most of these soldiers, do not care how many Indians die. It will only make it easier to control those who are left."

At that moment, Lieutenant Britt Claiborne rode up from behind and guided his horse close to where Cherokee Rose was sitting. "Hello," Britt said, running his gaze to all three.

A smile formed on Naya's lips as she noticed a soft glow on her daughter's cheeks. She leaned close to her husband and whispered so only he could hear, "I have to say that this journey is not *all* bad."

Walugo whispered back, "You are right, Naya. I like what I see happening between our girl and Britt. God does have a way of making even the worst things beautiful."

Cherokee Rose and Britt talked to each other about the cold wind, then she told Britt how much she admired his horse, a black gelding with a broad white blaze on his face and white stockings on all four legs.

"Blackie's a wonderful horse," the lieutenant said, smiling. "Ah…do you like to ride horses?"

"Yes, I do."

"Would you like to ride on Blackie with me?"

She smiled. "Yes, I would."

"I'll stop the wagon so she can move from the wagon to your horse," Walugo said.

"It's best you don't stop, sir," Britt said. "These other soldiers wouldn't like it. I can lift her up here without you having to stop."

Even as he spoke, Britt leaned from the saddle and extended his left arm toward Cherokee Rose. Naya steadied her daughter as she rose up into the curve of Britt's strong arm, and he quickly had her behind him on the horse.

Cherokee Rose put her arms around Britt's waist and smiled up at him as he looked back at her. He kept Blackie beside the wagon as they moved along the trail.

Moments later, another lieutenant named Jack Ayers pulled up alongside Britt and the girl. He gave Britt a dirty look, then quickly rode away.

Cherokee Rose leaned up close to Britt's ear and said, "That soldier didn't like me riding with you, did he?"

Britt shook his head. "No, but it's none of his business."

—⌒—

When the travelers stopped to make camp for the night, the air was quite cold.

After the evening meal, Britt came to where Cherokee Rose and her parents were sitting with some other Indians, talking. He greeted the group, then bent down to Cherokee Rose and said, "Would you like to take a walk with me into the woods over there? That is, if it's all right with your parents?"

Walugo smiled. "It is fine with her mother and me."

Cherokee Rose looked at Britt with shining eyes. "I would love to take a walk with you."

A bright moon was shining in the starlit sky as they walked along the bank of the small stream near where they had camped. Britt pointed to a large log lying on the bank ahead of them and said, "Would you like to sit down on that log?"

"Yes, that would be nice."

They sat down and talked for a while about the long journey still ahead of them. Cherokee Rose asked where the army might send Britt after the Cherokees were in Indian Territory.

He peered into her soft brown eyes. "You know what I wish?"

"Tell me."

"I wish I could stay right there in Indian Territory so I could be close to you."

Cherokee Rose felt a warmth spread through her heart. She drew a quick breath and said, "I wish you could, too. I—I am going to miss you terribly."

Suddenly, they were in each other's arms, and Britt kissed her tenderly. "Cherokee Rose, I cannot hold it in any longer. I *must* tell you."

"Tell me what?"

"I am in love with you. With all of my heart, I am in love with you."

She kissed his cheek. "And Britt, with all of my heart, I am in love with you."

At that moment, they heard footsteps on the rocky bank of the stream. They looked up to see two uniformed men approaching them in the moonlight. One was Lieutenant Ayers, and the other was Captain Douglas Holton.

As they drew up, Britt looked at them with steady eyes. Before he could ask what they wanted, Captain Holton said, "Lieutenant Ayers told me you had this Indian female riding on your horse with you today."

Britt met the captain's cold eyes. "He's right, I did."

"You shouldn't be fraternizing with a Cherokee woman, Lieutenant!"

Cherokee Rose felt a knot rise in her throat, and her heart began to pound.

seventeen

ieutenant Britt Claiborne rose to his feet. "It is none of your business who I fraternize with, Captain Holton. Just because you outrank me doesn't give you the right to tell me who I can spend my time with."

Lieutenant Jack Ayers stepped up closer to Britt, a scowl on his face. "I told General Scott about you having this Indian girl on your horse with you today, and he wants to talk to you right now. He sent me to get you."

"So why did you bring the captain with you?"

"It's none of your business who I fraternize with," Ayers said mockingly.

"The general is really gonna be upset when we tell him we found you kissing this Cherokee woman just now," Holton said.

"It's none of your business who I kiss, nor the general's!"

Cherokee Rose, still seated on the log, felt her face flush and her heart continued to pound.

"Have you lost your senses, Lieutenant?" the captain said. "Have you forgotten that these redskins are our enemies?"

Britt's jaw tightened and his fists clenched. Cherokee Rose reached up and laid a shaky hand on his arm. He looked down at her and saw the fear in her dark eyes.

She stood up and in a long, quavering sigh, let out the breath she had not known she was holding. "Britt, it is best if you go ahead and talk to General Scott. I will go back to my parents. I do not want you in trouble because of me."

The moonlight played across her apprehensive features, but Britt saw the love emanating from those beautiful eyes. Taking hold of her hand, he said, "All right. I will walk you back to the camp."

Holton and Ayers followed their footsteps as Britt walked Cherokee Rose back to her parents' wagon.

Walugo and Naya were not there at the moment. Britt took hold of her hand and said quietly, "I will come back after I talk to the general. Please don't worry. It'll be all right."

"I will be waiting," she said, forcing a smile.

She prayed as she watched Britt walk away between the two officers until the night swallowed his form in shadow.

―❧―

General Winfield Scott was standing beside the army wagon in which he slept when he saw the three men coming toward him by the light of the few fires that were still burning.

"Here he is, General Scott," Ayers said.

Scott nodded. "Fine. I want to talk to Lieutenant Claiborne alone, gentlemen."

"All right, sir," Holton said. "But before we go, we want to tell you that we caught Lieutenant Claiborne alone by the stream with the Indian Walugo's daughter. He was kissing her."

The general nodded. "I will talk to him about it alone."

When the two officers had passed from view in the night shadows, General Scott said, "I am appalled, Lieutenant! Why are you keeping company with that Indian girl? You had her on your horse with you today, right?"

"Yes, I did."

"And you were alone with her beside the stream, kissing her?"

"That's right."

"The Indians are the enemies of us white people, Lieutenant. You have no business doing this!"

Britt looked the general straight in the eye. "You asked a moment ago why I am keeping company with Walugo's daughter, but didn't give me a chance to give you my answer."

"All right. Let's hear it."

"General Scott, I am in love with Cherokee Rose."

"You *what*! You're in love with that Indian girl?"

"Yes, sir. Head-over-heels."

As Winfield Scott was trying to think of what to say next, Britt said, "Let me explain something to you, General. I am a quarter Cherokee. Cherokee Rose is half white. You've seen her blond, blue-eyed, fair-skinned mother."

"You're a quarter Cherokee?"

"My paternal grandmother was a full-blooded Cherokee. So what's wrong with the two of us falling in love with each other?"

General Scott wiped a hand across his mouth. "Well, since both of you are white and Indian, I…ah…I can't think of anything wrong with it. I will explain this to Captain Holton and Lieutenant Ayers, and tell them to mind their own business."

Britt smiled. "Thank you, sir."

Moments later, Cherokee Rose was standing alone beside her parents' wagon when she saw Britt coming toward her, weaving among the campfires. When he drew up, she noted the wide smile on his face, and said, "You look happy. It must have gone well with the general."

"It did. I told him I am a quarter Cherokee and that you are half-white, and I asked him what is wrong with the two of us falling in love. He said he couldn't think of anything wrong with it. He told me he would explain this to Captain Holton and Lieutenant Ayers, and tell them to mind their own business."

Cherokee Rose clapped her hands together. "Oh, Britt, I am glad it turned out so well! Praise the Lord!"

Time moved on, as did the travelers.

More Cherokees died along the way. Some were elderly people who had to walk more than their bodies could stand. Many others died from pneumonia, especially the elderly and little children. Some of the elderly succumbed to death simply because they had lost the will to go on living. Many of the Indians died from frostbite and gangrene, and once happy families were ripped apart as death took its toll.

It soon became evident that only the strong and resilient would ever reach the end of the trail. One day marched into another as the Indians' hopes and dreams of a brighter future faded more and more.

Winter came with freezing cold and the expected snow in western Tennessee. The columns of wagons, saddle horses, and Cherokees on foot moved slowly, covering only a few miles per day.

The food the Indians had packed in their wagons had to be rationed, and day after day, soldiers and Indians alike hunted game.

Each dawn they arose from their beds and bedrolls and trudged toward the vast unknown that lay ahead of them. At dark, they ate their meager meals and huddled together for warmth as they tried to lose themselves in sleep. Often, they awoke the next morning to discover that another family member had died in the night.

The Cherokee pastors, along with Layne and Sylvia Ward and many born-again Indians, did their best to comfort the grieving, and had the blessing of leading many of them to Jesus.

In the midst of all the sadness and sorrow, Britt Claiborne and Cherokee Rose found themselves falling deeper and deeper in love. Cherokee Rose often told Britt that she did not want the time to come when they would arrive in Indian Territory because he would be taken from her by his duty to the army.

In early January 1839, the soldiers and the Cherokees arrived at the east bank of the Mississippi River just south of Memphis,

Tennessee. General Winfield Scott went to the docks along the river and hired several flat-bedded steamboats to carry them across the river into Arkansas.

It took a few days to get everybody across the river, and when the columns of people, animals, and wagons were all on the west side of the Mississippi, a heavy-hearted Chief John Ross stepped up to General Scott and said, "General, I need to ask for your help."

Scott frowned. "What kind of help?"

"We have forty-one bodies to bury before we can move on. Would you help me find a place to bury them?"

"I will send some of my officers ahead to locate public land where the graves can be dug."

"Thank you, General. I will go tell the people that we will have the burials as soon as your officers find that land."

Chief John Ross was talking with Chief Calhondo and Chief Sequoyah on the riverbank when they saw a captain by the name of Horace Baxter coming toward them. As Baxter drew up, he said, "Chief John Ross, General Scott told me to tell you that we could find no public land in which to bury your dead."

Ross rubbed his chin. "I see. Well, I guess the only thing we can do is bury the bodies right here along the bank of the river."

Baxter nodded. "That's exactly what General Scott said to tell you to do."

Chief John Ross moved about the Cherokee camp along the west bank of the river and soon had over a hundred men with shovels, digging graves. Darkness fell just as they were finishing. Ross told them they would have the burial service after breakfast in the morning.

The sun had barely lifted off the eastern horizon the next morning, when all the bodies were placed in their graves. Pastor Jesse Bushyhead conducted the service.

When the service was over, Cherokee Rose, her mother, Naya, her Aunt Tarbee, and her grandmother, Nevarra, spent time comforting the mothers whose children had just been buried. They had the grieving mothers gathered near the graves, sitting on tree stumps and large rocks, with each of the comforters talking to a small circle of women. The one exception was Cherokee Rose, who was sitting on a tree stump, an open Bible in her hand, talking to Francisca, whose three-year-old daughter had just been buried.

Francisca's husband had been killed eight days previously by soldiers who thought he was running away, when actually he was running into a forest to help an old Cherokee man whose mind was failing him and who had strayed into the woods.

Cherokee Rose was showing Francisca passages of Scripture about salvation, and the young widow listened intently. When Cherokee Rose had shown her sufficient Scriptures to make the gospel clear, tears misted Francisca's eyes. She reached out, touched the Bible, and said, "I want to receive the Lord Jesus into my heart right now."

Moments later, after Cherokee Rose had led Francisca to the Lord, she took her by the hand and guided her to the other women and told them what had happened. Naya, Tarbee, and Nevarra, rejoiced in the good news.

Soon the women broke up their meeting and headed for the wagons. Francisca hugged Cherokee Rose, thanking her for showing her how to be saved, then hurried away to tell some of her friends that she was now a Christian.

Cherokee Rose lingered behind to pray, thanking the Lord for helping her to lead Francisca to Him. Wiping tears of joy, she then headed back toward the wagons. She had gone only a few steps when suddenly a rough-looking sergeant stepped out from behind a tree, blocking her path. She frowned and said, "Excuse me, Sergeant. I am on my way to the wagons."

A leer twisted Kenneth Middaugh's beefy face. As she started around him, he blocked her way and grabbed both of her shoulders. "I've seen you kissin' Lieutenant Britt Claiborne. Seems to me you must like kissin' white soldiers. How about a kiss for me?"

"Let go of me, Sergeant!"

Suddenly, Middaugh's lips were pressed to hers. Cherokee Rose twisted and groaned, trying to free herself, to no avail. The kiss was long, and when he finally released her, she saw a group of soldiers coming their way. When Middaugh glanced at them, Cherokee Rose darted away from him, running as fast as she could toward the wagons.

As she ran, she looked back over her shoulder to see if the sergeant was chasing her, but he was talking with the soldiers, who were laughing at whatever he was telling them.

Cherokee Rose hurried into the wagon camp and headed toward her parents' wagon. She saw Britt step between two wagons just ahead of her, and he smiled and spoke her name.

As Britt drew up to her, he frowned and asked, "Sweetheart, what's wrong? You look upset."

"I—I just had an encounter with one of the soldiers. I'm all right, though."

Britt laid a hand on her arm. "You don't look all right. What do you mean by an encounter? And who was this soldier?"

She looked up into his eyes. "Couldn't we just…let it go? I don't want to—"

"Somebody's done something to upset you. Now, what is it?"

Cherokee Rose took a deep breath, then said, "It was that Sergeant Kenneth Middaugh. He—he caught me alone out there in the woods and...well, he...he kissed me."

Britt's face flushed. "He's gonna pay for this! I don't care how big he is, I'll beat him to a pulp!"

Cherokee Rose shook her head. "No, Britt. Please. If you start a fight with him, you will get into trouble. You are an officer. The army will discipline you severely for starting a fight with an enlisted man. Please, just let it go."

"Let it go? I can't just let it go," he said. "But I don't want you any more upset than you are. I've got to tell him how I feel about what he did, but I promise, I won't start a fight with him. Okay?"

She nodded. "All right. I'll take you at your word."

Britt held her close for a moment, then said, "I'll go find him right now and get it out of my system."

Sergeant Kenneth Middaugh was standing at the side of an army wagon, talking to his close friend, Corporal Hank Rippy, when Rippy looked past the big sergeant and said, "Uh-oh, here he comes."

Middaugh turned and watched Lieutenant Claiborne coming toward him.

"You don't dare fight him, Ken." Rippy's voice shook. "He's an officer. You'll be in real trouble."

Middaugh shrugged his wide shoulders. "Let's see what happens."

Lieutenant Claiborne stepped up, his face grim. "Corporal Rippy, I want to talk to Sergeant Middaugh in private, please."

Hank nodded, glanced at his friend, and walked away.

Middaugh noted that Hank stepped around the end of a wagon close by and stopped, peering back at the scene. He was well within hearing distance of what was about to be said.

Middaugh met Claiborne's hard stare. "So, what's on your mind?"

"You know exactly what's on my mind, Middaugh. Don't play games with me." Britt stepped closer and fixed Middaugh with steady eyes. "Don't you *ever* go near Cherokee Rose again. I mean it. Stay away from her, or else."

"Or else *what?*"

"You figure it out, Sergeant. You'll wish you had never been born." With that, Britt wheeled and walked away.

Middaugh watched him until he passed from view, then looked toward the spot where he knew his friend had been hiding. Hank stepped out from behind the wagon, hurried to Middaugh, and said, "I heard every word. He sounds like he means business."

"Nobody talks to me like that and gets away with it," Middaugh said, the veins in his neck sticking out like cords of rope. "I'm gonna kill that smart-mouthed lieutenant. It may take some time to find the right time and place, but I'll find a way to do it when there's nobody else around. Mark my word, he's a *dead man!*"

eighteen

ord spread quickly along the riverbank about the confrontation between Lieutenant Britt Claiborne and Sergeant Kenneth Middaugh.

By now Britt was back at the wagon with Cherokee Rose, telling her that he had warned Sergeant Middaugh to keep away from her and that she was to tell him if Middaugh ever came near her.

Walugo's eyes were blazing as he said, "Britt, thank you for protecting my daughter from that snake of a sergeant!"

"He should be horse-whipped for accosting her that way," Nevarra said.

"And I would like to be the one to do it!" Chief Bando said.

Cherokee Rose looked at him and a slight smile curved her lips. "Thank you for wanting to protect me, Grandfather. It is a comfort to know that the most important men in my life are looking out for my welfare."

"I'm glad you're including me in that group," Britt said with a smile.

Cherokee Rose blushed, then said, "I would like to go talk with Francisca some more so I can finish what I started. We did not have time to talk much about what she can expect now that she is a follower of Jesus."

"I'll walk you to her wagon," Britt said. "I'm sure she can use all the help and encouragement you can give her about what it means to be a Christian."

Britt walked Cherokee Rose to Francisca's wagon, then headed back to where he had left the other family members. When he returned, Walugo stepped up close to him and said, "There is something I need to tell you."

Britt met his gaze and nodded.

"I am glad my daughter has fallen in love with you."

"So am I."

Walugo's brow furrowed. "But something is bothering me, Britt."

"What's that?"

"When we reach Indian Territory, you will be assigned elsewhere by the army, and you and Cherokee Rose will be separated."

Britt sighed. "This has been heavy on my mind, sir. I have been praying about it daily, asking the Lord to work it out for us."

Naya moved up to Britt and said, "I have been praying about it, too. It certainly seems that the Lord has brought you two together. It would be a shame for you to be separated for great lengths of time."

"I agree," Bando said. "Nevarra, Tarbee, and I will be praying, too."

As the Indians and the soldiers headed westward across Arkansas and the long, arduous days passed, more Cherokees died from typhoid, smallpox, and pneumonia. More graves were left behind on the side of the trail, and more tears were shed.

In the third week of January, the columns drew up to the wide Arkansas River just east of the city of Little Rock. As at Memphis, General Winfield Scott hired flat-bedded steamboats to carry them across the river. It took three days, with the boats making many trips back and forth across the river, to get everyone from one bank to the other.

Late in the afternoon of the third day, in one of the Cherokee wagons crossing the river, ten-year-old Yotok sat beside his mother, Susa, who was very sick with pneumonia. The boy's father, Kulsata, was at the bow of the boat, helping some soldiers water their horses from buckets dipped into the river below.

Susa's eyes were dull as she looked at her son and ran her tongue over her dry lips.

"Mother, do you want some water?" Yotok said.

The pallid-faced woman nodded and licked her lips again.

Yotok stood up and moved to a bucket of water that sat on the wagon's floor. He lifted the dipper, dripping with water, from the bucket and turned back toward his mother. "Here's your water, Mother."

Susa's head lay to one side and her eyes were closed.

Yotok knelt down carefully, trying not to spill any more water. "Mother. Here's your water."

Susa did not move.

Yotok touched her arm with his free hand. "Mother, wake up."

When she did not respond, the boy noticed that there was no rise and fall of her chest. He gasped and shook her arm. "Mother! Mother, please don't be dead! Wake up! Speak to me!"

Silence answered him.

The boy laid his head against his mother's shoulder and sobbed. Then, rising to his feet with tears still running down his cheeks, he made his way to the tailgate and dropped to the deck of the boat.

A few feet away, Corporal Edward Watson saw the boy go over the tailgate of the wagon and land on the deck. He rushed up to Yotok and said, "Hey! Children are not allowed out of the wagons when they are on the boat crossing the river. Get back in there!"

Other Indians nearby saw the tears on Yotok's cheeks and the pained look on his face as he broke into sobs and said, "My mother just died. I need to go tell my father!"

"I told you to get back in the wagon!" Watson said.

Yotok blinked at his tears, set his jaw, and headed along the edge of the deck toward the bow.

Watson breathed a profane word, dashed to him, and grabbed him by the arm, jerking him around. "I told you to get back in the wagon! Now do it!"

Yotok yanked his arm free, stumbled backward, and fell over the edge of the deck into the river.

Sergeant Alan Reed hurried to where Watson stood, watching the Indian boy bobbing and splashing in the water, crying out for help. Four Cherokee men who had been looking on hurried up to the edge of the deck.

One of them, whose name was Clodito, said, "I will dive in and rescue him!"

Sergeant Reed held up a palm toward Clodito, signaling him to stop. Then Reed looked at Watson and said, "It's your fault the boy fell overboard. I'm ordering you to go into the river after him!"

"I'm not riskin' my life to save a useless Indian!" Watson said.

Again Clodito started toward the edge of the deck to dive overboard, but Sergeant Reed shouted, "Hold it!" Then he dropped his hat on the deck and dove into the river.

The boat pilot heard the Cherokee men shouting to him that a soldier and a boy were in the river. When he looked to where they were pointing, he saw Sergeant Reed with the Indian boy in his arms. He quickly cut the engines and stepped out of the cabin. Two of his crewmen had heard the shouting and came running.

The pilot pointed to a large open box and said, "Grab one of those nets over there in the box!"

The crewmen dashed to the box and quickly drew out a rescue net equipped with a long rope.

Everyone on board now lined the side of the boat near its stern, where the soldier and the boy were bobbing in the water, with the boy clinging to the soldier's neck. The two crewmen who had the rescue net were running toward the stern as fast as they could.

Yotok's father, Kulsata, had learned from other Indians what had happened, and he hurried toward the stern of the boat, his eyes glued to the two figures in the deep river. The two crewmen dashed past him, carrying the net, and when they reached the stern, they tossed the net down to Sergeant Reed, who used his free hand to grab hold of it. Then he carefully placed the frightened boy in it, got a good grip on the rope, and shouted to the two crewmen, "Okay, guys, we're ready! Pull us up!"

Kulsata moved up close to the two crewmen as they slowly raised the man and boy from the choppy water toward the deck. "Need help?" he asked.

One of the two gave him a quick glance and said, "Grab onto the rope right here behind me!"

Yotok and Sergeant Reed were soon on the deck, amid the cheers of Indians and soldiers alike. Kulsata wrapped his arms around Yotok and wept with relief.

Kulsata turned to Alan Reed and said, "There is no way I can thank you enough for risking your life to save my son from drowning, Sergeant. Please know it in the language of my heart."

Reed smiled, caressed Yotok on the cheek, and said, "I know how it is to lose a son. My boy, Alan Junior, was eight years old when he drowned in the Smyrna River in Delaware. His little dog was playfully running away from him, from what we could tell, and the dog fell into the river. Alan jumped in to rescue him. He was alone and was not a swimmer. There was no one to rescue him. He and the dog both drowned."

"I am sorry for your loss, Sergeant. Again, please know my appreciation for what you did in the language of my heart."

The sergeant nodded. "I do know it, and thank you."

As the sergeant walked away, Kulsata turned to his friend, Clodito, who stood looking on. "Clodito, I was told that you were about to dive into the river to save Yotok just before the sergeant went in."

Clodito nodded.

Kulsata laid a hand on his shoulder and said, "To say 'thank you' is not enough. I want you also to know my appreciation in the language of my heart."

Clodito smiled. "Your heart speaks to my heart, Kulsata. I do know your appreciation."

Yotok was about to ask his father if he could talk to him alone, when Kulsata walked toward Corporal Edward Watson, who stood nearby with two other soldiers.

"I also know what you did to my son," Kulsata said, his voice rising. "And what you said when Sergeant Reed told you to dive into the river to rescue him!"

"You wanna hear it with your own ears?" Watson said. "I told him I wouldn't risk my life to save a useless Indian!"

Kulsata lunged at Watson, reaching for his throat.

The other two soldiers grabbed him, pinning his arms behind his back. One of them said, "We understand that you almost lost your son, Indian, and if it happened to one of our sons, we'd be upset, too. But you need to calm yourself down. So let's just head on back to your wagon. We'll be getting off this boat shortly."

Corporal Watson gave Kulsata a dirty look, spit on the deck, and walked away.

"Let's go," said the soldier who had just spoken to Kulsata.

As father and son were being ushered toward their wagon, Yotok broke into sobs and put his hands to his face.

Kulsata looked down at him, frowning. "What is wrong, son?"

Yotok looked up at his father through his tears. "Oh, Father, I don't want to have to tell you, but Mother is dead!"

"What? I know she is sick, but she could not—could not—"

"She is dead, Father," the boy said with quivering lips. "When I was with her in the wagon, she stopped breathing. She is dead."

Kulsata's pulse throbbed in his ears. "No! No, it cannot be!"

The boy took hold of his father's hand. "Come with me to the wagon."

The soldiers kept pace with Kulsata and Yotok as they ran to the wagon. When they reached it, Kulsata climbed in over the tailgate, fell on his knees beside his wife, and touched her cold skin. Noting her pale face and that she was not breathing, he began to sob.

One of the soldiers said, "I am sorry for your loss."

"Has she been sick for very long?" the other one said.

Kulsata looked at them through his tears. "For about three weeks. Pneumonia."

"We will leave you and your son alone now," the first soldier said.

As the soldiers walked away, Yotok climbed into the wagon, knelt beside his father, and stroked his mother's face.

A wail rose from Kulsata and echoed across the river.

After almost an hour of holding Susa's body and weeping, Kulsata took Yotok out of the wagon, sat him on a nearby bench, and tried to comfort him. Cherokees and soldiers kept their distance, but looked on at the heart-wrenching scene.

While talking to his son, Kulsata saw Corporal Watson passing by with some other soldiers. He jumped to his feet and shouted, "Edward Watson, I am going to kill you for what you did to my son!"

"I am sorry for your loss, Kulsata," a lieutenant with Watson said, "but I must warn you—if any harm comes to Corporal Watson, you will be very, very sorry."

Kulsata glared at the lieutenant, but did not reply.

"Do you understand what I am telling you, Kulsata?" the lieutenant said.

The grieving husband licked his lips and nodded.

"All right. Don't forget it." With that, the lieutenant and the men with him walked away.

"Father, Corporal Watson is bad," Yotok said, "but it is best that you not kill him."

Kulsata put an arm around Yotok and guided him back to the wagon. They climbed inside, and both father and son wept once again over the body of Susa.

nineteen

ll the soldiers, the Indians, their animals, and wagons were on dry land by the time the sun was lowering toward the western horizon. The story of Susa's death and of Yotok's near drowning spread quickly throughout the camp.

With the help of two other Cherokee men, Kulsata and his son were digging the grave to bury Susa on the bank of the river when Kulsata looked up and saw Layne and Sylvia Ward coming toward them. He tapped Yotok's shoulder and pointed to the Wards, saying, "We have visitors, son."

The other two men kept digging as Kulsata and Yotok stepped up to meet the Wards.

"Kulsata…Yotok…we wish to express our deepest sympathy in your loss," Layne said.

"Yes," said Sylvia, her eyes misty with tears, "please know that our hearts hurt for you."

Kulsata nodded. "Thank you."

"Could I talk to you and Yotok later, after the burial?" Layne said.

"Of course."

Susa was buried on the riverbank as the sun was setting. All the Cherokees who were physically able were in attendance, as well as Layne and Sylvia Ward. One of the shamans conducted the burial ceremony, as Kulsata had requested.

There was a golden glow to the west as General Winfield Scott led the columns of wagons, riders, and those afoot through Little Rock. People stood on the streets and looked on in wonderment as the crowd of soldiers and Cherokees passed through the city.

Soon they were moving along a road that headed west, and when they reached an open area, sided by a forest of tall trees a mile or so outside of Little Rock, they turned off the road and made camp.

While the cook fires were being lit, several officers moved through the camp and announced that General Scott wanted to have a meeting before supper, with everyone in attendance. Soon, the Indians were gathered in one place, and the soldiers stood on the fringe of the crowd.

General Scott stood before them and said, "I want you to

know that we are nearing your new homeland. At our usual rate of travel, we will be in Indian Territory in eight weeks, which will put us there by the third week of March."

The general ran his gaze over the faces of the Cherokees and saw the mixed emotions there. He pointed to the road they had just been on and said, "That very road is the one that leads to Indian Territory."

As all eyes turned that direction, Scott said, "All right, you are dismissed. Let's get supper cooked."

Moments later, Layne and Sylvia Ward happened to be walking by Kulsata's wagon and heard both father and son weeping. They stopped when they heard Yotok say in a tight voice, "Oh, Father, I miss my mother so much!"

For a few seconds, Kulsata could not speak, then finally choked out the words: "I miss her too, son. My life…will never be the same."

Layne stepped to the rear of the wagon and looked at the shadowed faces inside. "I know you are both hurting," he said when they looked at him with tear-filled eyes. "Is it all right if I come and see you after Sylvia and I have had our supper?"

Kulsata tried to smile. "That will be fine, Mr. Ward."

Meals were cooked and eaten all over the camp. Lieutenant Britt Claiborne had been invited to eat with Walugo, Naya, Tarbee, and Cherokee Rose. When they were finished, Britt said, "I will help you ladies wash the dishes, and then I would like to take Cherokee Rose for a walk."

Tarbee smiled at him. "I will work extra hard to make up for my sister's absence. You two go ahead and take your walk."

"It is hard on a man's pride, Tarbee," Walugo said, "but I will take your sister's place while we wash the dishes and clean up. I want these two to have some time together." He looked at the couple by the light of the nearby fire. "Go on and take your walk together."

"Thank you, sir," Britt said.

The moon was full and the sky was clear as Britt and the Indian maiden held hands and walked into the nearby woods. Soon they came upon an open area where the moonlight was bright and the stars twinkled against the dark sky overhead. Britt pointed to a large rock beneath a white pine tree. "How about we sit down for a little while?"

"Of course," she said, smiling up at him.

Still holding her hand, Britt helped her ease onto the rock, then sat down beside her. He looked into her dark-brown eyes and said, "Cherokee Rose, mortal words are weak vessels to convey how much I love you."

Cherokee Rose smiled back. "It is true for me also, Britt. There are not enough words in either the Cherokee or the English language to begin to tell you how much I love you. I—" Her eyes flooded with tears. She sniffled and put her head down.

Britt bent closer. "Is something wrong?"

She raised her head, palmed tears from her cheeks, and took a deep breath. "Yes, something is wrong. I...I am dreading our arrival in Indian Territory because you will then be taken from me."

He caressed her tear-stained face. "I'm still trusting the Lord to perform some kind of miracle so we can stay together."

She sniffed and blinked at her tears. "I am trying to trust Him, too, but the closer we get, the weaker my faith becomes. I'm...just so afraid to face the future without you."

"Well, perhaps I should tell you what's been going through my mind."

"All right."

"I've thought of taking you to whatever fort I will be assigned to when this journey is over. I want to marry you, and I'd like to have you with me but—"

She frowned. "But what, Britt?"

"But I cannot ask you to leave your family. Things are upset more than enough in their lives right now. It wouldn't be right to take you away from them."

Cherokee Rose turned her teary eyes to him. "Oh, Britt. I have felt it for some time, but this is the first time you have actually said you want to marry me."

His face beamed in the moonlight. "I do want to marry you."

"And I want to marry you, too!"

Britt folded her in his arms, looked into her star-filled eyes, then kissed her softly.

When she eased back in his arms, she said, "I have to ask you something."

"Mm-hhm?"

"Even if we could get past the problem of me leaving my family...as your wife, would I be welcome in an army fort? I am a half-breed, you know, but I look like a full-blooded Cherokee."

"Well, I suppose there could be a problem with that. I haven't really thought about it." Britt took both of her hands in his. "I don't have all the answers, but I'm well acquainted with the One who does. With God, all things are possible. I wish I could guarantee you that you would never have another heartache, and that this problem of our being together as husband and wife would work out as *we* want it, but that's not in my power. I'm signed up to be in the army for another five years."

She nodded. "But the Lord could still do a miracle for us if it was His will. I know He could."

"You are so right. If we submit ourselves, our desires, and our needs to Him, in His almighty grace, wisdom, and power, He will do exactly what is right and best for us. There may be some trials and problems along the way, and the answer may not be exactly what we think it should be. But if we pray hard and leave it up to our God, then whatever He does will be exactly right. And that is what we both want."

Britt planted a kiss on her cheek and caressed her face.

She smiled at him. "You are a wise man, Britt Claiborne. We will give it all to the Lord and watch Him work it out. And then we will know beyond the shadow of a doubt that it is right, and it is according to His will for us."

He kissed her cheek again. "God has given us this love for each other, and I know we can trust Him to make a way for us to be together."

She smiled again. "If I had to live my life without you, it would be hollow and empty. The Lord knows this, and He is not going to let that happen. Nothing is too hard for the Lord."

"That's my girl. The Lord brought us together, and He has His perfect will for our lives. Let's pray, trust Him, and watch Him work!"

They bowed their heads, and Britt said, "Ladies first. I'll pray after you."

Back at the camp, Layne Ward approached the wagon belonging to Kulsata and heard him say with a heavy voice, "I am telling you,

Yotok, there is still a blazing fire inside me toward that Corporal Watson. I want to kill him for being willing to let you drown."

Layne stepped up to the rear of the wagon and looked through the canvas opening into the shadows. "Hello, my friends. Is this a good time for us to talk?"

Kulsata's features were still flushed from anger, but he quickly made a smile. "Of course, Mr. Ward. Let us build a fire out here beside the wagon so we will be warm enough for talking in the cold night air."

Moments later, the three of them sat down around the small fire, and Layne expressed his sorrow over their loss of Susa. They both expressed their appreciation for his compassion, then Kulsata eyed the Bible in Layne's hand and said, "Are you going to preach to us?"

Layne grinned as he opened his Bible. "Not exactly. Do the two of you know what my work is among the Cherokee people?"

"You work at making Cherokees become Christians," Kulsata said.

"I cannot make anyone become a Christian, Kulsata, but I can show them why they need to be Christians so they can go to heaven when they die. This is the Book the Almighty God of heaven and earth gave to the human race. He tells us in here that we are guilty sinners before Him, but that He sent His Son into the world to provide salvation from the place He calls hell, so we can go to His home above the sky called heaven, and be with Him forever."

Yotok nodded. "We have heard this from some of the Cherokee pastors, Mr. Ward. It is about Jesus Christ, isn't it? And how He died on a wooden cross for us sinners and came back from the dead three days later, so He is alive to make Christians of us if we will let Him."

Layne smiled. "You have it right, Yotok."

Layne ran his gaze between father and son. "Then will you let me read it to you from God's Book?"

Kulsata nodded. "Yes. We will listen."

Layne then read several passages about the need for salvation and showed them how to receive the Lord Jesus Christ as their Saviour...which both of them did. He then read passages that would give them assurance of their salvation.

He was about to tell Kulsata that he had heard what he said to Yotok when he drew up to the wagon, but before he could get the first word out, Kulsata said, "Yotok, do you remember what I said before Mr. Ward came, about my desire to kill Corporal Watson?"

Yotok glanced at Layne, then looked back at his father. "Yes, I remember."

"Well, son, the Lord Jesus has made a change in my heart. I do not like it that Corporal Watson was willing to let you drown, but I no longer want to kill him."

A wide grin spread over the boy's face. "I am glad, Father. I did not want you to kill him."

"I heard you say that when I was moving alongside your wagon, Kulsata," Layne said.

Kulsata's heavy eyebrows arched. "You did?"

"Yes, and I am pleased that you no longer want to kill the corporal. You see, when the Lord Jesus comes into a person's heart, a big change occurs immediately, and then the person's spiritual life grows from there. No real Christian wants to murder someone, no matter what they have done to them. The Bible says that no murderer has eternal life abiding in him."

Kulsata smiled. "I am so different in my mind and heart than before. I am going to Corporal Watson and tell him that I had planned to kill him, but because I now have the Lord Jesus living in my heart, that desire is gone."

"That will be a tremendous testimony to what the Lord has done in your life, Kulsata." Layne took hold of the shoulders of father and son. "Now that you both are saved, I want to go and tell your other Cherokee brothers and sisters in Christ what has happened to you!"

The next day, before it was time for the wagons to pull out, Kulsata went to Corporal Edward Watson and told him that he had planned to kill him before the journey was over. But last night he had been born again by receiving God's Son, the Lord Jesus Christ, into his heart, and now, not only did he have God's promise that he would go to heaven when he died, he also had forgiveness in his heart toward the corporal. The desire to kill him was gone.

Some of the Christian Cherokees who were passing by had stopped to listen as Kulsata spoke to the corporal. They looked on in wonder as they saw the impact Kulsata's words had on Corporal Watson.

Watson told Kulsata he had heard the term "born again" many times in his life, but he had never understood what it meant. He asked Kulsata to explain how to receive Jesus Christ as his Saviour so he could be born again.

Kulsata said that Layne Ward showed him this from the Bible. He would take the corporal to Mr. Ward right now.

The group of Christian Cherokees followed Kulsata and the corporal to Layne and Sylvia Ward's wagon. They looked on as Layne showed Corporal Watson what the Scriptures said about the new birth and salvation, and led him to Christ.

Kulsata and Watson brought tears to many eyes when they embraced, calling each other "brother."

As the days passed, more Cherokees died from various physical ailments, some due to the cold January weather. More graves were left behind. It seemed to the Indians that there was no end to the "trail of tears."

Most of the non-Christian Cherokees had lost faith in their shamans, who had been unable to save any lives with their chants and magic.

With vengeance boiling inside him, Sergeant Kenneth Middaugh still waited for the perfect moment to catch Lieutenant Britt Claiborne alone and plunge the long-bladed knife he wore on his belt into Britt's heart.

One dark night, when the soldiers and the Indians were camped a short distance from the road, Britt and Cherokee Rose were sitting beside a fire Britt had built so they could stay warm while they talked. Suddenly Cherokee Rose gasped, and her hand tightened on Britt's hand.

"What is it, honey?" Britt said.

Cherokee Rose kept her eyes glued to a shadowed area a few yards away, straight ahead of them. "I…I—"

Britt focused on the same spot. "I don't see anything."

"It was…it was the shadowy figure of a man. He is gone, now. I think he saw me looking at him."

"Could you tell who it was?"

She thought for a moment. "I…I am not sure. It might have been that Sergeant Kenneth Middaugh. Britt, I have seen him passing by us in daylight at times, and the look in his eyes is not good. I think he still holds a grudge against you. I think he just wants to be a nuisance and maybe keep you on edge."

Britt nodded, still keeping his eyes on the shadowed spot.

"Could be, but I haven't seen any sign from him that he's carrying a grudge. But I don't trust him. I need to know if he ever follows you or makes you nervous in any way. You will tell me, won't you?"

"Of course," she said. "And you be careful."

"I will, sweetheart," he said, and kissed away the dread and fear from her face.

Suddenly, the shadow of a man rushed toward them. But as he came into the light of the fire, they quickly recognized Chief John Ross. He was visibly upset.

"Is something wrong, Chief?" Britt asked as he and Cherokee Rose both stood up.

"I want both of you to come to my wagon. Quatie is quite ill, and I want you to pray for her. Layne and Silvia Ward are already there. Sylvia says Quatie has typhoid, and I am very concerned because more Indians have died from typhoid on this journey than anything else. I very much appreciate your walk with the Lord, and your prayers will mean so much."

The three of them hurried toward the circle of wagons where John Ross's wagon was. Holding tightly to Britt's hand, Cherokee Rose's heart hammered in her chest, a whispered prayer on her lips.

As soon as they drew near the wagon, they saw Layne standing at the tailgate, watching for them, an alarmed look on his face. Layne stepped up to John and laid a hand on his shoulder.

"I'm so sorry, my friend. Sylvia and I did everything we could, but God has taken Quatie to her eternal home."

John's lower lip quivered as he stared at Layne. Then tears filmed his eyes. He looked at Britt and Cherokee Rose, then climbed over the tailgate into the wagon.

Sylvia was there beside Quatie's lifeless form, which was covered with a blanket up to her waist. Sylvia raised up on her knees, and with tears in her eyes, gently patted John's arm and said, "I am so sorry." She then headed toward the tailgate to let him grieve alone.

John knelt over the bed and drew his wife's upper body into his arms. Tears streamed down his cheeks as he cradled her close to him.

After weeping for some time, John drew a deep breath, let it out in a quivering sigh, and laid Quatie's body back down on the bed. He ran his hand over her hair and face, then took her hand into his own. He raised it to his lips and kissed her palm, then squeezed her fingers closed.

A certain peace settled over him as he gazed at Quatie for several minutes, then placed a soft kiss on her forehead and pulled the blanket up over the face he loved so much.

twenty

orporal Hank Rippy sat alone by a fire in the camp, his line of sight fixed on the spot where Sergeant Kenneth Middaugh had vanished into the nearby woods earlier. Numbers of other soldiers were gathered around campfires under the star-bedecked sky, talking.

Rippy wiped a coat sleeve across his mouth and wished the sergeant would return.

Suddenly, the corporal saw the wide form of his friend emerge from the trees and make a beeline toward him. As Middaugh came within a few yards, Rippy said, "Well? Did you find Claiborne and his redskin girl-friend?"

"Yeah," the sergeant grunted as he sat down on the other side of the fire.

"So…you kill 'em both?"

Middaugh shook his head. "Naw. The Indian gal spotted me before I got close enough. If I'd tried it then, Claiborne would've had his gun out and cut me down before I could've got to 'em." He sighed. "I'm determined, Hank. One of these days I'm gonna find a way to kill that no-good Claiborne."

"I sure hope you do, pal," Rippy said. "I sure hope you do."

The next morning, when Quatie Ross's body was buried, two soldiers were buried also. They, too, had died from typhoid.

General Winfield Scott stood over the two soldiers' graves, sadness framing his face, and said to the officers who stood there with him, "I wish, now, that we had brought a couple of medics along on the journey."

Chief John Ross, who was close by standing over Quatie's grave with Layne and Sylvia Ward, heard the general's words. Quickly, he stepped up to him and said, "I also wish you had brought medics on the journey, General Scott. Not only for the soldiers' sake, but also for the Cherokees'."

Scott's features stiffened. He met Ross's gaze, then turned to his officers and said, "Well, we'd better get ready to pull out." He flicked a petulant glance at John Ross, who was already walking back to his wife's grave.

The columns of Indians and soldiers moved on.

—᎒

One day, during the third week of January, a young Cherokee woman named Ferrisa was in the back of the family wagon, caring for her month-old daughter, who was very sick with pneumonia. Her husband, Desdo, was alone on the driver's seat. Also in the wagon was a young widow named Ninya, whose husband had been shot and killed by a soldier two days previously. Ferrisa and Ninya were close friends, and Ninya was giving birth to her first baby, with the aid of a midwife.

While holding her sick little girl in her arms, Ferrisa looked on as the midwife held up the newborn baby and said, "Ninya, you have a little boy!"

Though still in much pain, Ninya managed a smile, and said, "I will name him after my husband."

At the same time, Ferrisa's little girl coughed and gagged. The frightened mother patted the baby's back, trying to help her get her breath.

Only minutes after the midwife had the newborn baby boy dried off, wrapped in a small blanket, and had given him to his mother, Ferrisa's little girl died in her arms.

Ferrisa clutched the dead baby close to her heart and sobbed. Her husband heard the sobbing and stuck his head through the canvas flaps. "What is wrong?" he asked.

The midwife moved to him and said sorrowfully, "Your little girl just died, Desdo."

The agony of grief twisted Desdo's features. "I will stop the wagon and come to Ferrisa."

Two army officers were riding alongside the wagon, a lieutenant and a captain. As Desdo squared around on the driver's seat and pulled rein, the captain yelled, "Hey, what're you doin'? You can't stop that wagon!"

Desdo snapped back, "Our baby just died! I have to stop and go to my wife!"

Both officers pulled their revolvers, cocked them, and aimed them at Desdo. "You stop that wagon, and you'll die, too!" the captain roared.

Desdo kept his horses in motion.

"That's better," said the captain. Then he and the lieutenant rode on ahead.

The midwife stuck her head out the canvas opening. "I am sorry those soldiers are so heartless, Desdo. Ferrisa knows you tried to stop so you could be at her side."

Desdo nodded and bit down on his lower lip.

When the midwife sat down beside Ferrisa, she said with fire in her eyes, "I detest those wicked white men!"

Tears were streaming down Ferrisa's cheeks as she gave a short sob, then with a tight voice said, "If only we could have stayed in our homeland. We would be warm and comfortable in our cabins, and our children would not have to suffer and…and die." Fresh tears flowed, and as she clasped her dead baby tight to her breast, she wailed and broke into sobs.

In another Cherokee wagon a half-mile ahead of Desdo's, Zodi was at the reins while an elderly Cherokee woman tended to his seriously ill wife, Clodine, who had pneumonia.

Chief John Ross's wagon was the second one behind him. Riding beside Ross's wagon on his horse was Chief Sequoyah.

Three Indian men walked alongside the wagon that was between John Ross and Zodi.

Zodi's wagon was rocking back and forth on the uneven ground when the elderly woman appeared at the canvas opening with tears glistening in her eyes. She drew a ragged breath and said, "Zodi, Clodine just died."

Zodi pulled rein, calling to his team of oxen to stop. The wagons in that line quickly came to a halt behind him.

Zodi looked back through the canvas opening at his dead wife, who lay on a small cot.

At the same instant, a lieutenant named Lou Camden pulled up on his horse and growled, "Hey! Get that wagon going!"

Zodi looked at the lieutenant and said with a quavering voice, "My wife just died. I want a few minutes to go back into the wagon and grieve over her."

Camden whipped his revolver from its holster, snapped back the hammer, and rasped, "Do as I say, Indian, or you'll be buried with her! Get that wagon in motion!"

His face a mask of fury, Zodi stood up and started to lunge at the lieutenant. Camden's gun roared. Zodi took the slug in the midsection, buckled, and fell headlong to the ground.

The three Indian men who were walking beside the wagon just behind Zodi's dashed toward Camden, who was looking down at Zodi from his saddle. They grabbed him before he realized what was happening, and yanked him from the horse's back, slamming him to the ground head-first. When his head hit the ground, they heard his neck snap.

Suddenly, a half-dozen soldiers came thundering up on their horses, and the three Indians went down in a hail of gunfire.

The other columns of wagons and Indians on foot came to a halt.

Chief John Ross was out of his wagon and hurrying to the scene with Chief Sequoyah trotting his horse alongside him. When they drew up, Ross looked at the bodies on the ground as the soldiers bent over them. "Are they—?"

"Yeah, they're dead," one of the soldiers said. "All four of 'em. And so's Lieutenant Camden. These three broke his neck when they threw him off his horse."

At that moment, General Winfield Scott rode up, having come from the front of the columns. "What happened here?"

The same soldier who had spoken to John Ross gave the general his version of the incident, and Scott told the soldiers to pick up the bodies, saying they would bury them later.

While the bodies were being placed in an army wagon, John Ross and Sequoyah stepped up to Scott, and Ross said, "General, both Chief Sequoyah and I witnessed the entire incident. May we tell you what we saw and heard?"

The general drew them off to a private spot and listened while both chiefs gave him the facts.

When they had finished, Ross said, "General Scott, I am asking that you punish the soldiers who killed those three Indian men. They were wrong to shoot them down. They yanked Camden out of the saddle because he had shot Zodi, who was only asking for a few minutes to grieve over his dead wife."

Scott took a deep breath, let it out slowly, and said, "I'm sorry that Zodi had to die, but he should have obeyed Lieutenant Camden's orders. All the Indians must learn that when a soldier gives them an order, they must obey instantly, whether they like it or not."

Ross and Sequoyah looked at each other but said nothing.

"We'll bury the bodies when we stop for the noon meal," Scott said.

Two hours later, the travelers stopped for lunch. After the meal had been eaten, Indian men dug the graves for Zodi, Clodine, the baby girl who had died of pneumonia, and the three Cherokee men who had been shot down by the soldiers. General Scott assigned men in uniform to dig the grave for Lieutenant Lou Camden.

The Cherokees shed many tears for those of their own who were being buried.

General Scott's voice was heard above the weeping of the Indians, telling his men it was time to get moving again. Soldiers immediately began to shout for the Indians to make ready to get back on the trail.

An elderly Cherokee couple were standing over the graves of Zodi and Clodine, clinging to each other as they wept. They did not move when the loud voices of the soldiers gave the command for the Indians to get to the wagons and prepare to pull out.

A sergeant stepped up and said angrily, "All right, you two! Get to your wagon! Right now!"

The old man said to the sergeant, "My wife and I are Zodi's grandparents. Our son and his wife became very sick when Zodi was twelve years old. They died within just a few days of each other, and we took Zodi in and raised him. Can you not have mercy on us and give us a little more time to grieve over his grave?"

By this time, two privates were beside the sergeant, who said to them, "Take this old man and woman to their wagon."

One of the privates roughly grabbed the woman's arm, saying, "Let's go, old woman."

She tried to pull free, and the private gave her arm a jerk. "I said let's go!"

She cried out in pain and tried again to free herself from his grasp. The old man let out a cry and lunged at the private, hitting him with both fists. The other private stepped up and slammed a fist into the old Indian's left eye, knocking him down.

The old woman screamed at the private in the Cherokee language, and he slapped her face. When the man who had hit him lifted the old man to his feet, he had blood running from his eye socket. The privates forced the couple toward their wagon. The old man held a hand over his injured eye as he stumbled along beside his wife.

Another Cherokee man, who had been walking on the journey, saw what the soldiers had done to the old couple. He followed them to the wagon, then stepped up and told the elderly woman that he would drive the wagon for them. She thanked him, and he helped them into the rear of the wagon while the soldiers looked on.

As the columns of wagons, horses, and walking Indians moved out, the old woman bathed her husband's injured eye with cool water.

That night, when the travelers were camped in a wooded area, Lieutenant Britt Claiborne and Cherokee Rose were sitting on a fallen tree in the shadowed moonlight, wearing their heavy coats. They discussed the horrible events of the day for some time, then prayed together for God's help for the rest of the journey. They also prayed for the miracle they were going to need for them to be together after the Cherokees reached Indian Territory.

When they had finished praying, Cherokee Rose looked into Britt's eyes and said, "Oh, darling, I so desperately want to be Mrs. Britt Claiborne."

He stroked her cheek and said, "And I so desperately want to be your husband." Britt kissed her tenderly, then said, "I guess it's time to take you back to your wagon."

When they drew up to the wagon, Walugo smiled at Britt and said, "Unless I miss my guess, you two were out there among the trees praying together."

Britt grinned. "You are exactly right. We love to pray together."

"That's wonderful," Naya said.

While Britt and the family were talking together, in the shadows behind a nearby tree lurked Sergeant Kenneth Middaugh.

Middaugh decided that he would move farther back in the shadows and wait until Claiborne was walking back to the area where the soldiers were planning to place their bedrolls for the night. He would plunge his knife into Claiborne's heart when he was moving through the woods alone.

Soon, Britt told Walugo, Naya, and the woman he loved goodnight and began to make his way through the deepest part of the woods that surrounded the campsite. Moments later, he heard footsteps somewhere nearby, coming his direction. He caught sight of a shadowed figure several yards away, and then they passed each other. Britt recognized only that it was another soldier.

Sergeant Kenneth Middaugh slipped among the trees in the vague light of a quarter-moon, and soon he saw the shadowed form of a man coming toward him. Claiborne. Finally, he would have his revenge.

He turned, backtracked several yards, slipped behind a tree, and pulled his long-bladed knife from its sheath. His heart was pounding so hard in his chest, he was afraid Claiborne would hear him.

Middaugh listened as the footsteps drew closer, and peeked around the trunk of the tree. His target was in deep shadows, but he was drawing close.

Seconds later, Middaugh stepped into the man's path and hissed, "Now you die, Claiborne!" As he spoke, he plunged the blade into the man's heart, then yanked it out and watched him stagger, turn, and fall, facedown.

General Winfield Scott and Colonel Derrick Price, one of Scott's close friends, happened to be strolling through woods nearby, and by the faint light of the moon, they saw the stabbing take place.

Both of them pulled their revolvers and ran toward the spot, with Scott shouting, "Stop right there, whoever you are! We've got guns aimed at you!"

Sergeant Middaugh saw the guns reflect moonlight and froze on the spot.

Scott's eyes were bulging as he looked at the body on the ground, then focused on the killer. "Drop that knife, Sergeant!"

As the knife hit the ground, Colonel Price knelt beside the dead man and turned him over. "He's dead, General. It's Corporal Hank Rippy."

Middaugh started and looked down at the dead man. There was enough moonlight coming through trees to reveal the face of Hank Rippy.

Scott had his gun pointed at Middaugh's chest. "Why, Sergeant? I thought you two were friends."

Middaugh's breath caught in his throat, and he had no voice.

"You're under arrest, Middaugh," Scott said. "You'll pay for murdering this fellow-soldier."

The general and the colonel took Middaugh to the center of the camp, and Scott sent two men to pick up Hank Rippy's body and bring it to him. Middaugh was tied to a tree near where the soldiers were going to sleep for the night, and placed under guard.

The next morning, General Winfield Scott met with all his officers. Lieutenant Britt Claiborne was among them. Scott told his officers what he and Colonel Derrick Price saw in the woods the night before, and reminded them that such a crime called for the death penalty.

The hanging was announced to everyone, and Layne Ward tried to talk to Kenneth Middaugh about his need to turn to Jesus Christ for salvation, but Middaugh refused to listen.

While all the soldiers and all the Indians looked on, Sergeant Kenneth Middaugh was hanged on a tree limb. Graves had been dug already by six of the soldiers, and Kenneth Middaugh and Hank Rippy were buried side by side.

As Britt Claiborne and Cherokee Rose walked away from the graves, heading toward her parents' wagon, she said, "Britt, I've been thinking about Sergeant Middaugh stabbing Corporal Rippy in the darkness of the woods last night."

"Mm-hmm. What about it?"

"We both know that Middaugh carried a grudge toward you

for the way you confronted him after he forced himself on me that day. You know what I think?"

"Tell me."

"I think the sergeant was waiting to put the knife in you, but Rippy came along unexpectedly, and Middaugh mistook his best friend for *you*. Think about it. You and Rippy are built very much alike. The same height and the same body shape."

Britt pondered her words. "You know, honey, I think you're right. It was dark enough that he couldn't make out a face, but he *could* make out height and body shape. Poor Corporal Rippy just happened to be at the wrong place at the wrong time."

Cherokee Rose gripped Britt's hand and said in her heart, *Dear Lord, thank You for protecting Britt and keeping him from being killed.*

twenty-one

he travelers continued their westward trek, averaging five-and-a-half to six miles a day, as they had since first beginning their journey from North Carolina in October.

During the last week of January, several Indian children died from pneumonia or typhoid. Two Cherokee women died from complications in childbirth. More graves were left behind as more tears were shed.

On Saturday evening February 2, after having supper with Walugo and Naya, Britt Claiborne and Cherokee Rose took a walk together along the bank of a creek near the spot where the travelers had camped for the night. There was a half-moon in the sky, giving off its silver light.

They stood on the bank of the creek holding hands, and Cherokee Rose looked up at Britt and said, "Well, if all goes as expected, we will arrive in Indian Territory next month."

Britt nodded. "And when the Lord answers our prayers and makes it so we can be together, I will ask your father for permission to marry you."

She squeezed his hand and met his gaze in the dim moonlight. "The Lord is going to do that miracle for us, darling. I just know it."

"I do, too. He didn't lead us together on this journey just to tear us away from each other."

"Our wonderful heavenly Father has our lives planned out," she said, smiling, "and I have peace in my heart that He has His plan ready to put into action when we reach Indian Territory."

Britt smiled down at her. "I'm excited to see how He's going to work it out."

"And something else…"

"What's that?"

"When you ask my father for permission to marry me, I know he will grant it. Both he and Mother speak so often about how much they love you and admire you."

Britt's smile widened. "I'm glad they do. I love and admire them, too."

"Oh, Britt," she said, her eyes bright, "we are going to be so happy together!"

Britt wrapped his arms around her, kissed the top of her head, and hugged her tight, then they began to make their way back to the wagons.

When they drew near the wagon that belonged to Cherokee

Rose's parents, they saw Layne and Sylvia Ward there, talking to Walugo and Naya. Layne and Sylvia's eyes were shining with joy.

"Hello!" Layne said. "We've got some very good news we were just sharing with Walugo and Naya!"

"What is it?" Cherokee Rose asked.

"We just had the joy of leading Yonwi and his wife, Towanna, to the Lord!"

Cherokee Rose clapped her palms together and said, "Oh, praise the Lord! I have often talked to Towanna about her need to open her heart to the Lord, including three or four times since we have been on this journey, quoting much Scripture, sowing the seed."

"Well, it worked, honey," Sylvia said. "She was ready."

Cherokee Rose turned to Britt and said, "I want to go right now and tell Yonwi and Towanna how glad I am that they have become Christians."

"I'll go with you," Britt said.

"We would like to go, too," Walugo said.

They bid Layne and Sylvia goodnight, and in a matter of minutes, the foursome found Yonwi and Towanna sitting by a fire next to their wagon. The couple stood up, smiling.

Cherokee Rose dashed to Towanna with open arms. "Mr. and Mrs. Ward told us about you and Yonwi opening your hearts to the Lord Jesus!"

There was joy as Cherokee Rose and Towanna embraced and as Yonwi told Walugo, Naya, and Britt of the peace he now had in his heart.

The young ladies eased back in each other's arms, and Towanna's eyes were filled with tears as she said, "Cherokee Rose, thank you for all the times you explained the gospel to me. I'm sorry I waited so long to make Jesus my Saviour."

Cherokee Rose kissed her cheek. "I'm just so glad you settled the matter this evening!"

Walugo ran his gaze from face to face by the firelight and said, "We have all talked about how good it will be to get to Indian Territory and settle down in our new home." He let a smile spread over his face. "Well, just consider this! One day, as God's born-again children, we will all be in our heavenly home together with our wonderful Lord! And we will be together *forever*…where we will never see another grave!"

"Oh, yes!" Naya exclaimed. "No more graves, no more sorrow, no more crying, and no more pain!"

"How wonderful!" exclaimed Yonwi, taking hold of Towanna's hand. "I am so glad we both opened our hearts to Jesus before it was too late. And no matter how brief our time is on this earth, we will have all eternity in heaven together!"

"Thank You, Lord!" Towanna said, and then she kissed Yonwi's hand that was holding hers.

On Sunday morning, before the travelers pulled out for another days' trek, Layne Ward called for the Cherokee Christians to gather for a few minutes and sing a hymn together. Just before leading the crowd in singing, Layne pointed to a young couple who had never attended any services before, and said, "I want all of you to know that Yonwi and Towanna received the Lord Jesus as their Saviour last night."

There was applause and cheering, for many of them knew that Yonwi had always been a crusty sort, and they especially rejoiced in his salvation.

Soon the long lines of wagons, riders, and Indians afoot were once again moving westward.

That afternoon, two elderly Cherokee men who were widowers were walking together. One of them, Stanano, had become a Christian since the journey began. The other one, Flurido, had refused to listen when presented with the gospel, fearing he would enrage his shaman. The two men were using tree limbs as canes as they moved alongside one of the lines of wagons.

Suddenly, Flurido bent over, clutching his chest, and fell to the ground. Stanano used the tree limb in his shaky hand to ease himself to his knees so he could see to his friend. A soldier rode up on his horse, pulled rein, and looked down at Stanano. "What's goin' on?"

Stanano was studying Flurido's face and holding a hand in front of his open mouth. He looked up at the soldier and said, "My friend, Flurido, is dead. I think his heart stopped."

The soldier called ahead for other soldiers to go to General Scott and tell him they needed to stop. Within fifteen minutes, Flurido's body had been placed in one of the army wagons, and General Scott said they would bury the body when they camped for the night.

Some two hours later, Stanano was walking with two younger men, just ahead of Layne and Sylvia Ward's wagon. The missionary couple were talking about Flurido having died without the Lord when suddenly they saw Stanano stumble, try to steady himself with his tree-limb cane, then fall to the ground.

Layne pulled rein and hopped to the ground. He waved at the wagons behind him, signaling for them to stop. Soldiers were headed that way on their horses as Layne knelt beside Stanano.

The old man's glassy eyes were focused on Layne's face as Layne asked, "Are you in pain?"

Stanano licked his lips, choked a bit, and replied weakly, "Not…in pain. Just old and tired. I just prayed to my merciful God…to take me home to eternal rest."

Layne started to say something, but the words caught in his throat as he saw Stanano's mouth sag, his eyes close, and his body go limp. He felt the old man's wrist for a pulse. There was none. He placed his fingertips on Stanano's open mouth. There was no breath.

Layne stood to his feet as the soldiers were riding up, and whispered, "Thank You, Lord, that Stanano is now in heaven with You."

On Monday, the travelers were stopped to eat lunch in an open area next to a stream. While Yonwi and Towanna ate their meal together at their wagon, they talked about the joy they had in their hearts since they had been saved.

Yonwi chuckled. "You know, some of the Christian men have told me that I am a different person since I became a child of God. They say I'm not hard to get along with like I used to be."

"I will have to say that I have seen that, too," Towanna said with a smile.

"Was I that way with you, too?"

"Sometimes. But I never said anything because I love you so much. I admit, though, that having Jesus in your heart has made a difference in you."

"Well, praise the Lord. I am glad."

Soon they finished their lunch, and Towanna said, "Would

you take the bucket and get some water from the stream so I can wash the dishes?"

Yonwi chuckled. "Oh, this would be one of those situations where you found me hard to live with. I remember many times when you asked me to get a bucket of water for you, and I made some kind of excuse and hurried away. Well, that will not happen again."

Yonwi rose to his feet, picked up the nearby bucket, and headed for the stream. As he neared the stream bank, a crackling in the deep, dry grass and a sharp hissing sound brought him to a skidding halt. He could see the bulging black eyes and the flitting tongue of a coiled diamondback rattlesnake, the sound of its rattle filling the air.

Yonwi was preparing to ease back slowly just as the snake sprang at him with lightning speed. It struck his right leg just below the knee, the fangs cutting through his buckskins like the tip of an arrow. Pain like the sting of a hundred bumblebees shot up his thigh and down to his ankle.

Yonwi stumbled, let out a moan, and tried to hit the snake with the bucket, but the agile reptile avoided the bucket and slithered away.

Yonwi pulled up his pant leg and looked at the bite. The fangs had gone deep, and he was bleeding profusely. With a burning sensation in his wounded leg, Yonwi limped back toward the wagon, leaving the bucket on the ground.

Other Indians looked on as Yonwi limped into the camp and headed for his wagon. Towanna was just coming out of the rear of the wagon and saw him limping toward her. His pain was getting worse, and everything seemed to be turning yellow.

Towanna ran toward him, worry showing on her face. She

took hold of his arm, trying to steady him. "Yonwi, what happened?"

He licked his lips and put his hand down on his right pant leg. "I…I was bitten by a rattlesnake."

Her eyes widened when she saw the bloody spot on his pant leg. "Lie down on the ground and let me examine the bite."

Several Indians were looking on.

Just as Yonwi was easing himself to the ground, Lieutenant Britt Claiborne and Chief Sequoyah were passing by, headed toward the stream. They hurried to them and Britt asked, "What's wrong?"

Yonwi gritted his teeth in pain as Towanna pulled his pant leg up. "I was bitten by a rattlesnake just now, when I went to the stream for a bucket of water."

"I have experience with snake bites," Sequoyah said as he watched Towanna press her fingers around the bloody wound.

"Please! Help us!" she said.

Sequoyah pulled his knife from its sheath on his waist and knelt beside Yonwi, saying, "I will cut the wound open a little so I can suck out the poison."

Sequoyah put his mouth on the snakebite, sucked hard, then spit on the ground next to him. He repeated this several times, then looked at Towanna and wiped the back of his hand across his mouth. "I got all the poison I could, but I know there was already much poison in Yonwi's bloodstream. I just have to hope I got enough out."

Towanna dashed to the wagon and returned with a strip of cloth. She wrapped it around Yonwi's leg, covering the wound, then looked up at Britt and said, "Lieutenant, would you and Chief Sequoyah put him in the back of the wagon for me, please?"

"I'll carry him to the wagon," Britt said, and he bent down and hoisted Yonwi into his strong arms.

When Britt had Yonwi lying comfortably in the rear of the wagon, he turned to Towanna and said, "I'll go tell Cherokee Rose what happened."

As Britt was getting out of the wagon, Chief Sequoyah stepped up to the tailgate and said, "Towanna, General Scott is going to want all of us to be pulling out very soon. I will tie my horse to the rear of the wagon and drive it for you so you can stay back here with Yonwi."

She smiled thinly, worry showing in her eyes. "Thank you, Chief Sequoyah. I appreciate your help very much."

After a few minutes, Britt returned with Cherokee Rose at his side. She leaned over the tailgate and said, "Towanna, I will ride back here with you if it is all right."

Towanna nodded. "I would love to have you."

Britt helped Cherokee Rose into the wagon, then hurried away to be on his horse when it was time to pull out. At Towanna's request, two Indian boys filled buckets at the stream for her.

The columns of wagons, horses, and Indians on foot moved out moments later.

Yonwi was developing a high fever, and Towanna and Cherokee Rose bathed his face and wrists with cool water. When it seemed that the fever had dropped some, Towanna said to Cherokee Rose, "I will stay here at Yonwi's side. Why don't you relax a bit?"

"All right." Cherokee Rose crawled to the front of the wagon and looked through the canvas opening at Chief Sequoyah as he guided the horses along the trail.

He looked over his shoulder. "How does it look?"

"His fever seems to be down a bit."

"Good."

Cherokee Rose let her eyes drift to the long rows of wagons on either side of the wagon she occupied. As far as she could see, wagons were slowly moving along a slight rise, then disappearing as they dropped down on the other side. *I will sure be glad when this journey is over,* she thought to herself.

Turning around, she made her way back to the bed where Yonwi seemed to be sleeping. Towanna was once again bathing his face and wrists with cool water.

"You rest for a while now, Towanna," Cherokee Rose said. "I will keep the water on him."

The worried young wife shook her head. "Thank you for offering, my dear friend, but I cannot leave him. The fever is worse, and his breathing is so shallow and labored. I—I think it will only be a short time until our heavenly Father is going to take him home to heaven."

Cherokee Rose laid a hand on Towanna's arm.

"I need to be close to him, whether he knows I am here or not," Towanna said softly.

Cherokee Rose squeezed the arm she was touching and tears came to her eyes.

"I am so very thankful that as Christians we have our forever time ahead of us in heaven," Towanna said, "where all is perfect and time never ends."

At that moment, Yonwi stirred and opened his eyes. He looked up at his wife and said in a weary voice, "Towanna, I love you."

She started to respond when he breathed out a short breath, his eyes closed, and he went limp.

She turned to Cherokee Rose with tears in her eyes. Cherokee Rose took Towanna in her arms and held her.

After a while, Towanna eased back in her friend's arms, looked down at her husband, and said, "Oh, Cherokee Rose, I just thought of what Yonwi said to me that same night we were saved, when we were talking to you, Britt, and your parents. Remember?"

"Yes, I do. His words have stuck in my memory. He said, 'No matter how brief our time is on this earth, we have all eternity in heaven together.'"

Towanna broke into sobs, bent down, and embraced the lifeless form of her husband.

On the driver's seat, Chief Sequoyah had not heard the conversation between the two women, but his ears picked up Towanna's sobs. He looked into the back of the wagon and said, "What is wrong?"

Cherokee Rose moved toward him. Above the sound of the sobs, she said, "Yonwi just died."

With a heavy heart, he turned back and kept the wagon moving.

When Towanna's sobs became quiet moans, Cherokee Rose put an arm around her and said, "Yonwi's pain is gone, now. There is no pain in heaven where he is."

Towanna nodded, wiping tears. "Yes, and this gives me much comfort. Thank you for reminding me."

That evening, when the travelers made camp, Layne Ward conducted the graveside service for Yonwi. The Christian Cherokees spoke words of sympathy and comfort to Towanna.

When bedtime came, Cherokee Rose offered to spend the

night in the wagon with Towanna so she would not be alone. She gladly accepted the offer, thanking her friend for her kindness.

Britt squeezed Cherokee Rose's hand and said, "There are many things I love about you, Cherokee Rose, and one of them is your tender heart toward others."

twenty-two

he weary travelers continued their journey. Almost daily, more graves were dug for those who had died from disease and for elderly ones who could not endure the strain of it all.

Just a week after Yonwi had died, Cherokee Rose was riding once again with her parents on the driver's seat of the wagon. As usual, Naya sat between her husband and her daughter. It was a cold morning with a biting breeze that made the tall, brown grass bend and sway like the waves of an ocean. As the wagon rocked and bounced over the uneven land, Naya put a hand to her forehead and rubbed it. Her daughter noticed it, but she was too busy trying to catch a glimpse of the man she loved, should he happen to ride by, to think much about it.

Cherokee Rose let her eyes drift to the Cherokees all around her, noting that they had their collars turned up against the cold breeze, as did the soldiers who rode by on their horses. With her thoughts on Lieutenant Britt Claiborne, she moved her lips silently, saying, *"Dear Lord, we are getting close to Indian Territory. Britt and I will need Your miracle real soon."*

At that moment, she saw her mother put a hand to her forehead again.

"Mother, do you have a headache?" Cherokee Rose said.

Naya looked at her and shook her head. "No, dear."

"Then what's wrong?"

"I…I just don't feel well, honey."

Walugo turned to look at Naya as Cherokee Rose asked, "In what way don't you feel good, Mother?"

"Well…ever since I got up this morning, I have felt short of strength. And in spite of the cold air, my face feels a bit warm."

Cherokee Rose placed a palm on her mother's brow. "Mother!" she gasped. "You are burning up!"

"Do you feel dizzy?" Walugo asked.

Naya rubbed her forehead again. "Yes."

Walugo's head bobbed as if he had been struck with a whip. "Oh, no! You must have typhoid fever!"

With her heart pounding in her chest, Cherokee Rose cupped her mother's face in her hands and studied her skin. Red spots were forming on Naya's cheeks and on her ears.

Cherokee Rose turned Naya's head so Walugo could see her face, released a jagged breath, and said, "Look, Father! Look at the red spots on her face and her ears. It *is* typhoid fever!"

Walugo's face was pale. He nodded solemnly and choked out the words, "It…it has to be. I need you to take the reins so I can help your mother move into the rear of the wagon and lie down."

Cherokee Rose reached a shaky hand past her mother. Walugo placed the reins in her hand, then said softly to Naya, "Come, sweetheart. Let's get you on the bed."

Cherokee Rose looked over her shoulder through the canvas opening as her father carefully placed her mother on the bed in the rear of the wagon, doing his best to make her as comfortable as possible.

Once Naya was lying comfortably on the bed, Walugo kissed her hot forehead, telling her that he would send their daughter to her, then returned to the driver's seat and took the reins once again.

Cherokee Rose hurried into the rear of the wagon and poured water into a bucket from a small barrel. Trying to remain calm for her mother's sake, she dipped a cloth into the bucket and bathed her mother's face and wrists with the cool water while speaking in soft tones.

On the driver's seat, Walugo thought of what he had learned from a white man who once visited their village in the Smoky Mountains. The man had told him about a war in Europe that had taken place some thirty years before, wherein more soldiers died from typhoid fever than from battle wounds. Walugo swallowed hard, shook his head, and began praying quietly.

Inside the wagon, Naya had her eyes closed with her hand over them. "Mother, is your dizziness getting worse?" Cherokee Rose asked.

Naya reached up and massaged her temples, deep furrows creasing her brow. "Yes, honey. And I'm getting a headache, too."

She put her hands back over her eyes and said in a voice filled with pain, "The light is hurting my eyes. Would you close the flaps for me, please?"

"Of course, Mother."

Cherokee Rose quickly closed the canvas flaps at the tailgate, and the small space inside the wagon was darkened.

"Thank you, dear, that's much better," said Naya, massaging her temples again.

Cherokee Rose soaked two soft cloths in the cold water, wrung them out, then placed one on her mother's brow and used the other one to cool her face, neck, and wrists. Fighting back tears of frustration, she spoke to the Lord in her heart, begging Him to heal her mother.

When the travelers stopped for the noon meal, word quickly spread among the Indians that Naya was ill. Soon, many of them appeared at the wagon to see how she was doing and to wish her well.

Britt Claiborne had not heard of Naya's illness, but as usual, he headed toward Walugo's wagon after lunch to see Cherokee Rose for a few minutes before General Winfield Scott called for the columns to pull out.

As he hurried among the wagons, he was surprised to see a crowd of Cherokees gathered at the rear of Walugo's wagon. He could make out Walugo standing by the tailgate, talking to the other Indians.

Britt threaded his way forward among the Indians and said, "Walugo, is something wrong?"

"Yes, Britt," he replied, his face drawn. "Naya is very ill. She has typhoid fever."

Britt's features went gray. "Oh, no."

"Cherokee Rose is in the wagon with her. Would you like to climb in and see them?"

"I sure would."

Cherokee Rose had heard her father talking to Britt, and seconds later, as she was dipping a cloth in the bucket of water, she saw Britt climb over the tailgate and enter the wagon. She dropped the cloth into the water as he gathered her into his arms.

He held her close, then looked down at Naya, who was looking up at him with dull eyes. "Hello, Britt."

Britt bent low and said, "I'm so sorry to hear about your illness, Naya. Believe me, I will be praying for you."

Naya nodded. "Thank you."

Britt looked into Cherokee Rose's tear-dimmed eyes. "I know pull-out time is about on us, but how about we have a moment of prayer for her right now?"

She nodded, wiped tears from her eyes, and said, "Oh, yes."

Britt leaned down and laid a hand on Naya's shoulder as he led them in prayer, asking the Lord to heal Naya of the typhoid fever.

Just as he said his "Amen," the familiar sounds that signaled it was time to pull out met their ears.

Britt bent over and kissed Naya's brow, then kissed Cherokee Rose's cheek and said, "I will be praying as I ride. I love you both."

For the next two weeks, Cherokee Rose hovered over her ailing mother in the rear of the wagon as the columns moved westward.

On Saturday afternoon, February 23, General Scott rode along the lines of wagons and the few Cherokees who were still walking and told them they were now crossing the Arkansas border into Indian Territory. He explained that they still had many miles yet to go before they reached the other Cherokee tribes, who were situated near an army outpost called Fort Gibson.

Walugo made a half-turn on the driver's seat and looked through the opening in the canvas. "Naya…Cherokee Rose…did you hear what General Scott said?"

Cherokee Rose was kneeling beside her mother's bed. "Mother is too ill to speak, Father, but yes, we heard what he said. We are now in Indian Territory, but we have a ways to go before we arrive to the place where we will live."

"Yes, but it won't be long now!" With that, Walugo pivoted on the seat, facing forward again.

Cherokee Rose leaned over her mother and patted Naya's fevered cheek. "We are getting close. It won't be long now, Mother. You will be home soon."

Naya looked up at her with dull eyes, formed a slight smile, and nodded. Suddenly, she stiffened, gasped, and went limp.

Cherokee Rose felt for a pulse in the side of her mother's neck. There was none. Tears coursed down her cheeks and dripped off her quivering chin as she whispered, "You…you *are* Home now, Mother. You are in your heavenly Home."

Cherokee Rose gazed at the face of her precious mother who had loved her so much and taught her so well. "I am so grateful that you are in the presence of our Saviour, Mother. You will know only joy and contentment forever. One day, as our heavenly Father wills it, Father and I will join you in that place of eternal gladness and rest. I love you, Mother," she said, then bent down and kissed a pale cheek. She then stood up and used a nearby cloth to dry her cheeks.

Praying in her heart for God's grace, Cherokee Rose moved

through the opening in the canvas and slipped onto the rough seat beside her father.

As the wagon rocked and swayed on the rolling land, Walugo turned and looked at his daughter. She placed her hand over his, where it held the reins. A question formed on his rugged features, and Cherokee Rose nodded slowly.

Walugo peered into her dark-brown eyes, noting the redness around them. Tears welled up in his eyes.

She squeezed his hand and said with a tight voice, "Mother is with Jesus now, Father."

Walugo tilted his head back and looked up at the vast blue sky above. "It is as God has willed it, sweet daughter. It is as God has willed it."

Walugo wanted to stop the wagon and go to Naya's lifeless form, but knew he dare not. He set his tear-filled eyes straight ahead and kept the horses moving along the trail that stretched out ahead of him.

Cherokee Rose still had a hold of her father's hand. She squeezed it again and said, "Father, I must get off the wagon and find Britt. He must be told."

Walugo nodded. "Of course."

She climbed over the side of the slow-moving wagon, dropped to the ground, and ran up beside a mounted soldier. "Sergeant," she said, "would you know where I could find Lieutenant Britt Claiborne?"

The sergeant pointed forward with his chin. "I saw him maybe a couple dozen wagons up ahead about an hour ago, missy. This same line. He's probably still up there."

"Thank you," she said, and ran that direction. She counted wagons as she ran, and when she passed number nineteen, she saw Britt on his horse, riding beside another officer.

"Britt! Britt!" she called out.

Britt hipped around on the saddle and saw Cherokee Rose running toward him. He excused himself to the other officer, pulled rein, and quickly dismounted.

He could see tears in the young woman's eyes as he took hold of her shoulders. "Honey, what's wrong?"

"Oh, Britt, my mother just died."

He folded her into his arms and said, "Sweetheart, I'm so sorry." Britt held her for several moments, then kissed her forehead. "I want to go give my condolences to your father."

She nodded. "But first, I want to tell Towanna before we go to Father."

"Certainly. Let me put you on my horse."

Seconds later, Britt guided his horse to another line of wagons with Cherokee Rose riding behind him, her arms around his waist.

They pulled up beside the wagon where Chief Sequoyah was at the reins and Towanna was sitting on the driver's seat beside him. The chief and the young widow looked at Cherokee Rose and saw that her face was pale and tear-stained.

"Sweet girl, something is wrong," Towanna said. "What is it?"

"My mother just died. I wanted to let you know."

"Oh, Cherokee Rose, I am so sorry. I know how you must be hurting. When Yonwi died, you gently reminded me that his pain was gone and that he was in heaven with Jesus. At least you can take comfort knowing that your mother's pain is gone now too, and she is with Jesus."

Cherokee Rose blinked at her tears, but was able to manage a smile. "Thank you, Towanna, for reminding me of my own words."

—❦—

That evening, as the sun was setting under a clear sky on the western horizon, General Winfield Scott led the long columns of Cherokee wagons, riders, and the few who were still afoot toward their first campsite in Indian Territory. Before them was a shallow, widening valley, laden with thick stands of cottonwoods and willows. Wide grassy areas were laced with small streams glistening in the sunset.

When they drew up to the campsite the general had chosen, it had a grove of cottonwoods to one side and a brook that followed a grassy bank. Mockingbirds were singing somewhere off in the distance, and a raven croaked loudly overhead. The winter grass shone like gold as the top rim of the sun was about to drop from view.

Word of Naya's death had spread among the Cherokees, and when they pulled into the campsite, several men volunteered to dig the grave.

Twilight was fading over the land as Walugo and his daughter stood over Naya's grave with Lieutenant Britt Claiborne at Cherokee Rose's side. A crowd of saddened Christian Cherokees gathered for the graveside service, which was conducted by Layne Ward. When Layne had finished the service, he and Sylvia stood close to Walugo, his daughter, and Britt Claiborne as the Cherokees passed by, speaking comforting words to Walugo and Cherokee Rose.

As soon as the last Indian in the line had passed by, Sylvia put her arms around Cherokee Rose and held her tight, speaking compassionate words to her. Layne was speaking to Walugo, when Walugo suddenly embraced him and said, "Thank you for conducting the service."

"It was an honor to do so," Layne said. "It is good to see you holding up so well."

Walugo made a thin smile. "God helped me with a verse of Scripture."

"Wonderful. What was the verse?"

"Job chapter one, verse twenty-one. It was just after Job learned that all ten of his children had been killed by a powerful wind, and with love in his heart for God, he said, 'The LORD gave, and the LORD hath taken away; blessed be the name of the LORD.' I found great strength in this."

Layne smiled. "I'm so glad."

"Job was a real man of God," Britt said.

The others were nodding their assent when Britt ran his gaze between Layne and Sylvia and said, "For the sake of the Cherokees, I wish the two of you could stay here in Indian Territory."

"That is our plan—to stay right here," Layne said.

Britt's eyes widened. "Really?"

"Oh, yes. The Lord called us to work among the Cherokees, and we're going to stay here and do just that. I asked General Scott before we left the Smoky Mountains if this would be possible, and he told me that Indian Territory is open to missionaries."

"I did not know you were going to stay here," Walugo said.

"I thought that once we arrived at our new land here in Indian Territory, you would have to leave," Cherokee Rose said. "I am so glad you are staying."

Britt smiled. "Looks like none of us were aware of it, but I sure am glad to know you're staying. The Lord will continue to use both of you in a great way, just as He did in North Carolina."

—☙—

Late in the afternoon on Monday, March 4, the soldiers led the travelers into an open area surrounded by trees a short distance from the road.

Cherokee Rose and her father made their way down from the driver's seat of their wagon, which was next to one owned by a couple in their late sixties. The silver-haired man's name was Dosondo, and his wife's name was Lacrata. Dosondo was standing at the tailgate, calling for his wife to wake up and let him help her out of the wagon. When she did not stir, he climbed onto the tailgate and crawled to the bed where she lay.

Walugo and his daughter were now on the ground, observing the scene, when suddenly they heard Dosondo's loud wail. Walugo and Cherokee Rose dashed to the rear of the wagon, and when they looked in, they saw Dosondo cradling Lacrata in his arms, sobbing and begging her to come back to him.

Hearing Dosondo's weeping and wailing, a crowd of Cherokees and soldiers began to gather around. Among the soldiers was Britt Claiborne, who was headed toward Walugo and Cherokee Rose.

Suddenly the weeping and wailing stopped.

Walugo hopped into the wagon and hurried to Dosondo, who was lying across his wife's body. Walugo took hold of Dosondo and could tell right away that the silver-haired man was dead.

Britt was with Cherokee Rose at the tailgate, both of them looking on.

"Dosondo is dead too," Walugo said. "He must have died because he could not stand losing her."

Britt nodded. "That could be. When my grandfather on my father's side died, my Cherokee grandmother lived only a few weeks. Her doctor said she literally died of a broken heart. It looks like that is what happened to Dosondo."

Cherokee Rose looked up at Britt. "Darling, if you were to be taken from me, I most certainly would die of a broken heart."

Britt put an arm around her and said, "I would do the same if you were taken from me."

The young couple noticed Walugo smile at them as they clung to each other.

twenty-three

he next morning after breakfast, Dosondo was buried beside his wife in the same grave. One other adult and three children had died on the trail the day before, and their bodies were also laid to rest. When the graves had been filled in, leaving mounds of dirt to mark them, many tears were shed.

Soon the columns of wagons and soldiers and Indians on horseback moved out. So many Cherokees had died on the journey, there was now ample room in the wagons for those few who had been on foot. There were no more Indians walking.

Indians and white men alike were weary from the long journey, and the soldiers grew more short-tempered with the Cherokees as each day passed. Traveling under these conditions, the Cherokees felt the desperate need to get the journey over with so they could settle in and make Indian Territory their home.

As the Cherokees daily put more distance between themselves and their home in the Smoky Mountains, they were touched by the wildness and the loneliness of the vast rolling prairie that surrounded them.

Finally, on March 26, 1839, they arrived at Fort Gibson, which was located in the northeast section of Indian Territory, on the east bank of the Neosho River.

A unit of mounted military men met them and guided the rolling wagons to a spot beside the fort, where they were instructed to park the wagons in several huge circles. General Winfield Scott and seven of his officers approached the front gate of the fort, and were quickly allowed entrance by the guards. The fort's mounted men led Scott's soldiers to gather the North Carolina Cherokees in an open field on the edge of the Neosho River.

Inside the fort, General Scott and the officers with him were guided to the office of General Austin Danford, the commandant of Fort Gibson. Danford welcomed them and told them that there were three federal officials who had been there for just over a week, expecting their soon arrival. The general had his adjutant corporal go to the quarters of the government officials and bring them to his office.

Wilson Metzger, Aaron Copeland, and George Henderson entered General Danford's office, and introductions were made all around. Danford then explained that Metzger would address the Cherokees where they had now been gathered near the river.

Moments later, General Danford stood before the crowd of Cherokees and explained that President Martin Van Buren had sent three federal officials to welcome them when they arrived in Indian Territory. Danford then introduced Wilson Metzger and told the Indians he would now speak to them.

Metzger lifted his voice to make sure all the Indians could hear and told them that the tribes who had come earlier from Tennessee, Georgia, and Alabama were already situated in the Territory, their new and permanent home.

"I assure you, my friends," Metzger said, smiling as his eyes roamed over the dark Cherokee faces, "the other Indians here in the Territory like their new home. They are happy here."

While Metzger went on with his assurances that the Cherokees would also be happy in their new home, Chief John Ross left his place next to Layne and Sylvia Ward and stepped up to the other two government officials and introduced himself.

"Gentlemen," said Ross, keeping his voice low so as not to disturb the Indians close by who were listening to Metzger, "I would like permission to speak to my Cherokee people."

"Since you are a chief, we will allow it," Copeland said. "As soon as Mr. Metzger is finished, I will advise him of your request."

Some ten minutes later, when Metzger finished speaking, John Ross watched Copeland step up to him and speak into his ear. Metzger nodded, and Copeland turned and motioned for Ross to come.

When John Ross stood before his people, who were surrounded by the soldiers who had brought them to Indian Territory, as well as a few hundred soldiers of Fort Gibson, he said, "It is time for me to give my report concerning this long journey of we North Carolina Cherokees from our home in the Smoky Mountains."

Silence prevailed among both whites and Indians.

Ross's features were stony as he said, "Being the chosen leader of our people for this journey forced upon us by the United States government, I have kept a record of the deaths on the trail since we left North Carolina."

He choked up, then cleared his throat. Tears filmed his eyes as he said, "We have buried 4,239 Cherokees on the trail."

A low moan passed among the Cherokee people. Many heads went down and many shoulders were slumped as they mourned for their dead kinsmen.

"One of those graves back there on the trail has my wife's body in it," Ross said in a strained voice. "If we had not been forced from our homes back East, those 4,239 Cherokees would still be alive…including my wife."

Other than some more low moans and the sounds of sniffling, the Indians were quiet.

Chief John Ross glanced at Wilson Metzger and General Austin Danford. They seemed unmoved at his comments.

Ross went on. "My people, we are now where the white men say we can make our new homes. We are with the other brothers of what the white men call the five 'Civilized Tribes.' We are a strong and noble people. Let us raise our heads and stand brave and tall. We are not quitters! We will settle here and be a happy and prosperous nation!"

The crowd of Cherokees was silent. Then suddenly, there was a loud whoop from somewhere in the crowd, and they all began to shout and applaud in agreement.

A broad smile brightened Chief John Ross's face. "While we await the government's orders as to where in Indian Territory we

can build our new settlement and long-awaited homes, let us prepare ourselves to go to work!"

There was more shouting and applauding as Chief John Ross
turned and made his way back to stand with Layne and Sylvia
Ward.

General Danford motioned for General Scott to go before the
crowd, and silence once again prevailed as Scott stepped before
them. Making no comment about the Cherokees who had died on
the trail, Scott officially turned the North Carolina Cherokees over
to General Austin Danford and the soldiers of Fort Gibson, com-
menting that they were there to keep the Indians under control.
Scott addressed his men and told them they would have a meal,
then mount up and head back East.

As General Scott stepped aside, General Danford told the
Cherokees that the soldiers of Fort Gibson would take them, yet
that day, to the area where they would establish their homes. It
would be a few hours before they could head out.

Lieutenant Britt Claiborne was standing at the edge of the
crowd with Cherokee Rose and her father. Cherokee Rose was feeling shaky inside. Britt would be riding away soon.

At that same moment, General Scott stepped up to Britt and
said, "Lieutenant, I need to have a private talk with you right
now."

Britt nodded. "All right, sir." He turned to Cherokee Rose and
her father and said, "I will see you at your wagon."

Both of them nodded as the general and the lieutenant walked
away. Cherokee Rose had already been praying especially hard that
day for the miracle she and Britt needed from the Lord…and time
was running out.

When Britt and the general were alone beneath some cotton-wood trees on the bank of the Neosho River, Scott looked at him and said crisply, "Lieutenant, you're going to be in real trouble when we get back to our home fort."

Britt frowned. "What do you mean, sir?"

"I happen to know that quite a number of the soldiers you have accosted for being rough on the Indians are going to seek to have you dishonorably discharged from the army for your actions on this journey."

"Oh, really?"

"Yes, really. They are already talking about sending a message to President Van Buren, charging you with using your rank to abuse them. There are enough of them, Lieutenant Claiborne, that it could get pretty sticky. When it's over, you probably won't be in the army to get assigned to another fort."

Britt took a deep breath. "Sir, I had no choice but to get rough with those men when they were out of line. They were horribly brutal to the Indians. *They* are the ones who should be in trouble."

Scott shrugged. "Because there are so many of them, they will carry a great deal of weight with the president."

"I'm sure you're right, General. They certainly have me out-numbered."

The general rubbed his chin. "I...ah...I've been thinking about this situation for some time, lieutenant. It's quite evident that you and that Indian girl are stuck on each other."

"We've made no attempt to hide it, sir. Cherokee Rose and I are very much in love. We want to marry one day, but we've not made any solid plans because I'm still in the army and expect to get assigned to some new fort somewhere."

"Well, since I don't think you've got a ghost of a chance beating these charges that are going to be brought against you, I wanted to bring something up."

"All right."

"You are a quarter Cherokee, right?"

"Yes, as I told you, sir."

"Can you prove it?"

"I have papers with me that prove my Cherokee heritage. I carry them with other important personal documents."

"Would you be interested in staying right here in Indian Territory with that Indian girl?"

Britt raised his eyebrows. "Yes, sir. I sure would, sir!"

"Well, my boy, if you can prove you are a quarter Cherokee, I can take care of seeing that you get an honorable discharge from the army. Then you can apply to the Cherokee General Council to serve on the Cherokee police force right here in Indian Territory. They need men who can handle the job. In order to be on the force, a man must be at least a quarter Cherokee. Are you interested?"

"I sure am, sir!" Britt's heart was pounding. "Where in the Territory would I find the Cherokee General Council, sir?"

"I was here once before, you see, that's why I know about this police force situation, and I know the lay of the land. The Cherokee General Council headquarters are located in a settlement called Tahlequah, which is the new Cherokee national capital. It's eighteen miles northeast of the fort."

Britt stuck out his hand. As the general gripped it, Britt said, "Thank you, General! I will go there immediately and make application!"

"Hurry, will you? I've got to get my troops moving, but I have to know how it goes for you at the Council headquarters."

"The papers I told you about are in my saddlebags, sir. I'll ride like the wind both ways."

Britt ran to his horse, swung into the saddle, and galloped away, unseen by Cherokee Rose or her father.

General Scott went to have lunch with his men. When lunch was over, the other officers were eager to get on the trail, and told the general so.

He pulled out his pocket watch, looked at it, and said, "Men, we can't leave until Lieutenant Britt Claiborne and I have a few minutes of private conversation together. It's very important. Something came up, and the lieutenant is on an errand to the Cherokee General Council headquarters for me. He'll be back in about three hours."

One of the officers said, "Whatever you say, General. You're the boss."

Scott smiled and said, "We'll ride out once I've had a few minutes with the lieutenant as soon as he gets back."

In a little less than three hours, Britt Claiborne returned. He found General Scott alone and handed him the papers that showed he had been hired as an Indian Territory policeman..

Scott looked at the papers, smiled, and said, "Britt, I'll be sending your honorable discharge papers to you in care of the Council headquarters within a few weeks. I'll stop at one of the major forts on the way back East and take care of it."

Britt thanked the Lord in his heart for providing the miracle that he and Cherokee Rose had been praying for, then shook the general's hand and said, "Thank you, sir, for being such a help to me."

Scott smiled. "You and that pretty little girl have a wonderful life."

Britt smiled back. "We will, sir. We will."

twenty-four

eneral Winfield Scott and his troops had barely passed from view when several of the Fort Gibson soldiers rode their horses into the circles of wagons and told the Indians to gather once more to hear from General Austin Danford.

When the crowd of nearly eleven thousand Cherokees was gathered at the assigned field, General Danford rode up on his horse with a half-dozen officers beside him and dismounted.

Cherokee Rose was standing with some other young Cherokee women, looking on as the general stepped to a central spot before the crowd. She wondered where Lieutenant Britt Claiborne was, and also glanced around to see if she could locate her father. That familiar face was nowhere to be seen, but she figured he was with some of the other men. She did, however, locate her Aunt Tarbee and her grandparents, Chief Bando and Nevarra, several yards away.

General Danford ran his gaze over the crowd and said, "My plan, as I told you earlier, was for a number of my men to take all of you today to the area here in Indian Territory where you will be establishing your new homes. Some unexpected things have come up that have made it too late to make that trip today. You will camp for the night where your wagons are parked, and my men will lead you to your new homeland tomorrow. You will leave right after breakfast.

"It is my hope that all of you will be as happy in your new land as your Indian brothers and sisters are. You will have thousands of acres on which to establish your farms, and each family will be assigned a large section of land and will be given wood to build your cabins with.

"You will have to live in your wagons until then, and those of you who do not have your own wagons will be given tents to live in. The army will supply those tents, which we have in storage here at the fort."

General Danford then dismissed them, and the Indians, along with Layne and Sylvia Ward, made their way back to the wagons.

Walugo was with some of the other men at Chief Bando's wagon, talking about what General Danford had just told them. Cherokee Rose was at her father's wagon, talking to some women about the same thing. She was also thinking about the man she loved when suddenly her eye caught sight of Britt leading his horse between two wagons.

She noticed a broad smile on Britt's face, and she excused herself to the other women and dashed up to Britt as he drew Blackie to a halt.

"I've been wondering where you were," Cherokee Rose said. "You must have been riding somewhere."

"Yes, I have. General Scott sent me on an errand."

She cocked her head, studying the happy look in his blue eyes. "What are you so happy about?"

"Let's go to a private spot so I can tell you."

She walked beside Britt as he led Blackie, and they soon stopped under a cottonwood tree where they could talk without being heard by anyone else. They sat on a big rock, and Britt told Cherokee Rose what General Scott had talked to him about. Then he pulled some official-looking papers out of his coat pocket and said, "Look at these."

Her eyes widened as she noted that the papers were from the Cherokee General Council of Indian Territory. "That's where you've been?"

"Yes. Go ahead. Read what it says there on the first page about me."

She read the handwritten words and the official signature at the bottom, then she looked up at him, astonished. "You…you have been hired as a policeman on the Indian Territory police force?"

"That's right, sweetheart. The second page will explain that I'm going to receive an honorable discharge from the army. General Scott is going to see to that, and send me the discharge papers. The Lord has answered our prayers and performed the miracle we needed so we could get married and live our lives together!"

Hands trembling, Cherokee Rose cried, "Oh, praise the Lord!" and burst into happy tears.

Britt folded her into his arms. "It's official. We're going to get married very soon!"

She eased back in his arms and looked up at him through her tears. "I would really like for us to have my father's approval."

Britt chuckled. "We already have it."

"What?"

"After I showed General Scott those papers in your hand, I went to your father and told him what had happened. This was going on while the crowd was listening to General Danford over by the river a few minutes ago. Your father happily granted permission for me to marry you!"

Cherokee Rose wiped at the tears on her cheeks. "Oh, praise the Lord! Let's go to Father! I want to thank him!"

Moments later, as Britt and Cherokee Rose reentered the circle of wagons with Britt leading his horse, they saw that her grandparents and her Aunt Tarbee were standing beside Walugo's wagon, talking to him.

They all smiled at the couple as they drew up, and Chief Bando said, "Well, we are looking at the future Mr. and Mrs. Police Officer Britt Claiborne!"

Cherokee Rose giggled. "Oh, Father, you told them!"

"I could not keep from telling them, sweet daughter. We are all so happy for you!"

Cherokee Rose ran to her father and embraced him. "Thank

you for granting permission for Britt and me to get married."

"Honey," Walugo said, "do you remember that day at your grandparents' cabin when you were fifteen years old, and you were crying because you did not want to leave your Smoky Mountain home?"

"Yes."

"And your grandfather took you into his arms and told you that God was in control of our lives."

"Yes," she said, glancing at Bando. "And Grandfather also told me that nothing could come into the life of a child of God that did not first get past the great Shepherd who is leading us."

Walugo smiled. "And then your wise grandfather told you that the Lord must have a good reason for allowing us to be moved to Indian Territory, then he had you read Psalm 18:30 and Romans 8:28 aloud from his Bible."

As Cherokee Rose was nodding and smiling with tears glistening in her eyes, Walugo said, "Remember what you said after you read those verses?"

"Yes. I said I would trust my Lord better from then on."

"Dear daughter, your grandfather was so right. If the white man's government had not taken us from our home in North Carolina to bring us here, you would never have met Britt. God's way *is* perfect, and all things *do* work together for good to them that love God, who are the called according to His purpose."

Cherokee Rose had fresh tears flowing. She hugged her father, thanked him for reminding her of those truths, then hugged her grandfather and thanked him for showing her those verses.

When she let go of Bando, she turned to Britt, embraced him, and said, "You are God's gift to me!"

—❧

Early the next morning, a large number of mounted soldiers under the command of Captain Lawrence Kirkland led the North Carolina Cherokees southwestward from Fort Gibson across Indian Territory. Many army wagons were in the columns, also, as they carried tents for the Cherokees who would need them. Since there were no Indians walking, the wagons and saddle horses made better time than they had on the journey, and by midafternoon, the soldiers led them onto their assigned land.

As they traveled that day, they were surprised but pleased to see the rolling, grassy prairie, the great stands of trees, and the fertile farmland. They saw that many of the Indians who were already settled there had large herds of cattle in fenced pastures. Many streams ran across the Territory, providing plenty of water for their homes and farmland.

The tents were taken off the army wagons and set up in one vast area where the wagons were also parked in large circles. They would have one massive village, to be governed by all the village chiefs together, until the cabins for each farm could be built and they were living in their own smaller villages.

Captain Kirkland told them that the army would soon bring the logs for their homes, and the soldiers would also help them build their cabins.

That first night, Britt set up his private tent next to Walugo's wagon. He and Cherokee Rose sat together next to a small fire while Walugo was visiting with Chief Sequoyah at his wagon.

All over the massive area there was laughter around the campfires, something that had not been heard among the North Carolina Cherokees since they had been forced from their homes in the Smoky Mountains. Families chatted happily together, talking about the cabins and farms that would be theirs.

Chief John Ross sat at his own campfire, the aroma of strong coffee filling the air. He stared silently into the bright flames, his heart lonely as he thought of Quatie, whose body lay buried beside the long trail behind him. Soon his ears picked up on the laughter and happy talk going on around him, and he shook off his melancholy mood.

Although we have buried great numbers, he thought, *we are still a resilient nation. It is good to hear laughter and the people talking in great anticipation of our future here in Indian Territory. Yes, God has blessed us in so many ways.*

John looked up toward the starlit sky, a smile curving his lips. "I miss you, my beloved wife," he said, his throat tightening, "but there is still much for my people to accomplish, and accomplish it we will!"

At the small fire next to Walugo's wagon, Britt Claiborne and Cherokee Rose agreed that their wedding would be on April 28, the last Sunday in April, a little more than a month from now.

Britt looked around to see if anyone was watching them, and saw no one. He took the lovely young woman into his arms, kissed her tenderly, and said, "On April 28, 1839, I will become the husband of the most beautiful, most precious, and most wonderful woman in all the world."

The firelight showed her face flush. "And I will become the wife of the most handsome, most precious, and most wonderful man in all the world."

Britt grinned. "I think we should seal all of this with a kiss!"

They kissed each other, then held hands and looked into each other's eyes.

"Sweetheart, I don't know about you," Britt said, "but to me, it's already beginning to feel like we belong here."

Cherokee Rose lifted a hand and softly stroked his cheek. "I didn't think it would happen so quickly for me, but I really have found a place to call home."

For further reading about the Trail of Tears, we recommend the following books:

Ehle, John. *Trail of Tears: The Rise and Fall of the Cherokee Nation.* New York: Anchor Books, 1989.

Jahoda, Gloria. *The Trail of Tears.* New York: Henry Holt and Company, 1975.

Frontier Doctor Trilogy

ONE MORE SUNRISE–BOOK ONE

Young frontier doctor Dane Logan is gain-
ing renown as a surgeon. Beyond his
wildest hopes, he meets his long-lost
love—only to risk losing her to the Tag
Moran gang.

ISBN 1-59052-308-3

BELOVED PHYSICIAN–BOOK TWO

While Dr. Dane gains renown by rescuing
people from gunfights, Indian attacks, and
a mine collapse, Nurse Tharyn mourns
the capture of her dear friend Melinda by
renegade Utes.

ISBN 1-59052-313-X

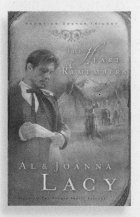

THE HEART REMEMBERS–BOOK THREE

In this final book in the Frontier Doctor
trilogy, Dane survives an accident, but not
without losing his memory. Who is he?
Does he have a family somewhere?

ISBN 1-59052-351-2

Hannah of Fort Bridger Series

Hannah Cooper's husband dies on the dusty Oregon Trail, leaving her in charge of five children and a general store in Fort Bridger. Dependence on God fortifies her against grueling challenges and bitter tragedies.

Angel of Mercy Series

Post-Civil War nurse Breanna Baylor uses her professional skill to bring healing to the body, and her faith in the Redeemer to bring comfort to thirsty souls, valiantly serving God on the dangerous frontier.

Shadow of Liberty Series

Let Freedom Ring
#1 in the Shadow of Liberty Series

It is January 1886 in Russia. Vladimir Petrovna, a Christian husband and father of three, faces bankruptcy, persecution for his beliefs, and despair. The solutions lie across a perilous sea.

ISBN 1-57673-756-X

The Secret Place
#2 in the Shadow of Liberty Series

Popular authors Al and JoAnna Lacy offer a compelling question: As two young people cope with love's longings on opposite shores, can they find the serenity of God's covering in *The Secret Place?*

ISBN 1-57673-800-0

A Prince Among Them
#3 in the Shadow of Liberty Series

A bitter enemy of Queen Victoria kidnaps her favorite great-grandson. Emigrants Jeremy and Cecelia Barlow book passage on the same ship to America, facing a complex dilemma that only all-knowing God can set right.

ISBN 1-57673-880-9

Undying Love
#4 in the Shadow of Liberty Series

Nineteen-year-old Stephan Varda flees his own guilt and his father's rage in Hungary, finding undying love from his heavenly Father—and a beautiful girl—across the ocean in America.

ISBN 1-57673-930-9

The Orphan Train Trilogy

THE LITTLE SPARROWS, Book #1

Kearney, Cheyenne, Rawlins. Reno, Sacramento, San Francisco. At each train station, a few lucky orphans from the crowded streets of New York City receive the fulfillment of their dreams: a home and family. This orphan train is the vision of Charles Loring Brace, founder of the Children's Aid Society, who cannot bear to see innocent children abandoned in the overpopulated cities of the mid–nineteenth century. Yet it is not just the orphans whose lives need mending—follow the train along and watch God's hand restore love and laughter to the right family at the right time!

ISBN 1-59052-063-7

ALL MY TOMOROWS, Book #2

When sixty-two orphans and abandoned children leave New York City on a train headed out West, they have no idea what to expect. Will they get separated from their friends and siblings? Will their new families love them? Will a family even pick them at all? Future events are wilder than any of them could imagine—ranging from kidnappings and whippings to stowing away on wagon trains, from starting orphanages of their own to serving as missionaries to the Apache. No matter what, their paths are being watched by Someone who cares about and carefully plans all their tomorrows.

ISBN 1-59052-130-7

WHISPERS IN THE WIND, Book #3

Young Dane Weston's dream is to become a doctor. But it will take more than just determination to realize his goal, once his family is murdered and he ends up in a colony of street waifs begging for food. Then he ends up being mistaken for a murderer himself and sentenced to life in prison. Now what will become of his friendship with the pretty orphan girl Tharyn, who wanted to enter the medical profession herself? Does she feel he is anything more than a big brother to her? And will she ever write him again?

ISBN 1-59052-169-2

Mail Order Bride Series

Desperate men who settled the West resorted to unconventional measures in their quest for companionship—advertising for and marrying women they'd never even met! Read about a unique and adventurous period in the history of romance.

#1	Secrets of the Heart	ISBN 1-57673-278-9
#2	A Time to Love	ISBN 1-57673-284-3
#3	The Tender Flame	ISBN 1-57673-399-8
#4	Blessed Are the Merciful	ISBN 1-57673-417-X
#5	Ransom of Love	ISBN 1-57673-609-1
#6	Until the Daybreak	ISBN 1-57673-624-5
#7	Sincerely Yours	ISBN 1-57673-572-9
#8	A Measure of Grace	ISBN 1-57673-808-6
#9	So Little Time	ISBN 1-57673-898-1
#10	Let There Be Light	ISBN 1-59052-042-4

Journey of the Stranger Series

One dark, mysterious man rides for truth and justice. On his hip is a Colt .45…and in his pack is a large, black Bible. He is the legend known only as the stranger.

Battles of Destiny Series

It was the war that divided our country and shaped the destiny of generations to come. Out of the bloodshed, men, women, and families faced adversity with bravery and sacrifice…and sometimes even love.

#1	A Promise Unbroken	ISBN 0-88070-581-7
#2	A Heart Divided	ISBN 0-88070-591-4
#3	Beloved Enemy	ISBN 0-88070-809-3
#4	Shadowed Memories	ISBN 0-88070-657-0
#5	Joy From Ashes	ISBN 0-88070-720-8
#6	Season of Valor	ISBN 0-88070-865-4
#7	Wings of the Wind	ISBN 1-57673-032-8
#8	Turn of Glory	ISBN 1-57673-217-7

CHEROKEE ROSE

Bring the story home.